TERMINALLY SAFE

A NOVEL

DANIEL MARTINEZ

For information about this title or to order other books and/or electronic media, contact the publisher:
Daniel Martinez Publishing (Costa Rica)
US Mailing Address: 6703 NW 7th Street
Suite # SJO-12708
Miami, FL 33126
dmpublishing@zoho.com

ISBNs: 978-0-9882677-1-8 (print)
        978-0-9882677-8-7 (eBook)

Printed in the United States of America
Cover and Interior design: 1106 Design

DEDICATION

To my sister

Sandra Noemi Martinez

She triumphed against innumerable adversities

And on her own raised two wonderful daughters

CHAPTER 1

The gargantuan earthquake at the bottom of the Pacific Ocean jarred the needles of hundreds of seismographic stations around the globe at exactly 3:22 early morning that Friday in November of 2003. Officials at the Broadband Array for Seismology in Taiwan and also those at the Australian National Seismic Network quickly identified the center of the seaquake as approximately 200 miles southeast of the Northern Mariana Islands and about 10 miles beneath the ocean floor. As they scanned more details of the data, they had an uneasy feeling that went far beyond their usual apprehensions when tremors would occur. For this was not just another seemingly random spot on the ocean floor but, the location of the deepest, most treacherous part of any ocean on the planet — the Mariana Trench, more than 36,000 feet below the ocean surface and stretching for about 1200 miles along the ocean floor. It is where the huge Pacific plate, moving ever so slowly in a northwesterly direction, rams the smaller Philippine plate with trillions of tons of quiet, persistent, unrelenting, and unforgiving force. The ever-vigilant officials quickly conjectured that the quake was due to the sudden slip of the Pacific plate under the other, lighter one, a colossal movement that, no doubt, instantly displaced millions of cubic kilometers of seawater, creating a devastating tsunami in the process. Immediately, the alarm went out to dozens of tsunami-warning stations all over the Pacific Rim.

As the calamity developed, U.S. Navy military intelligence officer and attack-helicopter pilot Troy Hamilton was enjoying a few days off, relaxing in his bachelor apartment near West 115th Street and Riverside Drive on Manhattan's upper West Side. In his middle 30s, Troy was tall and lean, with that workout hardness in every bone and muscle in his body. Originally from

Boston, he had joined the Navy after graduating from MIT, specializing in the military applications of computer and electronic technology. In the 10 years since he'd joined, he had advanced pretty well, and, five years previously, he had been assigned to sensitive intelligence operations and investigations around the globe — really, wherever the U.S. government found risks or threats to national security.

It was already about 3 o'clock on Thursday afternoon — a little more than two hours after the quake had hit in the Pacific — when Troy walked out of his apartment on his way to his usual long walk on Broadway toward downtown Manhattan. As he exited his building, he met up with Lilly Weinberg, his next-door neighbor up on the third floor.

"Good afternoon, Lilly. You are looking spritely and pretty, as always," said Troy as he kissed her on the cheek and got a whiff of her strong fruit-fragrance perfume. Lilly was a childless 80-year-old widow who lived alone and looked after Troy's apartment when he was gone for weeks at a time on his intelligence assignments. She believed he was a business consultant who was contracted by companies all over the world. Troy would regularly ask her to feed Arturo, his pet goldfish.

"Oh, you're just flattering me because you want to take me out to dinner again, Troy, I know you, you weasel." Her hands had slight tremors, but her mind was sharp, and her bright blue eyes still had a girlish gleam to them. Troy knew that she was only half-joking about the dinner thing, since she often complained about feeling lonely in her apartment and in the impersonal big city, for the old woman apparently had no friends or relatives anywhere. In fact, Troy had felt sympathy for Lilly ever since he had moved into that apartment five years before. And, for that reason, he often visited her and sometimes took her out to dinner at one of the many Chinese restaurants on Broadway.

"No, Lilly, I really mean it, your face looks brighter than those of the many young ladies there at Columbia. If you don't watch it, some young man will get enthralled by your spirit and sweep you off your feet!"

"I don't need no young man, Troy, as long as you keep taking me out to dinner or to Zabar's on 81st Street to buy some cheese. You know how I love to go shopping for cottage cheese with you!"

"Well, okay, Miss Lilly, I'll knock on your door soon, but if you need something in the meantime, well, just buzz me on my cell phone, okay?" And, with that, he said goodbye, and she entered the building.

Troy definitely felt that, as probably Lilly's only friend in the huge metropolis, he had some kind of moral duty to see to it that she was always comfortable. Troy did not see that, as he turned around to walk away, Lilly was watching him through the building's glass door, her eyes a bit glazed, her spirit a little bit saddened.

Troy felt his duty as a moral imperative, but that is not how the building superintendent saw it. Sneaky-looking and with bulging eyes that made him look like a frog, 40-year-old Antonio Colon, who lived with his loud wife and six disorderly children on the first floor, felt that Troy was cozying up to Lilly Weinberg to maybe inherit the $10 million that her retail-store-owner husband had left her. The super had not said anything relating to the widow's money to Troy, but he certainly gave him hateful looks whenever he saw Troy and Lilly together. In fact, it made Troy think that Antonio was feeling jealous of the relationship, as ridiculous as the idea may have sounded. Outside, Antonio gave him the usual sneer and blurted out, "Whatsa matter, big man? Can't get young woman in bed so you goes for the ones ready to die? Man, you should be sorry about youself."

"Sure, Antonio, you've got it all figured out. Just watch your step with Miss Lilly, and make sure you respond to her requests on time, or you're gonna have to deal with me when I find out. Have a nice day. And wash that ugly, greasy hair of yours. It smells like motor oil."

Troy walked east up the hill on West 114th Street, tall apartment buildings on either side, turned right on Broadway, and merged with the considerable crowd of familiar strangers and hundreds upon hundreds of stores on both sides of the street. Truly a cultural smorgasbord.

He had already walked past 96th Street, where the big subway express/local station lay beneath Broadway, when his highly secured and encrypted cell phone rang. Caller ID indicated just a code, which he knew was of military origin. *This is my time off. It must be big — it* better *be big, on a beautiful day like this*, he thought.

According to protocol, he answered the phone with a simple "Yes?" and waited for a confirmation code, which he quickly recognized and acknowledged. "Affirmative — this is Arpeggio 103," he said to identify himself. He received the corresponding acknowledgment from the other end. A business-like voice told him that Vice Admiral Christopher Ferris, Troy's immediate supervising officer in the U.S. Navy, was coming on line. Officially, Troy was in the Navy, but, for some intelligence assignments he would work with the Air Force, still under the direction of Admiral Ferris.

"Troy, I'm sorry to say this, but we have a very bad situation over on the Pacific Rim. Have you heard?" asked the Admiral, almost apologetically.

"No, what's up?"

"Killer tsunami, about three hours ago."

Troy was perplexed. *So what's that got to do with me? I don't do tsunami-relief work,* he thought. "I don't get it, Admiral. What's military intel got to do with that?"

"Troy, there is something very sinister going on with that seaquake and the tsunami, and I'd rather not discuss it — even on this secure line. We need you over here at Dover AFB, stat! I have ordered two choppers to pick you up at Kennedy Airport — they're also picking up some Navy support staff in New Jersey. You have one hour to get to JFK. As your commanding officer, I know you'll have no problem getting there on time, right?" Troy knew that the Admiral's question was rhetorical.

"No, sir. I'm always ready."

On the flight to Dover, Troy could not help but wonder just how an earthquake and tsunami could be called "sinister" — "dangerous," "devastating," "tragic," "deadly," yes, but not "sinister," no matter how many lives they could take. He figured he would know what the Admiral meant soon enough. He found a few moments to call Miss Lilly to advise her of his sudden business trip and asked her to go easy on feeding Arturo — he's a light eater.

The two mammoth Sikorsky CH-53E military helicopters finally arrived at around 8 o'clock that Thursday night at Dover AFB in Delaware. Because of the urgency of the situation, the Air Force was making its facilities available to Troy, the Admiral, and other support Navy staff. Little did anyone know at that point that this was to be the beginning of not just another military-intelligence investigation of imminent danger against the United States, but a colossal, worldwide undercover race against a threat so vile that even the continued existence of the entire planet Earth would be in question.

Military Police escorted Troy to Hangar 1301, where some special-operations offices had been rapidly configured for the briefing. Nothing fancy — some tables, chairs, two desks with phones, nothing hanging from the drab-grey walls, but plenty of overhead lighting, and the pervasive, oily-engine smell of the various older aircraft that had a permanent home in this hangar. The meeting space was quite chilly, since this corner spot did not have any heaters. Over the last several hours, electronics counter-intelligence agents had swept through the entire area to guarantee there were no bugs or other security leaks. Troy entered the briefing room, and, for the very first time in his career, he had not the slightest idea of what kind of problem he would be briefed about.

"Ah, Troy, a little late, but, heck, let's just say it was the damned New York traffic," quipped the Admiral as he motioned for Troy to sit. The Admiral sat, too, and waved his arm to dismiss the other security personnel in the tiny meeting room. Not knowing the real nature of the meeting, Troy was still in a good mood and responded to the Admiral.

"Well, I was happy with my few days off in New York, but I'm happy to be here, too."

"This damned military is causing me ulcers, Troy. I should be home relaxing with my wife and enjoying the fruits of my 35 years of service to this country. But, hell, I love America, and I'll tell my wife I'll be a few days late."

The beefy Navy Admiral, about 60 years old and with hardly any hair left, was a legend in military-intelligence agencies around the world. He had developed novel techniques for information gathering, useful also for counter-intelligence officers, but was also known to be quite stingy about sharing his methods. Foreign services knew about him because he was all too happy to acknowledge victories — after they had become obvious, that is. But, as he got older, he preferred to be in command of military-intel agents, as in the case of Troy.

"Okay, sir. Reporting for new duty. Tell me what you got."

"Don't know what to make of it, Troy," lamented the Admiral. "Don't know if this is a military-intel issue, but the Navy higher-ups don't want to take chances. Damn those higher-ups, Troy; they've got pensions coming up that're about three times the size of mine. They sit on their fat asses all day long. Well, they also go to ceremonies and all that crap!"

Troy thought it would be better to interrupt the Admiral. "On the flight here, I kept wondering about the tsunami but couldn't figure out what that's gotta do with me, with the military."

"That's why you're here, soldier. Reports indicate that the tsunami has already reached Indonesia, the Philippines, Taiwan, Japan, as well as hundreds of small islands in the Western Pacific area. Lots of destruction, thousands of lives lost. According to the Berkeley Digital Seismograph Network, the seaquake itself also caused major destruction in the large region west of The Trench."

"So, what's the sinister part, Admiral?"

"It's unbelievable, Troy. One week ago, our Naval Submarine Base in Groton, Connecticut, received a fax message from The European Advanced Earthquake Detection Center in London."

"So what's so sinister about that?" challenged Troy, with an air of frustration.

"Patience!" the Admiral retorted, with flared bull nostrils and penetrating eyes radiating the microwave heat of disapproval. He immediately composed himself. "The fax message indicated that the European Center had calculated that an ocean-floor earthquake was imminent within a radius of 250 miles from the Northern Mariana Islands in the Pacific. The document gave the date and the approximate time: 3:17 A.M., local Chamorro Time in that area."

Troy was shocked and couldn't quickly respond. "Admiral, they got the day and location correct, and they missed the time by only five minutes! This accuracy in prediction is unprecedented anywhere in the world!"

The two men just stared at each other and then at the floor, and then at each other again, digesting what had just been said and thinking of a possible explanation. "Admiral, I know of no agency in the world capable of making such uncanny predictions."

"Right, Troy. We all know the science of earthquake prediction is still in the dark ages. Hell, some agencies even depend on the changes in the behavior of farm animals to predict that an earthquake will soon happen. Some use toads, for God's sake! But this?"

"So what'd the sub base in Groton do when they got the fax? I bet they must have thought it was a joke or some stupid prank."

"Obviously, they thought it was ridiculous that an earthquake-monitoring agency would dare make such a highly specific prediction — down to the minute, mind you. They tried faxing back for more info, and they also called. No luck. Something about the calls ending up at the wrong place. They were baffled that no one had ever heard of that earthquake agency before, so they just ignored it after a couple of days."

"Well, Admiral, we cannot deny or ignore that their prediction was incredibly accurate. I can only conclude that the European Center has come across a very valuable method of prediction." As soon as he heard himself say that, he froze from the realization of the implications. His mind was whirling with all the possible scenarios, none of them good. Troy was now getting a feel for what the Admiral had meant when he referred to this event as "sinister."

Admiral Ferris was building too much anxious energy just sitting down, so he got up and paced the floor. "Yes, Troy, a very valuable method, indeed. Just imagine the military, economic, and political implications of some entity having such predictive power over earthquakes and the resulting tsunamis."

Troy's eyes were wider than normal, as one would see perhaps in a person who's in shock or in a daze or deep in thought. His brilliant military and logical mind was quickly assessing the nature of the unfolding events, comparing them with intelligence breaches that the United States had suffered in the past. Traitors like Aldrich Ames, Robert Hanssen, Nidal Hasan, John Walker — they had all inflicted damage against America, but this European Agency — could it use this prediction strategy to compromise the national security of the United States?

"You know, Admiral, it worries me to no end that the naval station could not make contact with this European Center. Was the fax sent to Groton a bona fide professional prediction, or was it sent as a provocative signal, a threat perhaps?"

"Troy, I sense we are in deep trouble. I have no doubt in my mind that the information contained in the fax message was meant to let us know that the sending agency, or whatever, has a technical capacity with enormous strategic advantages against which no military of any size can compete. I feel that, for the very first time in history, we have been cornered."

"Not so fast. I have yet to fail on a mission, and you know that I have several dozen under my belt. I love America, and military service is deep inside my heart. What plan did you have in mind, sir?"

"Gotta move fast, Troy, for we do not know what nefarious agency or terrorist group or government we are dealing with. I'm afraid to put this problem in the lap of the CIA over in Langley — they've had some pretty serious leaks lately in their London station, so it's up to military intelligence to tackle this one. The first step is to check out the earthquake-warning agency that sent us the fax — they indicated an address in north London. That's where you're going."

"I'll be ready in one hour, with all my gear. Will it be a commercial flight or a private jet?"

"The jet is waiting for you on the tarmac. Troy — another thing. I'm aware that you are not well versed in geophysics or seismology, so I am sending a highly experienced specialist along to help you interpret whatever technical crap the European Center may throw at you. She is Lieutenant Karla Bloomfield. And, like you, Troy, she is a decorated attack-helicopter pilot." Troy was taken aback, but tried not to show it. With that, the Admiral picked up the phone and ordered that Ms. Bloomfield be sent in.

"Come in, Lieutenant. This is the Troy Hamilton I told you about. Troy, this is Karla." They shook hands, sizing each other up as quickly as possible, and that began by noticing the firmness of the handshake. Troy knew instantly she would not easily acquiesce to playing second fiddle on this mission.

"Glad to meet you, Lieutenant Hamilton. Heard good things about you, but I gotta see that for myself. You know how some people often add fluff to just about everything they do," charged Karla as she gave Troy a smileless, penetrating stare.

"Yeah, I know what you mean. Luckily, I've never heard anything about you," retorted Troy with a cynical smile.

CHAPTER 2

Karla had studied geophysics and seismology at CalTech in Pasadena and had graduated second in her class. Upon graduation, she joined the Navy, more to please her father, who was a career military man, than anything else. She was a little on the upper side of petite, about 5'8", short, dark hair, brown eyes, and pretty facial features which were always hidden by her impending frown. Now in her early 30s, she had never really had any serious relationships because, she said, her love was the military. Her dedication to the Navy and her proficiency in her field were admirable, although colleagues often complained that she was difficult to work with.

Admiral Ferris wanted Troy and Karla to be comfortable on the long flight across the Atlantic, so he had commissioned a Gulfstream jet with spacious seating, lounging, hot-meal service, and a flight attendant. Troy and Karla chose seats facing each other for the task of discussing the mission. At first, they simply chit-chatted about the luxury and spaciousness of the aircraft — much better than a crowded commercial flight. *And no screaming kids, either*, Karla thought.

During a lull in the conversation, Troy took the opportunity to brief Karla on the details of what was already known about the incident in the Pacific. Not much, really, besides the fax and the accuracy of the prediction. She quickly grew impatient with his talk.

"You know, I am not stupid, Lieutenant," she charged.

"I know you are highly educated, Karla, so…" added Troy, but she cut in.

"So you don't need to talk to me in such a condescending manner. I can follow your descriptions via monologue perfectly well."

"Okay, okay. What's the problem? We're supposed to work together. I was just trying to make sure we're both up to date."

Karla gave him an icy look and fired, "'Up to date? Hell, you're already act-ing like you're the one in charge of this mission. Like hell you are! Keep in mind that I'm the seismology specialist, and nobody, but nobody is my boss in the field. Better get that straight!" Her upper lip stiffened and rose ever so slightly, but just enough to make Troy feel he was talking to a snarling Rottweiler.

"Listen, you may be the volcano specialist, but this mission is fundamen-tally an intelligence mission, and that's my field, and that's what we first need to concentrate on. Do you copy, Lieutenant?" stormed Troy.

"'Volcano specialist'?" mused Karla with a facetious and unfriendly smile.

"No, sorry, I meant seismologist." The slip-up robbed Troy of momentum and of some of the ammunition in his comeback. They both knew they'd better just give the volley some rest.

After a few hours, the Gulfstream made an uneventful landing in a secluded section of Heathrow Airport in the western part of London. As a security precaution, Troy and Karla took separate private-car service to the elegant Soho Hotel on Richmond Mews in Watford-NW London and registered under assumed names in separate rooms on different floors. They had previously agreed to get some rest and to start work later that evening.

As he lay on the bed for a short rest, Troy's analytical mind couldn't help but wonder if Karla had been deliberately paired with him to sabotage the intelligence mission. Was this more than a search for the origin of that seis-mographic fax message? Had some foreign government penetrated America's military intelligence and caused Karla to be assigned to him? Was Karla herself a foreign agent? He thought maybe all these theories were too wild to be true. On the other hand, he also knew that, in intelligence fieldwork, it helps to make paranoia your constant companion. It may save your life. It was now Friday, about 1 P.M. London time.

Back at Dover AFB, it was 8 A.M., and Admiral Ferris had already put together a small team of Navy intelligence analysts ready to provide Troy and Karla long-distance assistance as requested. Now that the Navy brass had had more than 15 hours to digest the particulars of the tsunami in the Pacific and the suspicious fax with the dead-on-target prediction, they were more convinced than ever that this was no legitimate seismographic predic-tion, but rather an outright and ominous threat against the United States. The full weight of the U.S. military would be mobilized if necessary, and all intelligence resources were put on standby, awaiting initial reports from Troy and Karla in London. Always committed to his duty, the Admiral had slept in a corner of Hangar 1301 that night. Not very well, though, since he'd had to endure the smell of engine oil and jet fuel all night.

Troy had been in bed less than an hour, his mind whirling, so he resigned himself to the fact that the tension of the mission was preventing him from fully relaxing. He got up and studied the scant information in the folder, again. He decided to call Karla down for a discussion.

"Hi, Karla, it's me. Why don't you come down to my room so we can go over the material and map out a strategy?"

"Here you go again. Why are we meeting in your room? *You* come to *my* room and bring the folders! I can explain what happened with the earthquake and tsunami a lot better than you can," responded Karla, almost with a growl, if you asked Troy.

"Listen, Lieutenant, you seem to have a chip of some kind on your shoulder. Maybe you were kidnapped by mountain savages when you were a kid or something. Maybe you're still feeling angry about that. But I'm getting tired of your neurotic insolence. Just come down to my room, now!" ordered Troy.

There was silence on the phone line for a few seconds. "I'll be over," she sighed.

Troy immediately began to feel sorry for the manner in which he had spoken to Karla. He was used to working intelligence missions alone and was not very adept at ordering colleagues around. He planned on apologizing when she came down.

Twenty minutes passed and no Karla. *She's playing games with me*, he thought. Ten more minutes. Then the phone rang. "Troy, come up, quick!" *Click.* It was Karla's voice — urgent and delivered in a whisper. Troy grabbed his 19-round 9mm Glock semi-automatic pistol and ran at full speed to the floor upstairs, his mind imagining the worst. After all, they were on a secret assignment of incredible importance to America, and the list of possible enemies on the other side included all of the world's professional cutthroats and assassins. However vile the threat, he knew his duty was to assist and protect Karla, in spite of how much she barked. In just a few seconds, he had arrived outside her door.

Not knowing what to expect, he placed his ear against the door and listened, but nothing. He crouched and tried to look through the paper-thin slit of light under the door, but nothing. An older Chinese couple who happened to be walking by in the hallway saw Troy peeking under the door and gave him a dirty look, perhaps thinking he was a degenerate pervert trying to catch a glimpse. He forced a smile, which came out quite sheepish. He knew that the seconds were ticking away, so he went to the next step, for Karla could be in mortal danger, with her chances of survival slipping away. He knocked softly on her door. No response. He knocked louder. Nothing.

At this point, Troy knew he had to go for broke. He chambered his single-action Glock. Since they had exchanged their extra key cards, Troy used his to quietly unlock the door. He pushed it wide open while staying low in the hallway, pointing his gun quickly in all directions inside the room, ready to fire at any and all threats.

"Over here, on the floor, by the side of the bed. Stay low," Karla warned, as she held her own military Glock in her hand. He crawled quickly and found himself next to her lying almost flat on the floor. "What's going on? Are you alright? Anybody in the bathroom?" asked Troy as he quickly scanned all corners of the room and pointed his weapon at the closed bathroom door. "I'm okay, glad you're here, nobody in the bathroom, but look at the window. Someone took a shot at me! Maybe he's still there."

Feeling that the worst was over, Troy got up and took a very cautious look out the window. There was a multi-story building not too far, so the shot had come from there, he thought. The window had a clean bullet hole, no doubt. To be on the safe side, he closed the two sets of curtains and shut the door. He checked the bathroom just to reduce his paranoia. "So, Karla, give me the details."

"I was arranging some of my stuff here on the dresser when, suddenly, I heard a crack and a buzz near my left ear. The dresser mirror I was facing developed a hole."

"What did you do then?"

"It took me a few seconds to turn around, and that's when I saw the hole in the large window. I grabbed my gun and went to the floor, expecting another shot. But, nothing more."

Troy walked to the dresser and moved it out of the way. On the concrete wall behind it was the clean hole made by the projectile. He fiddled with the hole, using Karla's nail file set until he was able to dislodge the spent bullet. "Looks like a 7.62×54mm round, Karla. Originally Soviet, NATO, too. Accurate and deadly up to 500 yards. Professional. Rifle round. Someone doesn't want us in London."

"Well, he's a damned coward, trying to take me out while my back is turned."

"We have a very serious problem. I'm pretty sure this is related to the work we came here to do. Someone or some agency means to hunt us down," warned Troy.

"But how did this hoodlum know we're here, that we're investigating the European Center? Does that mean we have a breach in Dover, or elsewhere?" queried Karla.

"Those are good questions, but I'm afraid I don't have any answers. One thing's for sure: It's starting to look like this European Center may be just the tip of some very dangerous foreign plan against the United States, and it's our job to figure out what that is."

"So, what now?" quizzed Karla as she re-holstered her weapon.

"We've got to contact Admiral Ferris in Dover to advise him of the attempt on your life, and we've got to leave this hotel as soon as possible. Someone out there knows where our rooms are, so we're sitting ducks here."

Troy hurriedly helped Karla re-pack her things. Then they cautiously went down to his room, closing the window curtains just in case, and locking the door with all its multiple latches. Within a minute, they had Admiral Ferris on the encrypted cell-phone line.

"Hello, Troy — glad to hear from you. How are you getting along with the pitbull?"

"It's okay. Someone attempted a hit on Karla while she was in her hotel room, through the window. High-powered 7.62mm round, of the 54mm variety. Few moments ago."

"My God! Was she hurt?" exclaimed the Admiral.

"No, she's okay. She's with me here in my room. But it was close. She heard the aerodynamic buzz of the projectile. Missed her head by maybe five inches. We figure that this mission is bigger than what we thought, and somebody does not want us here."

"We've got to get both of you out of there and into a London safe house right away. Let me speak with Karla." Troy gave her the phone.

"Hi, Karla. How are you feeling after that close call?"

"Okay, sir. It was a piece of cake. After the shot came through my window, I turned around, and I just made an angry face. Must have scared the damned coward away. Troy was a bit nervous, but I gave him a few words of encouragement. He's okay now. Performed well, sir."

That was not how Troy remembered the sequence of events, but he kept quiet and did not make faces. Surely, he did not want to antagonize her. The Admiral gave Troy the address of a CIA safe house on Hawley Drive on London's east side. He was told to go there with Karla right away. The Admiral gave him the clearance codes to be admitted, and he called the safe house to alert them of their arrival.

Karla and Troy checked out of the hotel separately, but they got into the same non-descript CIA vehicle that then took a very long and winding route to the safe house. They were tired when they finally arrived at around 8 P.M.

They were in a residential neighborhood, nothing extraordinary about the light-green, ranch-style house on the outside. Two short trees on the front lawn and various shrubs along the perimeter of the front lawn and the driveway. The vehicle entered the garage, and the door closed before anybody was allowed to exit the vehicle. Inside, it was another story. Cameras and thick doors everywhere, as well as what appeared to be a central room with monitors, all sorts of computers, and communications and radio equipment. There was also a very nice, well-equipped kitchen, like the one you would find in any family home. Except that this one had two rather large refrigerators.

They hardly had any time to place their belongings on their assigned bunks in the common sleeping area when they were advised to go to Room 5 for a conference video call with Admiral Ferris in Dover.

"Good evening, Troy and Karla. Can you see and hear me?"

"Perfect connection, sir," answered Karla.

"Good afternoon over there, Admiral," added Troy.

"I'm happy that both of you are safe now. I have counter-intelligence working feverishly over here trying to figure out what happened that blew the cover on your secret mission in London. Obviously, the information was relayed to some hostile operative who was waiting for you when you arrived at the airport."

"But very few people knew about this intel mission, right?" queried Karla.

"You're right, but some of them are practically civilian, like the seismology and weather guys who received that problematic fax in Groton. They would have known that it was relayed to Navy Intel here in Dover."

"Yeah, but, Admiral, the Groton guys could not have known that Karla and I were ordered to fly to London on this mission."

"Troy is right, sir. How did that info get out?" challenged Karla. "Are you saying that the bad guys have a mole at our sub base in Groton?"

Troy and Karla looked at each other with grave concern. *This is getting more dangerous by the hour*, they both thought.

"Well, Karla, normally earthquake and weather stations are not top-secret installations, but the Groton ones are connected to the submarine base. So I suppose that, yes, there has to be a mole there, unfortunately."

"We've got to move on, Admiral. I figure that Karla and I will check out that European Center address tomorrow morning. Eyes peeled for that madman assassin."

"Our counter-intelligence guys detected unusual movement and radio communications among some Iranian agents they've been shadowing, right before your plane left Dover and then again when your plane landed in London. We believe that they may be involved in that attempt on Karla."

"Iranian madmen, if you ask me, sir," Karla shot back.

"Another thing," advised the Admiral. "We've been checking that telephone number on the European Center fax — it's an Internet cafe. And the Center address is a small office building. Be very careful, and contact me if you have something."

Early next morning, Troy and Karla arrived at the European Center address — at the corner of busy Langford Road and Amherst Avenue in north London. Nice-looking brick building with several signs indicating that it was home to several businesses and private offices. The first-floor directory did not make any mention of a seismology center, and the other names on the list did not indicate anything related to earthquakes, tsunamis, volcanoes, and such. Just to be on the safe side, Troy and Karla went around and gave each business door a quick look — even stopped at a couple to ask about the European Center, but no luck.

"Well, maybe we should check the Internet cafe. That's where the fax came from," suggested Karla. Troy looked at his written notes and, in an assertive manner, motioned in a southerly direction. It had not escaped him that Karla was taking the lead in many instances. "About one block," he commanded.

I know where that is, thought Karla, *I have a map too, you know.* Her eyes and her stiff upper lip let Troy know that she was aware that he was trying to control her, or at least to act as her boss. But she kept her mouth shut in the interest of civility. Troy sensed that she was making the effort.

They quickly located the Cracker Jack Internet Cafe and approached the clerk at the cash register — youngish guy with long hair and a brilliant rose tattoo on his upper right arm, tattered T-shirt. Karla's eyes politely asked Troy if she could take the lead; his forehead gave the go-ahead.

"Excuse me, sir. We're from the airport baggage insurance agency, and we understand that, about a week ago, a person came here to fax a one-sheet message to a number in Connecticut, in the U.S. Were you the person who handled that fax?" Troy had not yet seen Karla smile, but, here, she did. *There is hope*, he thought.

"Yeah, yeah, I was here. I'm always here. Hell, I hardly sleep, so I'm always here, and even when I'm not here, I'm here, in the back room, taking a one-hour nap when I get the chance. So, he lose his suitcase or his bags or what? By the way, my name's Jenson."

"Nice meeting you, Jenson. Yes, something like that. Did he mention where he lived or worked, or maybe something else?"

"My, you are pretty. Sorry, but I'm always busy, or I would definitely ask you out. Well, the guy, I remember him good because he appeared nervous or spaced out on drugs. I don't do drugs — bad, bad. Been in rehab two times, arrested about three. He said he was in a big hurry and wanted me to hurry up on the fax. Almost totally bald, good dresser, though. Not like me — I'm not worth much. Kept looking out the big windows here. Really antsy type. Or maybe he was just hyperactive like me. You know, ADHD. Taking pills for that."

Troy stepped in and redirected him. "Did he say anything that would help us find him? It's very important."

"Matter of fact, yes. Very weird man, 'bout 40 years old, I'd say. He said if an American comes to look for him — wait, I wrote it down. Here. He would be at 14 Pemberton, flat 16. And my guess is that you're American, especially this delicious lady here. My, you lucky man! One day I want a pretty American wife just like her. Lucky, lucky."

"Oh, Jenson, you have been so helpful, and thanks a lot!" said Karla as they both waved him goodbye. Jenson blew her a goodbye kiss.

On the short walk back to their rental car, Troy and Karla tried to inconspicuously look in all directions, especially at tall buildings, in search of anything suspicious — well, in search of assassin rifle barrels and shiny scopes. They knew that just because no new shots had rung out it did not mean that they were not being watched. During the ride, taking the long way to hopefully lose any tail, they talked about the bizarre nature of the developing case before them. Why had the man who went to deliver the fax been so nervous? Why was he constantly looking out the window? Did he feel he was being followed? Why did he leave an address for an American? How would he know that Dover would follow up on the fax? Too many questions, no answers, and the more they thought about it, the more questions they had.

After about an hour they got to the Pemberton address in the crowded East Dulwich part of London, about south-central. Just to be on the safe side, they drove past the address a couple of times, and they parked about two blocks away. The white apartment building had three floors and looked well kept on the outside. The air in the area was filled with the aromas of pizza and fresh-bread, giving the neighborhood a friendly, homey ambience. Flat #16 was on the second floor. Troy and Karla made sure their weapons were chambered and ready to fire. They opted to keep them holstered.

They listened outside the door for a few seconds. Nothing. Troy knocked. Nothing. He knocked two more times. Then the door to apartment #15, facing #16, suddenly opened, and both Troy and Karla drew their weapons and pointed them at the man in #15. They were milliseconds from pulling their

Glocks' sensitive single-action triggers. "No, no, wait. I have no weapon —
don't shoot!" He did not appear threatening. He had almost no hair, as Jenson
had assured, and his hands were in full view. "Both of you are American,
right?" asked the stranger.

"That depends," grumbled Karla. "Are you the man who went to the
Cracker Jack Internet Cafe?"

"Yes. Thank God you're here."

"Just to get a bit more comfortable with you, tell us why you went there
and the details of what you did," demanded Troy.

"Come in, please. Get out of the hallway." Troy and Karla entered the flat,
did a cursory inspection, politely patted the man down, and then put their
weapons away.

"The answer, please," coaxed Karla.

"Of course. I sent you a faxed message. I sent you Americans at the Groton
Submarine Base a very detailed and specific prediction of an impending seaquake and tsunami near the Northern Mariana Islands, in the Pacific. I'm
sure by now you know we were off by only about five minutes."

"Why did you indicate to the clerk at the Internet Cafe that you were in
flat #16 when actually it is #15?" challenged Karla.

"I'm sorry about that, but I had to do it just in case they came to kill me in
the middle of the night," explained the man, with his lips now quivering. "For
your information, flat #16 is empty. I would not put innocent people at risk."

He was still trembling and had a look of terror and paranoia about him.
Yes, he did look about 40, tall, slightly overweight, dark brown eyes with circles
below them, and he was wearing very wrinkled brown dress slacks. Probably
part of the brown suit Jenson had described. His flat was very sparsely fur-
nished — just a bed, chairs and table, a very old television, and a few dishes.
His intelligent face seemed out of place in such a small and spartan apartment.

Somebody wants to kill this nice man? thought Troy. He and Karla had the
same thought at the same time and immediately began to move the table and
chairs away from the center of the room. The window had been providing a
clear shot for any would-be assassin.

Then Karla continued, "Okay, so what's your name?"

"Benjamin Thompson. I am a physicist and a geophysicist. You've got to
help me, and only your government has enough power to stop this horrible,
apocalyptic plan of theirs! Well, maybe nobody can stop them — then, we're
doomed. Excuse me — I don't even know your names!" Troy introduced himself and Karla, and said that they were connected with the Navy in Groton.

Just in case, he closed all curtains in the small flat and turned on the vintage RCA television set to create some ambient noise.

"Calm down. Breathe deeply several times, Mr. Thompson," whispered Troy in a reassuring tone. Remembering yesterday's hotel sniper shot, Karla kept looking nervously at the curtained window. *They don't have some secret scope that can see infrared through thick, dirty curtains, right?* She reminded herself that her semi-automatic was ready to fire all 15 deadly hollow-point rounds, if needed. The door to flat #15 had two locks, engaged.

"That's better, Mr. Thompson," continued Troy. "Now, tell us how you figure into all this."

"Five years ago, I set up a private company with my colleague and friend Jacob Graham. We met while studying physics at Lancaster University. Graduated together. We named the company Geophysical Dynamics Corp Ltd. Here in London. Not far, Wickham Street, in the Croydon area. Like me, he's in hiding, but at the Worcester Hotel in Birmingham. Said he would call himself 'Peter' — ah, um, I forget the last name. Only I know. Well, now you."

"And what does your company do, exactly?" Karla broke in, knowing that the topic was heading into her area of expertise.

"It has to do with Earth's plate tectonics and geophysical fluid dynamics deep in solid land or beneath the ocean floor. Hell — what does it matter now? We'll all be dead soon," lamented Mr. Thompson.

"No, Mr. Thompson. Things will be alright. Please continue," added Troy. Karla got a bit miffed, thinking that Troy had stepped into her lead. No stiff lip, though.

"For several years, we have been studying models of how the Earth's plates ram against other, adjacent plates. How they store huge amounts of potential energy when they snag each other and aren't able to move past one another. One day, the tension is so great that it suddenly and quickly overcomes the huge friction holding them together, and the plates swiftly grind and move against each other, creating a thunderous and catastrophic earthquake."

"Tell us something we don't know," interrupted Karla, surely feeling that this all was first-grade stuff for her. Troy gave her a disapproving glare. "And, by the looks of it, you created a method of accurately predicting these plate movements?" hissed Karla to help him along.

"That would be a great technical achievement to help humanity, but no," scoffed Mr. Thompson. "What we developed is a hundred times more technically advanced and, unfortunately, heinous. Pernicious, because we have lost control of it. It's sinister — it has no place in civilization. You see, they came…"

Just as instantly as a balloon bursts, Mr. Thompson's words were abruptly interrupted by an explosive hail of bullets coming from behind the closed door, wood splinters and dish fragments flying in every possible direction. Karla and Troy instinctively went to the floor and returned fire, pulling their triggers as fast as they could, their combined firepower approximating the action of an automatic military weapon. But the assassins kept pouring more bullets into the tiny room, even though they could not see what they were shooting at. Within seconds Karla announced to Troy that she had to reload, so he began shooting alternately at the left and right sides of the disappearing door to make up for it. Her spent clip went flying out, and she inserted a full one, chambered the first round, and resumed the awesome firepower of her Glock. While reloading, Troy noticed that Mr. Thompson had been slow in getting off his chair and onto the floor, so he grabbed him by the belt and pulled hard. A few seconds later all firing stopped. Troy and Karla quickly crawled against the wall that had contained the door, just in case the assassins were still there. They heard someone running away, but they were not about to follow. The door was practically gone, split into a thousand sharp splinters. From their positions inside the apartment, they could see pretty far down the hallway in both directions. Troy peeked out of the gaping hole where the door had been and saw that there was one motionless body, hand still on a pistol with an extended ammunition clip, probably for 25 or 30 rounds. Had a bullet-proof vest on, but he'd been hit maybe five times outside that zone.

"Are you hurt, Karla?"

"Naw, it was a walk in the park. How about you?"

Troy had bent over to remove the pistol from the assassin's hand when Karla noticed that the hand tightened around the gun and started moving in Troy's direction. She couldn't see if Troy still had his gun in his hand, so she quickly yelled, "Watch his hand!" Without hesitation, she fired one hollow-point round dead center into the assassin's forehead. He released the gun. Just in case, she used her foot to push it far away from his hand. She gave Troy a smart look that let him know that his failure to follow procedure had almost cost him his life.

"Thanks, partner," said Troy as he stepped back into what was left of the room to check on Mr. Thompson. Didn't look good. He wasn't moving. He had several wounds on his chest and arms. One bad one on his right cheek — a gaping hole at the back of his head. Just then, Troy noticed a flexible surveillance camera on the floor, by the door frame. That was what the assassins had used to peek inside the room, going through the small slit at the bottom of the door to gain visual access. While the three of them had been talking at the table, the bad guys outside the closed door were quickly calculating where they had to aim their weapons, without actually being able to see the target at the moment of firing. Crude and a lot more bullets, but their methods had proven deadly and effective, except for the expendable hit man on the floor.

They both looked around the room quickly and grabbed anything that might have intelligence value, including a picture of Mr. Thompson and his billfold. Karla took a photo of the dead assassin and then grabbed his wallet, phone, and passport. Troy noted that his gun was a 9mm CZ-82, standard arm of the Czech military. Quick photo of it, especially serial number. They couldn't help but see that flat #16 had about 50 bullet holes on the door and around it, and they remembered that Mr. Thompson had said he didn't want innocent people to get hurt. It had been a prescient decision on his part to have selected a flat across from one he knew would be totally vacant.

In two minutes, Karla and Troy were far from the apartment building. They were leaving behind a battle zone with two bodies and about 100 spent brass cartridges on the floor. At first, the police would surely think that it had been the scene of a drug deal that had gone brutally bad. But, in no time, a Scotland Yard investigation would add another complicating dimension to this labyrinthian case.

Since Troy and Karla feared that their rental vehicle was already under surveillance, they returned it to the agency and then took the Tube, changing trains various times to trip up any tail they may have gotten. It was then time for a restful dinner at a cheap restaurant on busy little Wye Street, near Thames Christian College. They entered Anwen's Cafe; the small place had about 10 tables and an even smaller counter service. The place was about half full, and the air was filled with a definite apple-cinnamon pie aroma — just coming out of the ovens. And that glorious fresh-coffee smell, like the one people can rarely get at home. They sat at a corner table, with a clear view of the entrance. After ordering, they discreetly changed the ammunition clips in their weapons to ensure that they were full to the max. No telling when they would have to again defend themselves against ruthless savages. It was time to talk about just what had happened that afternoon at flat #15.

CHAPTER 3

Karla went first, almost in a whisper. "Troy, these assassins, whoever they are, have incredibly good intelligence."

"I agree. They must be part of a state security or intelligence network. They cannot possibly be independent individuals or common criminals."

"How did they know you and I are working on the earthquake/tsunami case? How did they track us from Dover to London, and then to my exact hotel room?"

"It does seem we are up against something big, Karla. Very big. Something very ominous, malevolent. It's patently clear they don't want any survivors, any witnesses."

"I don't think these guys knew about the information that Jenson at the Internet Cafe had for us. They might have known where the fax originated, since Admiral Ferris suspects that someone in Groton leaked it, but maybe they never got around to asking the Internet clerk about it," Karla speculated.

"Yeah, that's a good theory. If that's true, then they were able to find Mr. Thompson when we were there because they followed our car. With the flexible camera tubing under the door, they made sure it was him," concluded Troy, keeping a sharp eye on the front door of the little restaurant. He was beginning to feel that maybe Karla and he were no match for these savage professionals, that it was just a matter of days or even hours before he and Karla would be killed mercilessly by these brutal murderers. But he was not about to share his defeatist thoughts with Karla the optimist, his partner who did not — even for a moment — hesitate to fire her weapon at close range to save his life. The least he could do was to take the bull by the horns and see this through so that they could both later say they served their country to the best of their abilities. Karla had confided to Troy that she needed more successful missions under her belt to advance her Navy career to the next level, that of Lieutenant Commander, level O-4.

Karla snapped her fingers. "Hello, Mr. Navy Intelligence — are you here at the table with me, or dreaming of someone else? Food's here, Lieutenant." Troy finished dissociating and brought his attention back to the here and now, back to reality, back to thinking about how to deal with an unseen enemy. *No more doubts — full steam ahead*, he thought.

"Okay, let's try to focus just on the nature of the leak here," said Troy. "All these leaks could be explained by just two factors. One is the possible seismology civil worker leak in Groton, and the second is the common network of spies and observers that all countries have in foreign lands."

"So, the seismology worker passed a copy of the important-looking fax document from the European Center to his handler somewhere in Groton, and, as a matter of standard operating procedure, the handler then relayed it to central headquarters in a foreign country," conjectured Karla, who, by now, was ravenously eating her steaming lasagna as if she had not eaten in days. Speaking with a full mouth and getting tomato sauce on her lips as a consequence, she added, "All this shooting makes me hungry, Troy. I don't know about you." Troy didn't say so, but he preferred to see tomato lips instead of stiff ones baring teeth. He chomped on his crispy fish 'n' chips, downing them with a Lees Vintage Harvest beer.

"That's right," agreed Troy. "Now, any intelligence analyst that was given this piece of intel in the foreign country would immediately realize the enormous value of what they had just received. Just imagine a seismology center making such an incredibly specific prediction about the occurrence of an earthquake at the bottom of the sea — even the exact time was provided! This would have enormous strategic value. My God!"

"So then he would pass that raw intel to his superior officer, who, in turn, would pass it to the intel chief," gurgled Karla as she kept wolfing down her dinner. "I would imagine that, within hours, this hostile country or terrorist group would put their observers and spies in and around Groton on high alert, and if they got a second piece of intel indicating that the fax had been officially passed on from Groton to Admiral Ferris of Navy Intel at Dover AFB, then Dover would also be put on the watch list. And especially so, since I am sure the spies who surround Dover AFB as a matter of routine happened to see that two Navy Sikorsky choppers had landed there, a highly unusual event."

"Yes. The interesting part, Karla, is that this hostile group had the fax and the address of the fake European Center a full week before we did, so we have to conclude that they checked and discovered that the European Center did not exist and that the Center's fax number was, in reality, the Cracker Jack Internet Cafe. Keep in mind that the Admiral also mentioned that our counter-intel agents detected unusual activity of Iranian agents before we left Dover and right before we landed in London."

Karla's eyes indicated she was deep in thought. "But why did Mr. Thompson, who admitted to us he sent the fax, invent this crazy European Advanced Earthquake Detection Center? That seems so unnecessary if he just wanted to communicate with some Americans."

"Yeah — that doesn't make sense. Unless…unless he was trying to buy some time. The prediction was for a week from the date of the fax. Maybe he thought that the seismographic station at Groton wouldn't take him seriously until after the prediction was deemed to be highly accurate. After all, the prediction would have to come from an earthquake detection center, and he didn't want to use a real center because he didn't want to smear their name," theorized Troy, who began to eyeball the glass cabinet containing the cinnamon-apple pies. He was already planning on ordering two slices and two coffees, even though they had not finished with their dinner.

"Troy, you know what? I am beginning to suspect that maybe there are two totally separate and independent hostile intelligence agencies, or terrorist groups, that have been involved in this case and in the events of the last several days. Those who have been trying to compromise or do harm to Mr. Thompson and his company may be only part of the story."

He spaced out for a second, deeply considering what she had just said, and exclaimed, "Yes, Karla, brilliant! Mr. Thompson and his company already had some type of threat before he sent the fax to Groton — the fax that was copied by a mole in the Navy seismology network — and surely the very first time the mole had read about an earthquake center making such accurate predictions! There being two separate and independent hostile groups explains a lot of things."

"So, Troy, to clarify this, let's label as 'Thompson's Enemies' the original group that caused problems for Mr. Thompson and his geophysics company, and we'll label as 'Groton Mole Group' the group consisting of the Groton seismology mole, plus all his associates who have been tracking us."

"Okay, makes sense and adds some needed order to the increasing complexity of this case," noted Troy. "Great idea."

"So, which group tried the hit on me yesterday? And why?" mumbled Karla. They both were totally silent for about a minute as their brains scanned every piece of available evidence to come up with an insightful answer or at least a working theory.

"It seems to me, Karla, that the Thompson's Enemies group had no reason to see either of us dead yesterday. To arrange a hit on us, they obviously would have to know about us first, and I don't believe they did. But if they did know about us, they would know we came to London to gather intel on the European Center fax, but especially to ask the directors of the center about the uncanny accuracy of their predictions. We know now that Mr. Thompson was terrified and in hiding, so the Thompson's Enemies group was looking for him. This group would want us to lead them to Mr. Thompson, so, consequently, they would not have wanted us dead. Well, not yesterday at the hotel, anyway."

"So that leaves the Groton Mole Group as the more likely suspect in the sniper shot yesterday, right? But why would they want either of us dead?" wondered Karla.

"Wait, I've got it!" Karla answered herself. "Once the Groton Mole Group was in possession of a very valuable piece of intelligence — the fax — they put Dover AFB under increased surveillance to detect any unusual movement and became aware that two agents — you and I — were sent to London to investigate. It seems to me that they knew right away of the incredible value of checking out and compromising a seismographic center with new techniques in earthquake prediction, so they began their own investigation immediately to see what strategic benefits they could reap. Therefore, you and I, in London, represented competition and a considerable threat to them. Obviously they sought to eliminate me or us."

"It's all starting to make sense. And the assassination of Mr. Thompson was carried out by the only group who would benefit by it — Mr. Thompson's Enemies Group. I think we were included on the hit list the minute the assassins confirmed with the flexible camera that the third person sitting at the table in flat #15 was Mr. Thompson. In that instant, the Group knew they had no further need for us — they had located their main target," summed Troy.

The tall, friendly waitress with the flowery apron and the 1950s hairdo arrived with the two pieces of hot apple pie and two cups of coffee. Troy certainly was getting full, but Karla was still going strong. She must have sensed the funny stare that Troy was giving her. "Don't look at me like that. I told you — it's all the bullets and commotion," she piped.

Now the second and final point for the night they needed to refine was the nature of the work that Mr. Thompson and his colleague Jacob Graham were doing. Mr. Thompson had told Troy and Karla that it certainly would have been a great technical achievement to develop a very accurate method of prediction, to help humanity.

But, no. What Mr. Thompson had added was more disturbing: "What we developed is a hundred times more technically advanced and, unfortunately, heinous."

Karla finished her apple pie. Troy was still working on his. "You know, Troy, Mr. Thompson alluded to something very sinister, very pernicious that was happening at his geophysics company. He said something about it not having a place in civilization."

"Yes, I got the impression he was talking about something really apocalyptic, and, judging by the firepower unleashed against him and us this afternoon, I would guess that these organized agents or terrorists will do literally anything to keep command of whatever Mr. Thompson created. Money, lives, and risk are no object. They are committed."

Karla picked up the ball. "I don't think Mr. Thompson was referring to just predicting earthquakes, Troy."

"So, tomorrow, we have to go over to Mr. Thompson's company to take a quick look, gather intel and such, and then we have to try to find Mr. Thompson's colleague, Jacob Graham, very early tomorrow at the Worcester Hotel in Birmingham," proposed Troy. "My guess is that the assassins are already looking for him to silence him forever."

Karla gave Troy a look that he knew meant trouble. "Okay, but I don't want you to make it seem you are giving me an order."

"I am simply making suggestions, Lieutenant Bloomfield."

"That's better," she replied, with an oblique look out of the corner of her eye.

They were starting to feel that their brains were getting fried from having to make logical sense of so much information. For the next few minutes, they just sipped their coffees, occasionally staring at a couple of lovebirds in their 20s, who were seated at another quiet corner. The couple apparently would forget they had food on their plates, and they would just stare into each other's eyes for the longest periods. *I bet they don't have to worry about assassins in their midst*, wondered Troy.

But, at another table, Troy spotted a second couple holding hands, sitting too close to each other, and playing with each other's hair. He looked in his 40s, she, in her 30s. Anybody would say they were madly in love, in love! But these were not husband and wife — this couple was too romantic to be that. No, they were lovers; their passionate fires were hot and burning like the glowing embers of a blacksmith's forging fire, fueled by two heavy-breathing bellows, Troy concluded.

Just then, Karla's eyes searched around for whatever it was that had captivated Troy's attention and, apparently, had put him in some sort of trance. She kicked him under the table and admonished him, "It's not polite to stare."

He came back to Earth. In fact, he was very surprised that his imagination had gone flying. Yes, it's not polite to stare, he knew.

"Karla, I know so little about you — just the quick one-page file I got on my phone while we were on the plane here. Bet you got my quick info, too, right?"

"Yep. But what do you want to know? You want to use it against me later?"

"Not at all. You saved my life, so I am indebted to you forever. Since we work together, I just thought it would be nice to know a little more than what those files divulged."

"I really don't like talking about myself because, if you haven't noticed, I have a hard time being personal. Just prefer to keep things at the professional level. We both know what our duties and responsibilities are, and if we follow those, there won't be any problems."

"But a moment ago, you said, 'Hello, Mr. Navy Intelligence.'"

"Well, just a moment of weakness. I'm back to normal."

"I love it when you let your defenses down, Lieutenant," crooned Troy, and, with that, they both looked in opposite directions to avoid each other's eyes.

Just then, two men in street jackets walked into the restaurant and took a table near the door — almost as if they knew ahead of time they would be seated there. Troy and Karla's demeanor changed instantly from cautious relaxation to almost high alert. It was obvious that, at all other tables, there was at least one woman sitting. Was this just a fluke, a coincidence? Troy and Karla knew from their intel training not to ignore coincidences, because, often, they do have meaning. They had already finished their coffee, so they paid the waitress. As they had already planned, Karla would walk about five steps ahead of Troy so that he would have a clearer shot if the two men were to attack her. Once she was outside, she would turn around and offer him the same cover.

They started walking, and the two men near the door kept their eyes on them. Both Karla and Troy had their hands on their weapons inside their pockets, ready to unleash a fury of bullets if it came to that. When they were both outside, they walked rapidly, looking over their shoulders frequently, but the two suspicious characters did not follow.

On Ingrave Street, they hailed a Black Cab and asked the cabbie to take them to the RE Hotel London Shoreditch on Hackney Road, near the financial district. Just in case they were being followed, they asked to be dropped off about two blocks from the hotel, and they walked around a bit before showing up without a reservation. They asked for one suite with two beds. Once in their room, they made sure all windows were locked, curtains and blinds drawn, door double locked. As an added precaution, they moved the sofa in front of the door to serve as a barricade. They took turns taking showers while the other one watched a bit of TV. Chambered and unholstered Glocks sat on their night tables.

"Good night, Karla."

"Pleasant dreams, Mr. Navy Intelligence." It was late Saturday night.

CHAPTER 4

In the morning, they had a full English breakfast, consisting of eggs, bacon, sausages, cornish potato cakes, toast, juice, and coffee. Now that there was daylight, they could see that the hotel breakfast area was rather nicely decorated with lots of antique vases, bottles, and coffee pots. It had maybe 20 tables, all full with tourists speaking incomprehensible languages. Well, Karla and Troy could make out maybe 10 of them, as was required in their training.

They had slept like logs in the very comfortable beds. Their suite was rather spacious, and they got to enjoy it just a bit since they basically had just been there to sleep.

After breakfast, they were mission-ready. Outside on the street, they saw the light Sunday traffic and beautiful apartment buildings, most of them no higher than four stories. Well kept and clean. The air smelled fresh in the early morning. After a short walk, they hailed a Black Cab again. "Wickham Street, in the Croydon area, please."

On the way there, Karla and Troy wondered just what they were going to find at Geophysical Dynamics Corp. After all, the two owners and brains of the whole operation would not be there — one was dead, the other in hiding in Birmingham. Since it was a very technical operation that had been run by two specialists in physics and geophysics, would Troy and Karla even know what types of machines or equipment they would be looking at when they arrived? Then, too, the assassins might be waiting for them. They both felt the classic gut churning associated with approach-avoidance conflict. But duty called.

The cabbie informed them they had just gotten to Wickham Street. Anywhere in particular? They asked him to just drive, but a bit slower. They kept a keen eye on both sides of the street, hoping that the company had a clearly visible outside sign. After about 10 minutes, Karla discreetly kicked Troy's shoe. He looked to her side of the street, and there it was — a small business sign above the front door. Traffic was getting heavier on this street with lots of stores and other businesses. They did not ask the cabbie to stop, letting him go for maybe an extra half-kilometer. Abruptly, they asked him to pull over, paid him, and got out.

Troy and Karla walked back, going around a couple of blocks, again, to lose a potential tail. They went into several stores. No sign of hostile agents. They got to Geophysical Dynamics, near the corner of Ballow Street, and, as expected, they found the front door locked. It looked like a rather large one-level building, mostly brick, good frontage on Wickham Street. They decided to check for a back entrance.

There was a wide alley in the back, wide enough to properly service the other industrial businesses there. It looked like a big mess, littered with trash containers and large shipping crates that nobody knew what to do about. It didn't help either that the garbage haulers were not careful when emptying the large steel containers, and abundant amounts of garbage had spilled on the ground. Neither the businesses nor the garbage haulers claimed owner-ship at that point, so it basically became orphan trash.

Karla was the first to spot the company's back entrance. Locked, too. They peeked through some windows but couldn't see anything interesting besides very messy offices. Without a second thought, she elbowed the glass portion of the rear door and broke it. In 10 seconds, they were in, Glocks in hand.

There were several small offices, all with drafting tables and assorted tools. Some offices had shelves and wooden tables with industrial electronic components such as heavy-duty power supplies, signal generators, enamel wire coils, relays and high-amp switches. What was peculiar was that all file cabinets and desk drawers were open, and many of their contents were on the floor. It was clear that someone had been looking for information.

Moving ever so carefully, with weapons ready, they located what appeared to be a large laboratory in another section of the building. Karla quickly spotted four independent seismographs in a corner, connected to four separate computers. This lab, with a very high ceiling, had some type of scaffolding structure in the center, full of pipes, copper and fiberglass tubing, wire coils of various sizes, and two eight-inch PVC pipes, about 15 feet long, arranged perpendicularly to each other. Judging from the many hanging electrical wires with connectors in place but connecting to nothing, it appeared that some components of this odd creation were missing. Neither Karla nor Troy could even guess what this machine was for, but, just in case, Karla snapped some photos of these scenes and then passed the miniature camera on to Troy, who thought some other devices there should be photographed as well.

At the other end of the long lab, there was a door marked SUPPLIES, and it attracted their attention. But when they opened it, they both instantly gagged at the horribly nauseating and putrid stench that assaulted their nostrils, so much so that they had to retreat from the door about 15 feet to let their stomachs settle. Neither said anything, yet they both knew what they would probably find at the bottom of those stairs.

In a drawer in the lab, they found some clean working rags which they completely soaked with water to cover their nose and mouth. Then they made a second attempt, going down the supply-room stairs. In the middle of the small room at the bottom lay three bodies, already bloated and ready to burst. Middle-aged men, wearing brown workshop aprons. All three appeared to have been executed by shots to the back of the head. Karla checked to see if there were any spent bullet casings, but there were none. There was nothing else down there of interest, so they quickly retraced their steps back to the front offices with the paper-littered floors. Still it took them a while to compose their stomachs, which were still working on the breakfasts they had just eaten.

"These three lab workers still had their lab aprons and work gloves on, so it seems to me they were murdered soon after they'd helped the intruders load some equipment into vehicles. All those dangling electrical wires and cables indicate that components were removed," opined Karla.

"Right. And I feel sorry for the three men downstairs. They were just doing their jobs working in the lab," sympathized Troy.

Karla warned, "So far, we have 4 dead bodies, Troy, and it's just by good luck that we are not among them, since the hail of bullets coming through the door in Mr. Thompson's small flat were certainly meant to wipe us out, too."

"Whatever it is, it's big. They have shown us that they will kill, without remorse, everything in their way. We must stop these cold-blooded savages."

"Let's get out of here before they decide to return to take something else. Time to go see Mr. Jacob Graham," ordered Karla.

Troy gave her a look and responded, "Well, let's hope he's still in one piece."

On Wickham Street, they got into a cab, which they asked to take them to several locations. After about an hour, they got out and walked the several blocks to a car-rental agency. Soon enough they were on the M40 Motorway on the two-hour northwesterly drive to Birmingham.

The drive afforded them an excellent opportunity to forward photos of all the intel they had collected in the past 48 hours to Admiral Ferris back at Dover AFB, with plenty of commentary and analysis. For the rest of the trip, Karla and Troy just chit-chatted. Admiral Ferris messaged back that he would contact them again ASAP.

An encrypted call came in when they were about 15 minutes from Birmingham. It was the Admiral. "Karla, I take it both of you are in good spirits, given the circumstances?"

"Yes, sir — it's like taking candy from a baby. We'll handle whatever comes our way, sir."

"Glad to hear that, Lieutenant. We ran a check on the assassin who died in the attack at Mr. Thompson's flat. CIA has an extensive file on this demon. He was a professional contract assassin from Iran. MI6, Israel's Mossad, and even Albania's State Intelligence Service have files on this guy — seems he's been killing people all over the globe for a long time."

"Admiral, I'm sure he's just one of many. What's your take on the three cadavers in the basement?" inquired Troy.

"We thought this was just going to be a clean intelligence-gathering operation, but it seems you and Karla have stumbled upon a very deadly conspiracy. With so many dead bodies, there's bound to be an extremely important plan in the works here. Something way beyond earthquake analysis and prediction. Proceed with extreme caution."

"Thank you, sir," said Karla. "But, sir, if you don't mind my asking, we are getting closer to the enemy, and we certainly need more firepower. Semi-automatic pistols just won't cut the mustard. What can be done?"

There was silence for a moment on the Admiral's end. "That's a very good point, Lieutenant. We have two safe houses in Birmingham. I will contact one that is able to meet you at a specified location and re-supply you with automatic weapons. Will send you a message within five minutes."

Troy looked at Karla and gave her a look of approval for making such a timely request.

They were in Birmingham, already on the A38, near Queen Elizabeth Hospital, when the message came in. Instructions indicated they were to go to a specific location within 20 minutes and meet an agent in a blue Ford sedan with a chalk mark on the front and the back. The transaction was uneventful; the agent gave them a large, black gym bag, very heavy, and he was gone. Troy opened the bag and found two bullet-proof vests, which they put on right away. There also were two Israeli Uzi submachine guns with shoulder holsters for concealed carry. One Uzi was chambered for .45 caliber, with a 16-round clip, the other for 9mm, with a 32-round clip. At the bottom of the bag was one Benelli M4 Super 90, 12-gauge, semi-auto shotgun, capable of blowing away a whole door with one blast. Only then did Troy and Karla realize how terribly outgunned they had been. They had come to London to ask some questions, but they had interrupted a ruthless conspiracy.

They traveled the fifteen minutes to the Worcester Hotel to locate Jacob Graham, Mr. Thompson's colleague. Karla and Troy knew only that he had registered as Peter. To make matters worse, Mr. Graham did not know they were coming to meet him. He was already overly suspicious, perhaps even paranoid, and in hiding. It was going to be tough to get him to let them in.

Beautiful yet simple, the Hotel Worcester had a gorgeous white-stone fountain in front, surrounded by various types of flowers and a couple of benches for the guests to enjoy the soothing sound of the dancing waters. Inside, the lobby was spacious, adorned with hanging plants, art reproductions, and plenty of seating for relaxation. Families with children coming and going gave the whole place a very friendly ambience. The coffee shop connected to the lobby filled the whole area with its magical, just-brewed coffee aroma. Hardly the place to transact the brutish business Troy and Karla had to deal with.

Troy entered the lobby first, Karla about 30 seconds later. He went to the sitting area; she went directly to the front desk. Karla had selected the younger attendant in the hope that she could cajole him more easily.

"Excuse me, er, Roger, but I came here to meet my client, Peter — if you know what I mean."

"Sure — and his last name or room number?"

"You know, I wrote it down, but I can't seem to find that little piece of paper. Just look in your register. He's there, named Peter, and as handsome as you. He doesn't like to wait, Roger. Please."

"I'm sorry, ma'am, but management has admonished us about letting this kind of, you know, transaction in this hotel, you understand," stuttered Roger, looking worried already.

Quickly changing her demeanor and strategy, she continued, "Oh, of course, Roger. And I am glad that you maintain high standards here — you are a young man of good principles. I am a private nurse, and I am here to give him his insulin injection. He phoned our clinic and said that he was feeling his sugar levels were getting high. You certainly would not want to be accused later of having rejected medical help for a guest, would you? So what's the room number? I'll be out of here in 10 minutes."

"Okay, it's 317. Please hurry. I hear that people can die if they don't get their insulin."

"You're a good man, Roger," quipped Karla.

Troy got up from his nearby comfortable seat and wordlessly met Karla by the elevator. *Nice job with the front desk clerk*, he thought, and his smile told her so. Her eyes accepted the compliment.

Troy knocked softly on door 317. No answer. He knocked again. No answer. Troy whispered, "Hello, Mr. Jacob Graham. We are from Navy Intelligence in Dover, Delaware. You're in grave danger. We're here to help." No answer. "We will step back from your door so you can get a good look at us through the door's peep hole." Karla thought she heard some noise inside. She gave it another try, in a whisper.

"Mr. Graham, my name is Karla Bloomfield; my colleague here is Troy Hamilton. We are here to help you. Do you have a question for us?"

All the while, Troy kept looking left and right on the hallway to make sure there were no other people approaching. Still, no answer.

"Come on, Mr. Graham, we know you're scared and wondering whether you can trust us. Ask us something, anything," reiterated Karla.

Finally, the voice in the room said, "Slip me an ID under the door."

Troy complied.

He returned Troy's ID. "So what do want with me?"

"We know you work with Geophysical Dynamics Corp, that you designed some incredible apparatus, that some very nasty people have been torment-ing you and your staff, and that you are in hiding. Are we correct so far?" prompted Karla.

"How do I know you're not here to kill me?"

Karla took the initiative. "You have a point — you don't know. I'll tell you what. We are intelligence officers, so we are armed. If I let you have my loaded service pistol, will that make you feel a bit safer?"

"Set it on the floor, resting against the door, and step away," mumbled Mr. Graham.

Troy and Karla knew that they could be as far as about 10 feet from the door and the fisheye lens of the peep hole could still catch of good view of them for Mr. Graham. For his comfort, that is. The door opened slightly with the chain still secured, and the gun was retrieved by a trembling hand. If this play did not pan out, Karla would be out of her gun and would have to account for that in Dover. They both approached the door.

"It's loaded, Mr. Graham. Don't put your finger on the trigger. It's very sensitive," she warned.

"Now, unlock the door, and step back. You can point the gun at us, if you wish, but don't put that finger on the trigger. We will step in very slowly," advised Troy.

"Come in."

They entered ever so slowly and closed the door behind them. Finally, they were face-to-face with Jacob Graham, probably the only human left on Earth who could shed some light on this murderous mystery full of ruthless assassins.

Jacob appeared to be in his early 40s, balding, about 5'11", stocky, unshaven, wearing rumpled clothes and wire-rimmed glasses. He looked like a worried mathematics professor who had secluded himself to work quietly but passionately on Fermat's Theorem about the Pythagorean formula.

The room was tidy and clean. Th bed was made, beige curtains were drawn, carpet looked well-kept. Ivory-colored walls gave it a bright look. There were some files and folded blueprints on the dresser. It smelled a bit musty, probably from the lack of ventilation.

Karla and Troy sat at the table, Jacob on the bed, with the gun still pointing toward them, finger resting on the slide, not on the trigger.

Karla started to explain. "Thank you, Mr. Graham, for letting us in. We are not here to hurt you. We've come to help you. Like we said, you are in grave danger."

"Yeah, but how's Ben doing? He's hiding out in London," interrupted Mr. Graham.

Troy responded. "I am sorry to tell you that Mr. Thompson is dead. We were talking with him at his Pemberton flat when two or more assassins shot through the door and killed him. We returned fire quickly, but Mr. Thompson had already been hit."

Mr. Graham looked at the floor momentarily. "That is terrible. He is, was, my good friend." A few moments later he continued, with a worried look creasing his forehead. "So does that mean I'm next?"

"It's a matter of time. These savages are not common criminals. They are well-connected and have huge resources helping them. They probably represent some hostile foreign government that will stop at nothing," Karla explained.

"I told Ben not to trust that foreign-looking businessman who came to our lab about three weeks ago, claiming he was interested in investing in our private company."

"But investing in what, exactly?" asked Troy.

"He was dressed like a Londoner businessman, but he asked too many technical questions. It gave me the impression he already knew far too much about what we were trying to do."

There was a firm knock on the door.

In an instant, Troy and Karla drew their Uzi submachine guns, went to the floor, and ordered Mr. Graham to get on the floor on the far side of the bed. They were ready to unleash fiery hell at the intruders. But Mr. Graham whispered, "Cool it — I think it's the lunch room service I ordered."

And it was. Mr. Graham told the room-service person to just leave it outside and charge it to the room.

He returned the pistol to Karla, comfortably convinced they were not there to harm him in any way. But this tense little false alarm at the door reminded Troy and Karla that they were very vulnerable there in the hotel. They had already asked the Admiral earlier in the day if they could take Jacob Graham to a safe house there in Birmingham, given the ferocity of the attack against Benjamin Thompson the previous day, and he had approved. Karla discussed the plan with Mr. Graham, and he quickly agreed.

Now, how to get him to their car? The rendezvous location with the safe house agents was at a cemetery about 30 minutes away. Karla decided to go out first to bring the car directly to the front entrance of the hotel.

Four minutes later, Troy and Mr. Graham left the room, walked downstairs, and got into the car with no incidents. Then they sped away. Troy spotted the black gym bag in the back seat. *Karla thinks of everything*, he mused.

Karla was driving at moderate motorway speeds to the meeting place on the northeast corner of Handsworth Cemetery, when, suddenly, two sniper bullets in rapid succession came through the windshield — one high, one low, in the center area between Troy and Karla. Immediately Troy glanced at the back seat, but, fortunately, Mr. Graham was sitting directly in back of Karla, and the bullets went right through the back seat.

"Troy, did you see where they came from?" shrieked Karla as she attempted to keep control of the car after being shocked by the bullets. Troy unholstered his .45 caliber Uzi and glanced at all the vehicles in front of their car, but he couldn't see anything suspicious. "No, nothing. Just a white van far ahead of us, maybe 100 yards."

In the back seat, Mr. Graham started screaming, "Oh, my God, we're all going to die! We're all going to die! God help us!"

"Just stay down!" Karla ordered.

"Anything, Troy? Where are these damned bastards! Fucking cowards!" She began to accelerate in the hope of leaving the problem behind, but three more shots hit their car in the area of the front fenders and the rear quarter panels. Now they were desperate and almost in a panic, for they couldn't locate the sniper or snipers. They both felt it was just a matter of time before the bullets hit their mark. Other vehicles soon began to go to the shoulders or exit altogether to avoid the deadly drama unfolding on the motorway. All, that is, except for a red van about 50 yards behind them.

"Accelerate, accelerate — I think they're in the red van behind us!" screamed Troy, and Karla floored the gas pedal, the 6-cylinder engine growling like a furious lion. In the back seat Mr. Graham was whimpering and praying, asking God to take all three of them out of this horrible situation.

The car's engine was roaring at full RPM to leave the red van behind, with Karla looking left and right and every which way to plan and anticipate any steering moves she might have to execute on a second's notice. That second came too soon, for they both saw that the white van ahead of them had no glass on the two rear windows and that there were two rifle barrels now sticking out of them. She steered the car sporadically left and right to make it a more difficult target, then hard right, soft right, but the van in the rear was catching up. Karla steered with her left hand; in her right, she now had her 9mm Uzi, which she brought into action with a volley of bullets, spent casings flying off in formation. Her bullets found their target and peppered the rear doors of the van ahead. Troy, too, decided it was time to fight back, and he risked leaning out the passenger window to unload a full automatic procession of hot bullets at the van in the rear, but they were now shooting back at them with automatics.

The situation was getting desperate. How could they handle very hostile enemies upwind and down?

Troy thought of something. He got the Benelli shotgun from the rear and quickly loaded it with military-grade, magnum 12-gauge, 00 buckshot, brutal enough to cut down a tree in one blast. Karla slowed sufficiently to permit the rear van to catch up, then swerved to the right and braked hard, like their lives depended on it. As the red van aligned with Troy, he was ready, and he blasted the driver through the van window five times in quick succession, as fast as the shotgun reloaded itself. Troy could see that the inside of the van had turned crimson red from the vast amounts of blood and dripping human tissue that had exploded in the process. Most of the van's door had also disappeared due to the hellish and unforgiving effects of the 00 magnum buckshot, and the van quickly came to a stop way behind them.

Karla could barely process the swiftness of the many things that were happening around her, but she did notice that the two snipers in the forward van were still shooting at them — the windshield already had five holes on it, and the car radiator was spewing high-pressure steam. Surely it had been hit at least once.

She yelled, "Troy, the radiator's been hit — we can't go much farther!"

"Find a way off this road, now!" Troy screamed back.

Instantly, Karla swerved to the left, hit the curb hard, went flying about five feet off the ground, landed on a grassy area, and spun around maybe twice. Within a few seconds, she regained her bearings and quickly got on the exit ramp coming off the motorway. Again she floored the gas pedal as Troy warned, "Those damned bastards stopped the white van. Wait — yes, they're turning around and heading this way!"

This time, their car did not roar; there was no more steam coming off the engine. "We have to get out of this car and seek cover, maybe within one minute," urged Karla.

They noticed that the exit ramp had brought them to a dilapidated industrial area. No choice. Karla drove the car around a building that looked like a factory, looking to maybe hide it quickly. She went into a truck-loading area, and all three of them ran from the vehicle into the factory.

"Mr. Graham, here's my gun, loaded and ready to fire. You have 19 bullets. Try to keep count. You have no choice. Keep your finger off the trigger until you are ready to fire. Shoot only if the enemy is within 10 yards and coming toward you. Do you understand?" spelled Troy in an urgent tone. Mr. Graham was trembling, but he nodded his head in agreement.

Karla quickly determined that they needed to know how many assassins were in the van, so they selected strategic windows up on the second floor. Five mean-looking, muscular men got out — two had sniper rifles, and the other three had weapons that appeared to be Czech CZ-Scorpion submachine guns, reliable and accurate, adopted by many military services around the world. With automatic weapons like that, these cutthroats had a clear advantage. Yes, they did look like Iranians. In fact, like Iranians angry that their comrades-in-assassination had been wiped out. They were bent not just on killing their prey but on killing them with vengeance, with hatred, with pleasure, with a deep primal need to destroy and eradicate something from this Earth. These were the savage assassins from hell. Who had sent these fiends?

Troy and Karla knew they were the underdogs — and by a wide margin. So they figured their best chance was to take the offensive. They quietly took posts on the balcony of that second floor and waited for the five hit men on the ground floor to walk into view. And when they did, Karla and Troy opened fire with a continuous barrage of bullets from their fully loaded Uzis. Almost instantly, the assassins returned fire with their Scorpion automatics, and the small factory area was suddenly permeated by the sound of five machine guns simultaneously spewing bullets at a combined rate of 3000 rounds per minute — a deafening roar that made even the sturdy metal floor vibrate.

Bullets were ricocheting all over the place, so there were impact pieces of wall and ceiling floating and falling and bouncing. Windows were shattering and raining dangerous shards of glass.

One assassin lay motionless on the floor, but the two snipers were now behind roof-support columns, taking deadly accurate aim at their prey on the balcony, a mere 30-yard shot. As soon as Troy and Karla lowered their heads, two rounds, about one second apart, whizzed above them and impacted on the wall behind, creating lunar-type craters the size of large, flour tortillas. From the sound of them, each projectile was big enough to take down a raging rhinoceros.

They saw the attackers walking up the steel stairs that led to the second floor, taking turns firing in automatic mode to provide cover. It was time to retreat. Troy, Karla, and Mr. Graham ran toward the far end of the second floor, where they had spotted another set of stairs. Karla led while Troy provided the back-door cover, firing sporadically behind him to delay the advance of the Iranian assassin squad.

The stairs proved to be a challenge because they appeared to go to a level that was between the first and second floors, not visible from either. They soon got to a heavy steel door that they were able to secure behind them. Now they were worried because they could not hear the assassins. Since they were at a grave disadvantage, they had to get out of the factory building as soon as possible. Soon they located an open window that was about 12 feet off the outside ground and decided that this was their way out. Troy hung his Uzi's sling around his shoulder and jumped first. At that exact moment, one sniper's bullet from another section of the L-shaped building reached him, and, when he hit the ground, he was already stunned or dead. Karla and Mr. Graham retreated from the window under a new barrage of automatic fire coming from the same direction. They weren't exactly sure if Troy had been hit by a bullet or if he had hit his head when he landed, but he wasn't moving when they retreated.

Troy came to after just a few seconds and checked his body. The sniper's .308 caliber high-powered bullet had hit and penetrated his Uzi all the way through, coming out the other side, and delivering the rest of its kinetic energy to Troy's protective vest. That impact had knocked the wind out of him. Immediately he knew that his Uzi had been destroyed, so he dumped it.

Now unarmed, he quickly scrambled to find cover as bullets were hitting the ground just about a foot from where he was. Large, steel trash containers offered the best protection. But he needed to get back inside to help Mr. Graham and Karla. He found a ground-floor window unlocked and climbed in.

As he quietly crept along hallways and machine rooms, he came upon a large collection of wood pallets stacked neatly about ten feet high, and, through the spaces between them, he could see the back of one of the snipers in a shooting position, pointing at the second-floor balcony. Having no gun, he had to improvise, so he grabbed a large, adjustable crescent wrench and quietly but quickly made headway to attack the sniper from behind. With the wrench high in the air, he advanced quickly. He would have delivered a fatal head blow to his enemy, but he did not take into account that his shadow arrived there before he did, enough to allow the Iranian to block the blow with his huge lumberjack arm. The struggle for life and death was on.

Troy still had the wrench tightly gripped in his hand, so he delivered two more blows that struck the assassin on the arm again and then on his ribs. In defending himself, the madman had dropped his sniper rifle, so now he went after Troy with his huge bare hands. The two combatants exchanged many blows to the chest and face, so, pretty soon, they were both bloodied and breathing heavily. Time was on the assassin's side, since his associates would hear the commotion and come running. Troy had to exert maximum effort to try to finish the battle even though he was fighting mostly a defensive battle, trying heroically to avoid a body grip by this bear-sized killing machine. The assassin gave Troy a lucky punch to the jaw that sent him dazed to the floor. The madman then straddled Troy and kept beating him on the face, creating a bloody mess. Troy felt an object under his hip, and, yes, it was the wrench — his last chance because he did not have the strength to get this monster off. He reached for it and swung it with all his remaining strength, striking the assassin on his left temple with the heavier, jaw end of the wrench. Troy slithered out from under the now-limp-but-still-moving body. He turned him over and straddled the enemy, and with a fury he did not know he had in him, he beat his face over and over again with the wrench, until it was no longer recognizable. He got off and sat against the wall, breathing as if he had just run five desperate blocks to catch the last train on a snowy night.

He was spitting blood, had two loose teeth, his vision was slightly blurred, he had a ringing in his ears, his nose was gushing blood, and his hands were trembling. He had never come this close to sure death. But where was Karla?

After he got up, he looked for the rifle the sniper had been using but found out that it had fallen and gotten stuck in a deep groove on the cement floor, a channel that guided the steel wheels of the mobile crane in that production area.

So he slowly continued his search in that level of the factory. He seemed to get a bit better with every passing minute. Surely his military physical training was helping him to cope with the brutal beating he had just endured.

Within about two minutes, he came to another section of the factory and heard some voices. He still had the crescent wrench. He got closer. It was Karla's voice, and she was responding to one of the killers. Troy felt immediately that this could not possibly be good. "Come on, you American bitch. Where is that Mr. Graham, the earthquake genius? We saw all three of you. Where did you hide him?"

"I'm telling you the truth. We were all running in different directions, and I don't know where he went!"

"Why is it that I don't believe your pretty lips?"

"This has gone far enough. If I knew where he was, I would gladly tell you so that I could go home. Believe me."

"We were told to bring him in alive. He has all the knowledge we need. So I guess I am going to have to convince you to tell me where he is, you American no-good whore."

From his hiding position, Troy asked himself why Karla was even answering questions. She must have been subdued. And something bad was about to be done to her.

Troy took a peek at the room. Karla was kneeling in the middle of the dingy, foul-smelling room, her shoulder bleeding from what appeared to be a six-inch cut. Her tormentor and interrogator was standing behind her, with his gun in one hand and a deadly-looking curved knife in the other, a knife like the one used to swiftly remove all the innards in cattle slaughter houses. Her safety vest had already been removed and was not visible anywhere.

"Let me see if I can jar your memory a little bit, worthless slut. Take off your blouse."

"Look, I already told you — I don't know where he is!"

The power-hungry maniac, infuriated by her non-compliance, swung the curved knife swiftly at her other shoulder, this time cutting into her about nine inches. Her skin and flesh quickly parted on both sides of the deep cut, and Karla let out an agonizing scream.

"You will obey me, bitch. Don't make me cut up your American face. Now take off that blouse." Karla complied. She was now kneeling, in her bra, with blood running down both arms and her back.

Troy wanted to do something, but at that distance and with only that wrench, he felt completely powerless.

The ruthless sadist walked in front of Karla. "Let's see now. Not bad. Mmm — I might have some plans for you after this is all over. Now, where is the scientist?"

"Please, please believe me when I tell you I don't know. Please, I have no reason to lie to you," pleaded Karla.

"American bitch, do you know what the next step is? I am going to cut the back strap of your tit-cover with this knife. I am going to play with your tits for about a minute. And then, if that does not work, I will slice you between your legs. Lots of blood, you die quickly — believe me. Done it before."

Troy had had enough. He took a gamble and stepped out into the room.

Immediately pointing the gun at Troy, the assassin exclaimed, "Ah, soldier boy, you want to hurt me with that wrench? Drop it or you die right now." Troy complied and said, "Look, you have to believe her when she says she doesn't know. Not even I know where Mr. Graham went. Just let her go. She's just a stenographer. Take me instead."

"Do you think I am that stupid? Kneel down, soldier boy. I am going to tie you down, and then I will show this American whore what it feels like to have a real man inside her. And when I finish, I will thrust this knife between her legs and give it a couple of turns. It's quick, it's fun. I like to watch the squirting blood."

It seemed rather hopeless. Troy had played his only card, expecting to get Karla released. No luck. Now both of them were captives.

Just then, Mr. Graham crept from between two large crates where he had been hiding, and, as the beast was unwinding some rope, he pointed the gun, placed his finger on the trigger, and fired one single bullet into the back of the madman. He fell on his back, fully conscious but stunned by the impact, his abundant muscles having stopped the bullet before it penetrated too deeply. Karla quickly got up, grabbed the gun from Mr. Graham, and stood at the feet of her tormentor.

"'American bitch,' eh? You mother-fucking, worthless cockroach!" And, with that, she blasted five quick, explosive rounds into his face and seven more into his crotch. "No more sadistic abuse of women, you piece of shit!" Troy and Mr. Graham just stood by, stunned by Karla's indignant ferocity.

She was still trembling when it was all over, for never in her life had she mentally prepared herself to be inevitably raped and to have her insides butchered by a curved steel blade. The preparation itself was almost like the real thing — traumatic, disgusting, and nauseating.

Karla was trying to compose herself when she looked at Troy's bloody face and asked softly, "Lieutenant, what happened to you?"

"Met up with one of them, big guy, about 275 pounds. He had me on the floor, pounding away at my face, as you can see, but I hit him with a wrench. He won't bother us anymore."

Mr. Graham picked up Karla's torn and bloody blouse from the floor and handed it to her. "I'm sorry, Karla. I didn't want to shoot him, but, at the same time, I felt I had to take some action."

"Don't feel bad, Mr. Graham. You probably saved our lives. You did the right thing," she replied with a painful smile and gave him back Troy's pistol.

As she was trying to put her blouse back on, Karla's attention was immediately commanded by the two painful knife wounds on her shoulders and back.

Troy took a close look at them and suggested, "These cuts look deep enough to require stitches and some antibiotics. We'll have to get you to a doctor pretty soon." He took off the T-shirt he was wearing under his blue shirt, cut it into two pieces, and placed them on her wounds to help stop the bleeding and to provide some chaffing protection from the blouse.

"Look, we really don't have much time. The other assassins surely heard the gunshots and must be coming this way. We gotta get out of this factory now," Troy insisted.

Mr. Graham suggested to both of them, "Both of you are in bad shape and can't run fast enough to get away away from these bad guys. I can't run too fast, either. My legs are trembling and are feeling like noodles. Shouldn't we at least try to see if the guy on the floor has the keys to the van?"

Troy checked, but nothing. Took his wallet as potential intelligence material. He thought of the other thug, the one he had finished off with the wrench. Soon they had made their way to that area, and Troy promptly advised both Karla and Mr. Graham not to look at the face of the dead assassin. Mr. Graham complied, but Karla wanted to see how Troy had defended himself against this gorilla-sized attacker. It was a bloody mess, unrecognizable as a face. Looked more like a smorgasbord of different chopped meats, colorful vegetables, and extra tomato sauce — just like a medium-sized pizza with everything on it. *He deserved it*, she thought.

"We got 'em!" exclaimed Troy as he pulled out a set of keys from the man's pocket. Pulled out the wallet, too. But they heard metal clanging, perhaps on the stairs, and not too far away. They had to hurry. Well, they slowly hurried.

Even though his vision was slightly impaired, Troy got behind the wheel of the van, Mr. Graham got in on the front passenger side, gun still in hand, finger not on the trigger. Karla wanted the entire back seat to herself to lie down. The stinging, burning pain of her cuts was getting intense; her blouse was now soaked with blood.

"Karla, are you okay?" Troy asked.

"Sure, Troy, it was like child's play," she mumbled softly, her voice trailing off into a whisper.

Troy asked if everybody was ready, for he knew that the roar of the starting engine would alert the remaining two assassins. He started the engine, put the van in reverse, and started moving away from the building. Just then, two steel doors on a delivery ramp burst open. It was them!

Just as Troy put the van's transmission into drive, the two attackers opened fire with a barrage of bullets from their automatic sub-machine guns, hitting the accelerating van everywhere and causing windows to explode and spew flying glass all over the inside. The impacts inside the van sounded like *ping, ping, ping, ping.* Dozens of times. He swerved left and right to make it more difficult for the assassins to take good aim, but he could already feel that perhaps one or both of the rear tires had been hit and were deflating rapidly. *Maybe five minutes*, he figured, so he drove in a direction where they could ditch the van and grab a cab.

In three minutes, the van's rear tires were completely flat, and the vehicle was fishtailing at a high speed. He wanted to put as much distance as possible between the madmen and the van, but he also knew that every passing minute increased the chances that he would lose control of the vehicle. Two simultaneous processes — one good, one bad — and he had to find the right balance between the two. Finally he parked the van in an inobtrusive space behind a building in a very populated business area, and they hailed a Black Cab.

While in the cab, Troy called Admiral Ferris in Dover, explained briefly what had happened, and requested an emergency pick-up by safe-house personnel at some location — a sort of friendly extraction. After about a minute, the Admiral gave Troy the location of a park where military agents would pick them up. Karla was getting worse, and quickly.

When the safe house vehicle showed up at the park, both parties exchanged passwords. Karla, Troy, and Mr. Graham had to wear black hoods over their heads to preserve the secure location of the safe house. While in the van, Troy had to hold Karla since she had already become too weak to sit upright by herself. Soon they were inside the safe house, surrounded by heavily armed Navy and CIA personnel. Finally, they could feel safe again.

Mr. Graham started whimpering. "I have never felt so totally terrified, so near the end of my life."

CHAPTER 5

It had been pre-arranged to have a military doctor on hand to treat all three visitors. Triage procedures required that Karla be treated first. She needed about 20 stitches on her two cuts, antibiotics, strong analgesics, and transfusions to replace the blood she had lost. Troy was quickly treated for abrasions and contusions on his face. It was his macho ego that had suffered the most from the beating he had taken. And Mr. Graham needed very little — just alcohol, iodine, and a few bandages for his various cuts due to flying glass.

This Birmingham safe house was much like all others. Various meeting rooms, kitchen, an electronic communications center, and maybe three bedrooms, including one general one with bunk beds. Those in charge had obviously consulted with an interior decorator because all wall colors were soft and pleasing, and they blended well with the curtains that covered the non-windows.

After dinner, the CIA on-site safe house coordinator, Braxton Millstone — short, never married, in his 50s, and slightly paunchy — introduced himself, welcoming all three to his "well-run" safe house.

"I certainly hope all of you have been well taken care of here. Rule #1 is no cell phone calls, for security purposes. And, just in case some of you forget that rule, there are signal jammers in all areas of this place. If we detect that you have attempted to use your phone, we will take it away from you whether you like it or not. And I see we have a female on board. No sexual contact, no romantic scenes, no hand-holding, no low-cut blouses, no sitting with your legs open so others can see your undergarments, and no lipstick — it entices others to behave immorally and fail in their duty. Please, ma'am, be modest. And that goes for the men, too. When you go to the urinals, please refrain

43

from trying to catch a glimpse of the private parts of someone who might be using the adjacent urinal. I know how easy it is to get the urge to peek, but control yourself. Respect their privacy. I'm in charge here, so you are going to live by my rules as long as you are a visitor here. The rest of the rules are clearly posted on several walls throughout the house. You have been cleared to be here for 48 hours, but you must leave before then if possible. I will see you again tomorrow morning for a short meeting. Enjoy your evening."

Agent Millstone's monologue was in character, for he was known for his brashness, lack of interpersonal sensitivity, and strange adherence to some weird sexual code meant to rid the agency of what he believed were rampant sexual improprieties and sinfulness. Originally assigned to the very important London CIA station, he'd blown many field assignments because his need to control others above anything else had gotten the best of him. After many of his colleagues secretly complained that he was unwittingly putting their lives in danger, the station chief had re-assigned him to this safe house in Birmingham. Here, he could nourish his delusion that he was king, controlling others to a great degree, and expressing his long-standing subconscious sexual repression as a moral imperative to do what was right for the agency he so loved. Many agency officers considered him a borderline, but functioning, psychotic, and wondered just how he could have gotten into the CIA training program at Langley to begin with. They figured he must have had some other powerful kings in Washington pulling strings at the CIA on his behalf.

Niether Troy, Mr. Graham, nor Karla could not believe that this man was in charge of the safe house. Worse, how could he possibly still be part of the CIA? Whispering among themselves, they voiced the opinion that it would be foolhardy to divulge any information about the current case to him. They tacitly agreed not to reveal anything.

They relaxed in the lounge area for a while, nursing their wounds and pain. Sitting in an oversized easy chair, Karla gave Troy an oblique look.

"What is it, Lieutenant?" queried Troy, feeling there was something to be concerned about, for he knew that look.

"Thanks for trying to save me back there at that factory from hell, but I have never been a stenographer and never will, Lieutenant Mr. Wrench!" she rebutted.

"Yeah, I know, but it was worth being a stenographer for just a few seconds while Mr. Graham finally got the nerve to come out shooting, wouldn't you think, Lieutenant Shoot-'em-in-the-Balls?" Troy fired back, with a smirk. That produced a half-smile from Karla, but her eyes were saying, "I don't take no shit!" She turned.

"Mr. Graham, do you have a family, wife, kids?" asked Karla, grimacing a bit from her pain.

"Divorced, no kids. Married young, spent too much time at the lab, so she got tired of me. Given my current circumstances, maybe I should have gone into architecture or pharmacy. And you, Karla?"

"No, never married. The Navy is still my first love. Right now, it may not seem like it, but I love what I do. I love seismology."

"How 'bout you, Troy? Do you have a wife or kids?" he continued.

"Me? No, never married. My work takes all my time. All I have to take care of really is just Arturo." Karla glanced at him with a concerned look, which she quickly tried to disguise.

"I thought you didn't have any kids," she challenged.

"Yeah, I don't. Arturo is my dear pet goldfish. He's all I've got," lamented Troy, as his eye contact with Karla became somewhat uncomfortable and he looked at Mr. Graham instead.

"Oh, that's great — a goldfish!" gushed Karla. She immediately heard her own words and wondered why she thought it was great when she really did not care at all about fishy-smelling pets. And she was not trying to be polite, either.

Suddenly, a grave look came over Mr. Graham's face. "I really think we need to talk about the problem." Troy and Karla took a quick and suspicious look around the lounge; they closed the door.

"Okay, let's start with the nature of what you do. How in the world were you able to get your earthquake prediction so damn accurate? That is unheard of!" exclaimed Troy.

"No other seismographic center in the world comes even close! When they predict, they say something will happen in the next few years," Karla added.

"It's not what you think. It's not prediction," said Mr. Graham as he looked at the wall but was really staring into space.

Troy and Karla were confused. *Isn't it a prediction when someone states that something will happen at such and such time and date, and then it happens?*

"We don't follow. Mr. Thompson sent a fax to our Naval Submarine Base in Groton, Connecticut, predicting one full week ahead of time the ocean-floor earthquake that became a reality just about three days ago. You knew about the fax, right?" asked Karla.

"Yes, we discussed it. We were desperate to get your government's attention, and that is why we added that thing about the European Advanced Earthquake Detection Center in London. We invented that part."

Still confused, Troy demanded, "Well, explain why your totally accurate prediction is not a prediction."

"Very simple. We didn't just predict the earthquake — we deliberately caused the earthquake at that exact moment and at that precise location."

Karla and Troy heard what Mr. Graham had said, but they didn't understand it. Or maybe didn't hear properly, or they misheard. It was as if Graham were speaking in Chinese. They would have reacted in the same manner if he had said, in all seriousness, that he had just converted an ant into a fully grown giraffe. Simply incomprehensible.

They just stared at him and at each other. This was Karla's field, so she jumped in. "You're saying that you deliberately caused an earthquake — and precisely where you wanted to?"

Mr. Graham looked at the floor and then nodded.

"But, that's not possible. I'm sure you know about the Earth's tectonic plates and how their abrupt movements is what causes earthquakes. Now, you tell me: How are you going to move these gargantuan plates, which weigh almost as much as the moon? It's just not possible!"

"Karla, I know it's hard to believe, but why do you think these cutthroat assassins are after us? They are the ones who forced us to produce that quake. They were there. They told us where they wanted it. They told us at what time they wanted it. They personally witnessed the first man-made underwater quake. They know this is real, and they want the technology at any cost!"

And with that explanation, Karla and Troy started to believe what Graham was saying. It was like August 1945 and the dawn of the atomic age when an awesome, destructive force was unleashed upon Hiroshima and Nagasaki. It had the potential to bring an end to life upon the entire earth. That never-before-heard-of cataclysmic force had been devised and harnessed, and it would alter the course of civilizations. And now, here, again, was the dawn of a new device, not for the good of mankind, but for the precise destruction of entire continents. How could the Earth itself survive when entire sections of it are summarily being destroyed?

The conversation slowed to a crawl as Troy and Karla remained stunned by what Graham was saying. Scenarios, mostly having to do with Armageddon, played in their heads, with a country carrying out the total annihilation of an entire enemy continent and its culture by creating a surgically planned earthquake. It would take minutes to carry out. No military force on earth could counteract that. Whatever country had this device would be the undisputed and absolute ruler — there would be no need for accords, or treaties, or even diplomacy. International law would become irrelevant. Any country or continent not complying with demands from the ruler would be annihilated in minutes. Never had apocalypse been so real, so close in the near future.

"Mr. Graham, I was beginning to think of you as a personable and responsible human being, but what you're telling us right now makes me feel you are, in fact, a monster. What have you done? What the hell were you thinking of?" exclaimed Karla. Troy now knew for sure that Admiral Ferris back in Dover had had the right gut instinct in saying that something very sinister was going on.

"I can't blame you for feeling that way, and you are right to condemn me. As things stand right now, I feel I don't even deserve to live because of what we have created, although that was not our original intent."

"Well, explain yourself before we turn you in to the FBI. You are responsible for the deaths of hundreds of thousands of innocent people! You deliberately killed these innocents! You caused billions of dollars of damage and untold pain and suffering for millions of survivors!" screeched Karla.

"Look, you're right. We — or I, now that Ben Thompson is dead — am responsible for this horrible calamity, and, if you want to prosecute me, please do so. I would not contest any of the charges and would actually welcome the death penalty. I really don't deserve to live. I'm sorry. This thing got out of hand. Been thinking of suicide but also thought that it would not be fair — your courts must have the opportunity to judge me."

"You're damned right, Graham. You and I both studied geophysics and seismology because we felt we could use that knowledge to better mankind — not to destroy the Earth. I still can't fathom your motivation," complained Karla.

"There's nothing I can add to help reduce our guilt or responsibility."

"So now, tell us — what does your device do?" quizzed Karla.

"Many years ago, Thompson and I studied the tectonic-plate theory of earthquakes. You know, how the giant plates on which continents rest are forever moving against each other, and how they oftentimes snag each other, and then the forces build up. Well, when the built-up force is too great, the opposing plates suddenly release and shear each other at the point of contact, which can be thousands of miles long. This sudden release and movement is transmitted to the surface and is felt as a devastating earthquake."

Karla seemed bored with his elementary explanation, but she thought it best not to say anything, since the lecture might be educational for Troy. "Okay. Continue, Graham."

"About two years ago, Thompson and I figured that the real cause of earthquakes was not that the plates release but rather that they release suddenly. So naturally we wondered if there was a way to cause the plates to constantly release, gradually, so that they never have to snag and build up destructive pent-up energies. With our model, there would never again be an earthquake.

Only imperceptibly small and natural movement, like the rotation of the Earth. No more destruction. We wanted to help the people of the world."

Just then there was a knock on the door, and Millstone walked right in. Everybody prepared for another sermon. "Glad to see you all are socializing, but just a friendly reminder that we have about one hour left until our 'lights out' for visitors. Through the years, we have found that this policy is sensible, since most visitors are here because they are living under stress. Sleep is good to help your body recover. The floor manager will show you your bunks, but there will be a separate bedroom for the lady, just in case some of you tend to get horny at night. We will not tolerate any improprieties. Enjoy your evening."

Karla just rolled her eyes. *He is hopeless*, they all thought.

Troy responded to what Graham had said before Millstone walked in. "So, in actuality, you were working on a method or technique of allowing tectonic plates to move constantly and ever so slightly, without snagging?" cited Troy. Graham nodded.

"That seems like a monumental task," Karla interjected. "Some plates can be as thick as 75 miles and rub against another plate for a length of a thousand miles. A quick calculation will tell you that the abrasion area would be about 75,000 square miles. The static and dynamic friction, Graham, would be absolutely enormous — heck, inconceivable by the human mind."

"Thompson and I were well aware of that. We weren't trying to go against that enormous frictional force you just mentioned. That would be like trying to drag a huge box, 75 miles wide by 1000 miles long, filled with boulders, across a sandpaper floor. It's not going to happen."

"So if you did not go against insurmountable friction, how did you figure to move one plate against the other?" interrupted Troy, with an air of frustration.

"And, Troy, not only move a plate, but they chose the biggest plate on Earth, the colossal Pacific plate pushing and crunching under the Philippine plate, deep beneath the ocean floor, under the Northern Mariana Islands," elaborated Karla with a sense of astonishment.

"Look," spoke Graham in a professorial manner, "you seem to be arguing why theoretically this is not physically possible and are forgetting that we already did it and that hostile agents or governments are out to kill us for it."

Karla and Troy remained silent for longer than usual. *Graham is right. We should not argue against the facts before us*, they thought.

"Let me explain," Graham continued. "As a physicist, I also have a background in lasers, neutrinos, and alpha-gamma ray generators. Even a small quantity of radioactive polonium produces enough particles that, when focused many millions of times, can penetrate through the entire Earth."

"Get to the point," Karla rudely interrupted. She was also worried that Millstone the Psychopath might soon return with another moral lesson.

"Sorry — I thought you wanted details. Okay, we have developed two complementary devices, separated by about 100 miles on land, that shoot neutrino and other radioactive rays, many times amplified, to a spot deep where the plates rub, and they create intense heat to melt away the two plates' leading edges so they do not snag. Advanced satellite guidance directs the coordinated movements of the two laser-like flows of particles so that they travel along the entire collision area of the two plates. Thompson and I named these two coordinated devices Geo-1 and Geo-2."

Troy and Karla were nonplussed, maybe not really believing what Graham had just said, but they remembered his admonition: Facts are facts.

Troy broke in. "Do you realize the incalculable military, strategic, social, political, and economic implications of what you have created?"

"Originally, we just wanted to slowly release the tension of the plates so that the movements were very small and maybe imperceptible, but these goons who showed up forced us to raise the power of the magnification to create a very rapid release of the snag, thereby causing a very large and abrupt movement of the plates — what happened in the Pacific."

"Tell us about 'the goons.' How did that come about?" asked Troy.

"About three weeks ago, an Iranian-looking man showed up at our lab, saying he had heard of some devices we were trying to produce…"

"Was he one of the men who were shooting at us?" Karla questioned.

"No, I would have recognized him. He said he wanted to invest in our company, but, as I said before, he was asking a lot of questions — and the right ones, too, as if he knew a lot about what we were doing. Said his name was Bitor Spinelli. He didn't look Italian to us. Was short, stocky, in his early 30s, appeared to have a three-day beard."

"Did he eventually invest?" asked Troy.

"We didn't get that far, and we doubted he really had that intention. After two days, Thompson and I decided that there was something fishy and sinister about him, so we told him we really were not looking for investors. His demeanor changed, like a Jekyll-and-Hyde, and he pulled out a gun, with a silencer."

"Did he say he would shoot you, kill you, or what?" queried Karla, eager to get more facts a lot more quickly.

"Certainly. He told us that he killed people for a living and that he would kill us as easily as he would squash a cockroach if we didn't do as he asked."

"What did he want?"

"He wanted Geo-1 and Geo-2, and our assistance in swiftly releasing the increasing tension between the two plates at the Mariana Trench in the Pacific. Thompson told him that it would be catastrophic to apply too much power, because then the release would be very quick. and an underwater earthquake would result."

"And what'd he say next?" uttered Troy.

"'That's the whole idea.'"

"We told him we could never do something like that. His face changed from sinister to diabolical. He asked us to call in one of our lab workers. We called Jim, who came in and sat near the couch where we were — we thought he would interrogate him. Without any warning, he shot Jim in the eye. The wall behind him was covered with blood and brain tissue slithering down. It was shocking. We were nauseated."

"I take it you then agreed to carry out his wishes?" Karla asked.

"Yes. Unfortunately, yes."

"These two devices, Graham — where were they at the time the seaquake was produced three days ago?" inquired Troy.

"After they killed Jim, we disconnected Geo-1 and -2 from the lab and all the monitoring equipment attached to them. As per their instructions, we put them in crates. He brought with him four assistants, also Iranian-looking."

"Do you know where the crates went?" continued Troy.

"Yes, of course — we had to be there to set them up and to calibrate everything for that specific satellite position. We took one to Gloucester, west of London, and the other to Crawley, south of London. The goons were there with us, but they said they had other associates near the Northern Mariana Islands to witness the earthquake and to check the time."

"So, Graham," interjected Karla, "I take it you then programmed Geo-1 and -2, and, at the exact moment, they sent what? A beam of neutrinos or gamma rays, or what?"

"Yes, basically. The particles in Geo-1, the lead device, are amplified millions of times, and they penetrate the ground in England, guided by satellite coordinates to a specific spot in the Mariana Trench. Simultaneously, Geo-2, the reactance device, also sends a complementary stream of powerful reacting particles that will collide with the stream of Geo-1 at precisely the assigned location, the Trench. This particle collision creates a temperature as hot as the sun and melts away the rubbing surfaces of the plates. Millions of times per second, the intersection of these two streams is readjusted by onboard computers to cover pretty much the entire area of contact between hostile tectonic plates."

Karla then asked Graham, "And what do Geo-1 and -2 look like, so we can recognize them if we see them?"

"They're not pretty or elegant. About the size of a large cabinet. Base is about 1.5 × 1.5 meters, with a height of about 2 meters. Lots of copper tubing, heavily insulated wires, three 30-cm copper-enamel wire coils, several sealed electronics boxes, two control panels with switches, and two 29-cm-diameter vertical pipes covered with heavy aluminum shielding, among other things. Each weighs about 225 kilograms."

Troy had a very worried look. "Can these assassins operate the devices?" He was afraid of the answer.

"Definitely not. Too complex. These machines require technical skills and knowledge like Thompson's and mine. Besides, all electronics are totally covered by a protective, non-conductive, semi-hard gel. Any attempt to remove it to decipher the components will damage the circuits."

Karla and Troy breathed a sigh of relief. It didn't last long.

"However, if Geo-1 and -2 are sent to a hostile government, their electronics and nuclear-particle-accelerator specialists will eventually figure everything out. So, it is just a matter of time."

"What's your best guess as to how long it would take?" asked Troy.

"Give it three weeks. And Armageddon will then be upon us."

"One thing is puzzling me, Graham," said Karla. "How did you and Thompson get away from these killers?"

"It wasn't easy. We were deathly afraid — they were always armed. But after Geo-1 and Geo-2 were programmed, we saw an opportunity to escape when one of them went to the toilet and the other one was drinking vodka at the table. Thompson faked that he was going to drink from the bottle but instead used it to strike the face of the guy sitting at the table. Two of his teeth went flying, and he fell to the floor. We ran out the front door just as the guy on the toilet came out and sent a hail of bullets in our direction. We could hear the buzz of the bullets all around us, but we did not stop. For about two hours, we hid in a wooded area while he went up and down the streets in his vehicle, searching. Both of us were trembling from the terror."

Karla asked, "Did you go back to the lab?"

"No, we immediately went into hiding. Thompson tried to warn your government by sending the exact location and time of the earthquake to your Groton Navy base. Obviously, no agency took that fax seriously."

Troy got up, walked around a bit, sat down and said, "It's clear we have a very serious situation on our hands, and we have to act quickly before those two devices leave England and end up perhaps in Iran or North Korea. God help us if they make it out."

"What's the next step?" stammered Karla.

"Graham will give me the exact location of the two places where the devices were activated, and we need to get there to destroy them. Humanity is just not ready to properly utilize machines like these, even if they were meant to do good and not evil."

"For now, let's all get some sleep. We will take on these bloodthirsty barbarians in the morning. Without a doubt, by now, their leaders know that *we* know, so they are regrouping with a lot more psychopath assassins and firepower. They have the mother lode. Let's hope that Geo-1 and -2 are still in the country, or the end of Western civilization won't be too far off!"

CHAPTER 6

Monday morning None of the three had slept well. It wasn't just that they had had a brutal Sunday, with all the shooting and blood and desperate escape measures. It wasn't just the ringing in their ears from the dozens of bullets that exploded from their guns and from the guns of the assassins. And it wasn't the painful injuries they had suffered. They were thinking about the viciousness of the assassins who had come after them, seemingly willing to take any and all risks to kill all three of them and to maintain possession of Geo-1 and -2.

Graham wasn't sure just what his role would be from this day on, since Troy had indicated, and rightly so, that the most urgent goal was to destroy the two devices before their technical specifications could be deciphered and duplicated by an enemy government or terrorist organization. Or worse, that these very machines would soon be used to destroy countries or even continents. It would not be easy to accomplish this search-and-destroy mission, for the devices would certainly be under heavy guard, by perhaps even a small army of sadistic cutthroats, Graham thought.

But he also knew that he was in mortal danger as the only surviving inventor with all the technical specifications of these earthquake-producing machines — all safely stored in his brain. Merciless Iranian mercenaries could kidnap him, ruthlessly torture him until he revealed all the technical details, and then dismember him into a thousand pieces so he couldn't reveal the details to the British or American governments. But if he couldn't go home, where could he go? His life was practically over. He might as well be prosecuted for his responsibility in the Mariana Trench seaquake and tsunami, and summarily given a lethal injection. Death would be painless and quick.

After a light breakfast, Troy requested a private meeting with Millstone. He wasn't looking forward to it, but he needed some supplies and a favor concerning Mr. Graham.

"Good morning, Troy," gushed Millstone as if he were talking to a long-lost relative he was very fond of. "I hope everybody slept well. I know I did — I like to sleep in the nude. It makes everything feel so fresh in the morning, if you know what I mean."

Troy responded simply, "Glad to hear that, Sir."

"So, tell me — what did you want to talk about? I'm in charge here, so if you need something, just say so."

"You may have guessed already that we are working on a highly classified mission here, and we need to send Mr. Graham to the States urgently — his life is in great danger here in England."

"Certainly. Is he being sought by a jealous girlfriend or something? Last night, did he behave? I hope he did not try anything immoral, especially with that female. Sometimes I think that, when people get strange urges in the middle of the night, they can even open locked doors by just touching the doorknob with a warm spoon — you know, one that you have placed on your naked navel for about five minutes."

Troy was aghast at what he was hearing, not knowing if he should contradict what Millstone was saying. He opted to ignore his ramblings and continue the conversation, if that was at all possible.

"Yes, sir, I know what you mean. No problem — everybody behaved last night. Will you be able to do all the paperwork to get Graham airlifted to Dover AFB as soon as possible?"

"Yes, there is an express train that goes to Dover, no local stops at all. Takes about five hours, I think. Your man Graham will be safe there. There is good security on that train — no perverts are allowed. But let me ask you, since you look like a reasonable young man. Do you ever, and I mean ever, get the feeling that there is another person living inside your body? Just be honest — it's just a question."

"You mean like a part of you wants to do something, but another part of you wants just the opposite?" asked Troy to clarify the question, although he sensed that Millstone was referring to something very disturbing.

"Well, no, I mean another real person, a full person, someone who can come out of your body at night, for example, someone who can lie there on your bed and even talk to you," added Millstone.

Troy was beginning to feel the hairs on the back of his neck stand up. Something was seriously wrong with Millstone, and he was not about to leave Graham in his care. Troy had to find another quick solution.

"No, sir, I have never had that experience, but I know many people who do. It's quite natural." Troy did not want to rile him, lest the provocation hasten some impending breakdown. But what this all meant was that he needed to warn Karla and Graham — and that they needed to leave rather soon.

Very promptly, the other staff afforded Troy the opportunity to have a private video call with Admiral Ferris in Dover. Troy gave him as many details as possible about the case, including that they needed to fly Mr. Graham to Dover, preferably in a private jet, and that he needed to be placed in protective custody there at the base. He also asked for new weaponry, including rocket-propelled grenades, better bulletproof vests, and an armored passenger car. Things were going to get really nasty.

The Admiral asked about Karla. "How is she doing after her stitches? Is she up to the task?"

Troy pepped up right away. "Yes, Admiral, she's still sore, but I spoke to her this morning, and she is ready and willing. She's got a lot of fire in her. She's a big asset — glad to have her on our team."

Even as they were talking, the Admiral was already directing his staff in Dover to immediately get the equipment that Troy had requested. About ten minutes later, the Admiral said, "Okay, hold on, Troy, I have a confirm here. Yes, confirmed. The American Embassy in London will place your car and equipment in an underground garage not far from there. When you get to London, call the special telephone number we gave you to get instructions on the location of your car and on how to get Mr. Graham to the Embassy. Any questions?"

"No, Admiral, we've covered everything. Oh, there is one thing. The coordinator of this safe house, Braxton Millstone, is on the verge on having some type of breakdown. It is my belief that the staff here are in danger. His higher-ups should look into this," whispered Troy.

One hour later, the three of them again were asked to place the hoods over their heads, and a vehicle took them from the safe house to downtown Birmingham, where they got a Black Cab for the two-hour ride back to London. During the ride, they tackled the thorny issue of prosecution for Graham.

Karla opined, "Now that we understand exactly how that earthquake came about, we feel somewhat ambivalent at the thought of charging you with murder."

"Yes, and you understand that this needs to be decided upon by civil and military courts in the U.S. and in England. I'm not sure what they'll do. Karla and I can testify that you saved her life, so that can be a mitigating force against your prosecution," added Troy.

"I am grateful to both of you. But now I feel that my soul is not clean anymore because the fact remains that I programmed those two devices that killed so many people. Certainly I appreciate your gracious help, but I want the courts to judge me and to execute me if that is their will."

Troy asked the driver of the Black Cab to drop them off at a location he knew was a few blocks from the American Embassy in London. He made the required phone call and was given the location of the car that he and Karla would be using. They were told to wait in the car and that a second vehicle would be picking up Mr. Graham for transport to the Embassy.

They went to the underground garage and got in their car. Soon enough, an unmarked vehicle showed up, and, as per protocol, they exchanged code words.

Both Karla and Troy shook Mr. Graham's hand. "Good luck. We'll ask the Admiral in Dover to give you some details just to keep you updated on our progress." Then the vehicle drove away with Mr. Graham, fate undetermined.

CHAPTER 7

While still in the underground garage, Karla and Troy prepared the weaponry that Admiral Ferris had provided them through the American Embassy. Sig-Sauer semi-auto P226 9mm handguns, with extended magazines. This time they also got what they had requested: Heckler & Koch MP7, 4.6 × 30mm cartridge sub-machine guns with 40-round mags. Karla had mentioned to Ferris that they needed more firepower, and the H&K provided 850 rounds/min. Also in the trunk they found two Colt M-16 assault rifles with 30-round clips, plenty of ammunition, night-vision scopes, and some explosives.

Nice car they got this time — a silver 4 × 4 Range Rover SUV with armor plating all around to protect against the savages they would surely encounter again, this time with even more powerful weapons, no doubt. Troy got behind the wheel, drove out of the garage parking, and was soon on the A23/M23 toward Crawley. Soon Karla barked, "Hey — why do you have to take the wheel? I don't want to get stuck reading stupid maps and giving you directions!"

"It just so happens that Graham gave me detailed directions to the secret locations where Geo-1 and -2 were taken, that's why," Troy rebutted.

"You can just as easily instruct me where to turn if I were the driver," Karla continued.

"Okay, how about this? I drive to the Crawley location and you to the Gloucester one. Will that satisfy your testosteronal urges?" he suggested. Troy immediately knew that maybe he should not have said that. Not to someone like Karla Bloomfield.

Her upper lip stiffened up, and she gave him the look. "And what do you mean by that, Mr. Sir?"

Troy had to think really quickly, especially since he had not seen her upper teeth in quite a while. "You don't have to feel that I am trying to control you. You'll get your chance on the way to Gloucester — if we're still alive, that is."

"And the testosterone?" Karla miffed.

"I really didn't mean that. I was using that term as a metaphor for defensiveness, that's all," Troy whimpered.

"Well, good, because I almost thought you were meaning to imply that I was half-woman, half-man just because I tell you what I want."

"No, Karla, anybody can see you are 100% woman — no mistake about that." She thought for a moment what he had meant by '100% woman.' Was he making a reference to her prominent breasts? The more she thought about it, the more she was dying to know but preferred to put on a bland face. For the moment.

"I'm glad we got that straight. Now, back to the plan. Why are we first going to Geo-2 in Crawley when it would make more sense to first destroy Geo-1 in Gloucester?"

"I figured that time is of the essence, and we have to destroy one of the devices right away. The one in Crawley is closer, that's all. Do you see it differently?"

"Let's just go with your plan for the moment," she noted.

They were already on the extreme southern outskirts of London, past the Farthing or Fairdean Downs, along a peaceful stretch of woods. Their Rover drove beautifully, masterfully, and silently along the motorway, radio playing some soft classical music, which Karla had selected and Troy didn't mind. Who would have guessed that in that graceful vehicle were two intelligence officers, armed to the teeth, on a risky and deadly mission, who might have had maybe just one hour to live?

Sometime later, in the southern end of Crawley, they got off the M23 and onto Horsham Road. About one kilometer later, they were at Black Hill Wood and turned left onto a dirt road, as Graham had specified. Not too many homes. No vehicles on the road here — too many trees. Could be ambushed easily. They made sure their weapons were loaded and chambered. All windows up, just in case. Adrenaline gushing into the veins. Eyes, ears on full alert. They felt like they were driving into Satan's lair.

About three kilometers down this quiet, isolated dirt road, they came to a bend, and there it was: One hundred meters further to the right, a white farmhouse with a huge, never-painted barn on the left. From their position, they could see various farm machinery — a tractor, power tiller, a large sprayer, and a variety of other smaller, tractor-driven machines. In front of the farmhouse was a small corral, maybe for one horse. Weeds here and there indicated that perhaps this place was not being kept up as well it could have been.

Karla advised Troy that maybe they should hide the car in their current position and walk the extra 100 meters, just in case. Troy replied, 'I'm glad you phrased that in the form of a suggestion, Lieutenant."

Yes, Lieutenant Sir, it was a suggestion — and don't let your estrogen get the better of you!" *Okay, she's feeling better*, Troy thought.

Fully armed with the handguns, submachine guns, and their Colt M-16 assault rifles, they locked the Rover and took one step, when, suddenly, they heard a zip-whirr-crack sound, and a large limb just over their heads broke and fell not one yard to their right. They both knew instantly that it had been a sniper bullet. They had been waiting for them.

Troy and Karla quickly hit the ground and hid behind a large oak tree, assuming the shot had come from the farmhouse. Whoever had taken the shot most probably had a high-powered scope and was already aiming at either side of the tree. Troy used a small mirror with a long handle that he carried for such an occasion to get a glimpse of the house without poking his head out.

"There is some movement at one of the upstairs windows, far right, but I can't make out what it is," warned Troy.

"I guess we'll have to split up and try to get closer," suggested Karla. On the count of three, they ran out simultaneously, but in opposite directions, to the next tree available for cover. About halfway there, Karla heard the whirring sound of a bullet zip past her head. *That was close, but nothing can stop me*, she thought. *We'll get this sombitch!*

Using their in-ear tactical radios with scrambled signals, they changed strategies, with Karla shooting an automatic volley of bullets at the window with her M-16 while Troy made a longer zigzag run toward the house. Then he provided cover while she made her run. They started thinking that there was only one hostile shooter. Or maybe it was a trap.

Soon they both had their backs against the house. Karla tossed a concussion grenade through a window, knocked down the front door with her big boot, and entered the house firing bullets in all directions, just in case. No response. Troy followed while she kept her eyes on the stairs going to the second floor. He quickly checked all the rooms on the first level and gave the all-clear by radio. Nothing much there. Old furniture, beat-up sofa, lamps with no shades, dirty floors. House looked unkempt. But the kitchen appeared relatively clean with fresh dirty plates in the sink. There was blood on the kitchen floor — it was gooey, not flaky, and there was lots of it. It was time to tackle the most dangerous part — going up those stairs.

Troy picked up a small vase and tossed it upstairs so that it crash-landed on the second floor. A single bullet rang out. So maybe the bad guy did not have an automatic weapon. Karla stayed at the bottom of the stairs providing cover while Troy slowly went up the creaky wooden steps. That made his heart race even faster. Slowly, he advanced, staying clear of the many family photographs hanging on the stair wall, and each step signaling his position relative to the second floor. He truthfully expected that the madman would suddenly appear in a desperate suicide bid to fire one bullet into him. How can one defend against someone who does not care if he lives or dies? Besides the unwanted creaking, the place was deathly quiet. Had the guy rigged his door with explosives?

Finally at the top, Troy could see there were four doors, one with a bullet hole. He figured the assassin fired through that one, but he could have changed rooms after he'd fired. Now he provided cover while Karla slowly made her way up the stairs. He was surprised that his face and shirt collar were all wet with terror perspiration, but Karla looked crisp. Very crisp. And that was in spite of the 20 stitches on her shoulders and back. *She probably does not realize how much danger we are in*, he thought, to make himself feel better at the comparison. And just as they were preparing to blast the door that had the bullet hole, another door behind them swung open, and two bearded, ugly-looking men started shooting their automatic weapons in Karla's direction. Troy and Karla had barely enough time to get out of the line of fire, so when they shot back, their bullets were way off the mark. Both quickly jumped out of a window, expecting to drop one full floor, but they landed on the roof of the porch. They quickly jumped off as a hail of bullets followed them, and they went back inside the house on the first level.

At that point, the two men with automatic weapons were coming down the stairs, shooting, but Troy and Karla quickly were able to neutralize them with fierce fire from their M-16s. After the bodies rolled down the stairs, everything became quiet. Smoke and dust everywhere, but deathly quiet. Was there a third man upstairs? Karla quietly looked out of several windows — nothing moving outside. They signaled each other to remain absolutely quiet. They could even hear the drip-drip of the kitchen faucet all the way to the living room area. The need for total silence meant they could not even change the magazines on their M-16 rifles, so each made a mental note that they had to be ready to pull out their Heckler & Koch submachine guns from their shoulder holsters at the first sound of the familiar click indicating their M-16 clips were empty. Surely, saving two to three seconds could be a matter of life and death under these conditions.

After about three minutes, they heard a muffled crunch upstairs and were able to estimate about where above the first-floor ceiling the third man was located. Karla and Troy fired their weapons into the ceiling until they were totally spent. They took out their H&K subs and ran upstairs, kicking down the door without hesitation. They came within milliseconds of shooting the man slumped in a corner. He was fully alert but was grimacing from the pain of a bullet that had struck him in one buttock, traveling from the bottom upward. Karla made sure he had no weapons. There was a great deal of blood on his trousers.

"We killed two of your buddies. Are there others here or in the barn?" demanded Karla with a stern look. The man replied there were no others. "You'd better not be lying to me, or I'll have to put a bullet right here," she warned, as she pressed the machine gun into his testicles. His look of terror made her think that maybe he was telling the truth. So Troy went quickly to check on the other rooms in the house. He again looked out all the windows. Nothing. All okay.

In a way, it had turned out better than planned, because now they had one of the assassins with information. It was time to interrogate Gorgin.

He was about 5'10", very muscular, black hair, short mustache, unshaven, very black, menacing eyes, poorly maintained teeth. Tattoos on both hands — looked like dragons. Smelled like he hadn't taken a shower in several days. His clothes were military green camouflage. Just to be on the safe side, Troy tied his hands to a heater steam pipe there in the room.

"Gorgin, do you know who we are?" queried Troy in dead monotone.

The wounded man looked Troy in the eye and said, "You Americans are really stupid if you think I will say anything, you scum!"

"Gorgin, you don't realize that you really don't have a choice here. Your two friends are dead, but you're alive, and, if you want to continue being alive, you will talk to us. So, again: Do you know who we are?" repeated Troy.

"Fuck you both, especially the bitch who put the gun to my manhood. I will kill her for this!"

That must have been a trigger for Karla, for she ran from across the room and slammed the butt of her M-16 across Gorgin's face, causing three rotten teeth to fly within a splatter of blood toward the wall. "It's your mother who's the bitch, you fucking larva " she exclaimed. It took about 30 seconds for Gorgin to realign his mouth and spit out the bountiful blood — and an extra tooth.

"Go ahead, decadent streetwalker — I am not afraid to die!" he mumbled.

"But I'm sure you don't like pain." And, with that, Karla slammed her boot, full force, against his testicles. He had been sitting on the floor in a corner, but he just led out a whimper and keeled over, unable to vocalize his extreme pain. They gave him about 10 minutes to recover some semblance of functioning. Karla kept checking on the windows.

Barely whispering, as he was trying to regain his breath, he said, "We know who you are: The two detectives who are investigating the earthquake company."

"And why were you shooting at us when we approached this house?" Karla pointedly asked.

"My boss said you two might come here to investigate. He told me to shoot you, that you should not check the barn."

"So what's in the barn?" asked Troy.

"Nothing, now. The weird-looking machine was there, but now it's gone."

"Whom do you work for? What government or terror group?" growled Troy.

"Does it matter, Mr. Policeman? We just proved that we can destroy large parts of your world at will, like we did in the Pacific. I was in charge of taking care of that scientist who programmed the machines here and in the other city…"

"You mean Gloucester?" interjected Karla.

"So, you know. Well, it does not matter. While he was programming the contraption, I was wearing a cap with a hidden video camera and was able to get all the codes and procedures. Ha. We don't need that stodgy scientist — we can do it all ourselves. Ha-ha-ha, you stupid Americans!"

Troy was really fuming that this enemy combatant was so arrogant and was not displaying any respect toward them. But worse, if he was right, then this terror group already had the codes and programming procedures, things that Mr. Graham said would take a long time to decipher. Worst of all, Gorgin was proudly stating that they now had the ability to destroy any part of the world, at will. What Karla and Troy did not yet know was the true motive that drove and inspired Gorgin's group. What did they want?

Karla, too, was privately getting riled up at the self-confidence of this man sitting in an unflattering position in the corner. She had a fleeting thought of putting her whole weight on his hip to crunch his bloody buttock — *That should be agonizingly painful* — but decided against it, because, after all, her job was military seismology and not interrogation. Still, the lives of millions of people could well be on the line, and the fruits of this interrogation could determine if they lived or died. She was fully aware that she could not ignore or avoid the decision before her: Do whatever had to be done to extract beneficial information from this enemy, or fail to protect the lives of millions of innocents who would surely die horrible deaths by drowning or by being squashed by toppling buildings.

It took her only about two minutes, exploring the depths of her heart, reading her sentiments about why she had become a military Navy officer. She quickly remembered how these assassins had mercilessly killed Mr. Thompson in that hail of bullets in flat #15 in London and how they had murdered the three workers in the Geophysical Dynamics lab, each with a heartless shot to the back of their heads, and left to rot in the supplies room. Another one of these monsters had cut open her back, down to the bone, and threatened her with sexual assault. Yes, evil had to be resisted. She knew what she had to do, even though it would also be painful for her soul.

She walked in a straight line to Gorgin, who still displayed a cynical smirk, and in her most threatening Rottweiler face said, "Look here, you toilet amoeba, my colleague just asked you a question. Answer it immediately, or you will soon be in a lot more pain. Whom do you work for?"

"I wonder if you are that forceful in bed, too? Do you do spankings?"

Karla exploded and, without any further warning, fired two shots from her 9mm Sig-Sauer handgun into his lower leg. His cocky attitude instantly evaporated as he was now consumed by the intense pain of a lower leg broken in two places.

He was writhing and twisting and grimacing with insufferable pain for a few seconds. Troy added, "You still have one good leg, but not for long. She wants to shoot you again. Answer the damned question before she goes for your arms, too. You know I can't stop her. She might even shoot me!"

"You win, Americans. Don't shoot anymore, and I will tell you."

"We already have some information, so, if you lie to us, we will know, and she will ram an ice pick deep into your ear. You will feel it inside your brain without really dying. Now, talk."

"In London, there are about 12 of us, all from Teheran in Iran. We handle assassination assignments as given to us by the organization."

"What is the name of the organization?" snapped Troy.

"In English, it is 'Blue Sparrow.'"

Karla asked, "And your leader?"

"If I tell you, I would be a traitor."

"Seems to me, Gorgin, that you and your two dead buddies at the bottom of the stairs have been abandoned here by them on this dead-end mission. They took the important thing, the machine, and you are left here to guard an empty farmhouse. It's clear that *they* are the traitors. Now, who's the leader?" insisted Karla.

Gorgin was undecided, clearly worried. But he kept an oblique eye on Karla — *Who knows what she might do?* Still stalling, still worried. In a split second, Karla pulled her 9mm from the holster, and Gorgin blurted out quickly, "Sanjar! We know him only as Sanjar."

"Describe this Sanjar. What is his mission? Where can we find him?" demanded Troy.

"None of us knows what he looks like. We normally carry out hits, but this time they paid us to take these two machines from the laboratory in London. Before we left, we took the three workers there to the basement, and we terminated them. Sanjar had sent us the message that there were to be no witnesses."

Karla and Troy continued with a barrage of questions, and it became clear that the members of Gorgin's group were assassins, not necessarily politically motivated. He had mentioned that nobody had ever seen Sanjar, if that was his real name. Over the next few minutes, Gorgin appeared weaker, maybe from the loss of blood. They had to hurry with two last important questions.

Karla asked him, "So if you have never seen Sanjar, how do you get instructions for your next assignment?"

"That's easy. An Englishman named Hugh Mitchell, a hotshot at Fernwood International Bank and Trust in Brussels. Pays good."

Troy told Karla that he thought he'd better take a quick look at the barn to see if they had left any evidence, but Karla said that, since Troy was doing so well with the interrogation, she should go instead.

Karla left, and Gorgin continued answering questions, although he was definitely getting weaker. In the span of about eight minutes, Troy had asked maybe ten more questions, which Gorgin appeared to have answered truthfully. But on the last one, Gorgin had closed his eyes. Troy took his pulse — there was none. He had bled to death.

Troy whispered Karla's name into his tactical radio. No response. He whispered again. Nothing. Something was definitely wrong; he had to hurry without making any noise that might alert the enemy, if there were still any around. While still inside the farmhouse, he made sure all his weapons had full ammo clips in them. Then he peeked out the back door.

The unpainted barn was about 50 yards from the back of the house, with a nice stone-covered path leading to its two huge front doors. It had the customary door up on the hayloft and the pulley system to transport the bales in or out, up or down. Troy couldn't see any movement; nothing seemed out of line. He again whispered, "Karla, Karla." No response, not even static. He used his rifle scope to see if anyone was looking at him from within the loft area but nothing showed up, so he made a quick zig-zag run to a spot behind a water tank on the right side of the barn. Something was definitely wrong with Karla.

He carefully walked along the barn's huge, right-side windowless wall that led to the back. There was a regular-sized door. It was closed. But something caught his eye. About 10 yards from the back of the barn was a body under some machinery. His heart dropped as he had to quickly consider that it might be Karla's. Then his nose confirmed it couldn't be Karla's, for the stench was acidic and nauseating, and the body was covered with maggots. It was the body of a man, dressed in farming clothing. He had a clean, round hole in his forehead. Probably the owner of the farm. It lessened Troy's guilt feelings about Gorgin having bled to death upstairs.

The next step would be quite risky, for he knew that old barns have very squeaky door hinges, yet he did not have much time to think. What if Karla had been stabbed and was bleeding to death? He had heard no shot. He would be an easy target coming through the door, but there was no other way.

Troy pulled the door open and rapidly rolled on the floor to get inside. He heard the zing of a bullet fly past him, then a second bullet. Clearly both had come from a silencer-fitted weapon. He sought cover behind a massive wooden beam supporting the hayloft. The shooting stopped.

There were plenty of farm machines inside the barn that afforded good cover for Troy, so he started crawling under one, then another, trying to get a position on the shooter or shooters. It was then that he saw the situation he and Karla were in. A gruff-looking, slightly underweight assassin was holding on to Karla with his arm tight around her neck and a gun barrel pushing against her cheek, deforming it in the process. Troy changed positions, but he still could not get a clean shot to the head. Besides, Karla's tormentor wisely kept moving just enough to make the shot very risky, even if Troy could work up the confidence to take it.

"I can see you now. You must be Troy Hamilton, right?" asked Karla's kidnapper.

"And who are you?"

He repositioned himself, "They call me Kamil, but that's not important. Listen, Troy, there has been a change in the plan. We were supposed to kill you both. But not anymore. Got a message from my director, and, now, we just want Jacob Graham, the scientist. So you give me Jacob, and I give you back your girlfriend."

"I am not his girlfriend, you filthy maggot!" mumbled Karla as well as she could with the gun barrel still deforming her mouth.

"Shut up, woman — I am talking!"

"Kamil, let's talk about this. You sound like a reasonable man," suggested Troy, still trying to get a better position for a lethal head shot.

"Oh, I am very reasonable. I will not kill this angry woman even though I want to, and you just give me Jacob Graham. Let's get going before my director changes his mind and I have to kill both of you. I kill her first."

Kamil was not nervous at all. In fact, he seemed to be taking the situation in stride, perhaps fully confident that he controlled every aspect of it. Like the others, he was a paid assassin who just followed orders and had little emotional or ideological attachment to the assignment. Maybe that is what made him even more dangerous — he could think clearly and coldly about what needed to be done.

And he had been thinking. Troy saw that there was a long rope tied to one of Karla's ankles, the other end of which was tied to the slow shaft of a reciprocating electric water pump. It was not just to keep Karla tied down. It was meant to slowly pull Karla into the pump's gears as the shaft turned and wound the rope around itself. But why would Kamil have done that? If he wanted to kill her, he could simply shoot her. What was his plan, and how could he quickly turn on the electric pump?

Troy was full of uncertainties and unknowns — too many, he thought — to make a final decision to shoot Kamil. He needed more time to figure out something. "So why do you have a rope around my colleague's ankle?"

"It's my insurance, in case you try any tricks," Kamil responded with a smirk. And just then Troy saw that Kamil was standing next to a thick cable with a small box that had a green and a red button. Yes, it was the start button for the pump, and it was just inches from Kamil's hands.

Just then, there was a vibrating sound coming from near one of Kamil's wrists, so faint that only he and Karla heard it. Kamil looked at his wrist and read some type of text message: GRAHAM DEAD. COULD BE HOAX. CHECK STATUS WITH PRISONERS. IF TRADE NOT POSSIBLE KILL THEM BOTH.

"Troy, it looks like luck just ran out for you and the woman. The director says that Graham is dead. You know we want him alive. So, is this a ploy by your superiors?"

Troy was thinking that it was the assassin network who was playing a trick, but, just then, he felt a message come in on his communicator. He got a terrible feeling about it. But the important thing was to let Kamil believe that Graham was okay, even if he was already dead.

"Just to make sure, I will call my superiors," claimed Troy, just to cover up that he had to attend to the message. He retreated a bit for better cover and saw what the message was: CALL ADM FERRIS STAT!

He dialed the encrypted number and said, "Admiral, this is Troy. I have to whisper. What's the problem?"

"Terrible news, Troy. Mr. Graham was shot and killed as he was coming out of the American Embassy there in London a few moments ago. It must have been a devastating military round. Head was completely blown off. The only thing left attached to the body was the neck and the lower jaw with teeth. Ghastly sight on those photos. I'm sorry."

He didn't know what to think. Poor Mr. Graham. He had worked so hard to create something to benefit the whole world, but all that it had brought so far was cadavers everywhere. And to make it worse, the enemy always seemed to be two steps ahead of Karla and Troy. Something was very, very wrong.

"Very well, Admiral. Try to keep a lid on this. Will brief you later."

Troy knew he couldn't reveal to Kamil that Graham was indeed dead, so he played along to buy more time. At any moment, Kamil would be getting another message confirming Graham's assassination, and, within seconds, he would be putting a bullet into Karla's head. There was little time to consider all possible intervention options.

"You were right, Kamil. My superiors were trying to fool everybody by making it seem that Graham had been killed. But they've abandoned that plan. So we can still do the trade."

"I have a better plan. This is taking too long," complained Kamil, and, with one swift swing of his handgun, he struck Karla on the head, and she dropped totally limp. Kamil crouched down quickly and pressed the green electric-pump switch. The thick shaft started to pull in the rope attached to her ankle. It was easy to see that, in less than a minute, first her leg and then her whole body would be pulled into the rotating shafts, pulleys, and gears, and she would be shredded like a corn flakes box under a roaring lawn mower.

"So drop your weapon now, and come forward with your hands up. There is still time to shut off the electric motor!" demanded Kamil.

Troy had no choice but to hope that Kamil would shut off the motor as soon as he came forward. He dropped his M-16, raised his hands, and approached Kamil. "Now, quickly, turn off the motor! It's pulling her in!" exclaimed Troy.

The assassin seemed to be taking his time. Then, apparently, he felt the vibration of his message device, because he said, "Just a moment, Mr. Troy, I have another message coming in."

It was do or die for Troy and Karla, for surely within two to three seconds, Kamil would have a confirmation that Mr. Graham indeed had been assassinated, and he would immediately terminate them both.

Kamil's attention had been diverted to the message, and Troy, against all odds, jumped in his direction and barely managed to land a weak punch to his face. But it was enough, and Kamil dropped the handgun. The two men wrestled on the ground and punched and kicked, and, within a few seconds, both were bloodied about the face. Troy was trying desperately to keep an eye on the shaft and how close Karla was to being shredded, but his first priority was to finish off his opponent, or they would both die.

Troy was muscular and well trained, but so was this animal he was up against. Kamil was thin but fast, and he knew how to land very painful karate blows, which Troy was not able to duplicate. In one quick look, Troy saw that Karla's leg was less than 24 inches from the shaft and gears. He had to do something drastic, and fast. While he was under Kamil and being pummeled mercilessly, Troy put his arms around Kamil's neck, and, with all his diminishing strength, he pulled him forward all the way so as to place Kamil's nose inside his mouth, and he bit as hard as his teeth could stand. Troy felt a big, loose object inside his mouth, a disgusting object that needed to be spit out immediately. So while Kamil was holding his nose-less face in agony, Troy grabbed his head and gave it a bestial twist. Something cracked, and Kamil dropped totally limp.

Seconds counted. Troy didn't have time to check on Karla. He just raced to the red button and slammed his open hand against it. The noisy but deadly electric pump came to an abrupt stop. He then dragged himself to the edge of the pump, where the rope had pulled Karla. She was still limp, and there was blood where the maniac had struck her on the head with his gun. Her damaged boot was already making contact with a few gears and pulleys. Some blood there, but not a lot. He cut the rope and wearily dragged her away a safe distance from the gears. At a snail's pace, he went to get his M-16 and then slumped down next to Karla, who was breathing okay. He was spitting blood, his lips felt like they were balloons, and he was wet with perspiration and blood. He just had to catch his breath. Everything hurt.

After about ten minutes, he started feeling a bit better, and he attempted to revive Karla by calling her name and moving her shoulders and arms. Totally limp. After two more tries, she started coming back to life. It took her a few moments to reorient herself, but then she touched her bloodied head where the assassin's gun had struck her. She quickly remembered that they had been in a life-and-death situation and saw that the kidnapper was dead.

"What happened, Troy?"

"Kamil here was threatening to kill both of us, so I managed to get close enough to punch him, and, well, he punched me, too, as you can see, but I finally did him in and cut you loose. And how are you feeling?"

"Oh, fine. I just managed to sleep through the whole thing — no problem. You should have woken me up during the action. Thanks for taking care of everything. My foot hurts, though."

He took off her torn boot and saw that her foot had some abrasions and cuts. Nothing serious, but her sock had really been ripped by the teeth of the gear that had almost cut off her foot. He thought it best that her foot with all the open wounds not be exposed against the flapping and torn leather of her boot, so he exchanged socks with her and gently put her boot back on.

"We need to clean up a bit back at the farmhouse and get out of here soon, Lieutenant. More guys may be on the way," advised Troy. They quickly located Karla's M-16 in the barn and walked slowly to the house. There they found some first-aid paraphernalia in the bathroom, including some analgesics for the pain, and were able to clean up. Ten minutes later, they were in their Rover on the way back to London And this time, Karla had quickly gotten behind the wheel and handed Troy the London map.

CHAPTER 8

The first order of business was to decide where they should go in London. Karla opined that maybe they should take a roundabout route to some small restaurant where they could map out a strategy. Troy agreed.

"Listen, I am concerned. What's this I heard about Graham? Is he okay?"

"He's dead, Karla. Admiral Ferris informed me that he was shot as he was coming out of the Embassy. He doesn't know what to make of it."

"That doesn't make sense. I thought these cretins we just fought off at the farmhouse wanted him alive. Why would they suddenly decide to kill him?"

"We need answers, and fast," fumed Troy.

The London countryside was beautiful, peaceful, with lots of open sky one could not normally see in the city. Karla and Troy passed by dozens of farms with huge horse fencing to let the animals take their spirited runs. Farmhouses typically had stone walls, steeple-shaped roofs, and various numbers of gables — leading into cozy rooms where one could snuggle up to a favorite easy chair to read a romance novel and such. At least that's what Karla privately imagined.

But Troy's mind started comparing his crowded living conditions in Manhattan's upper West Side to the expanse of farmland here on the outskirts of London. New York offered a cultural extravaganza, hundreds of bookstores, and thousands upon thousands of interesting little stores and restaurants along Broadway, but especially in Greenwich Village, Tribeca, and SoHo. He also was fully aware of the grass-looks-greener-on-the-other-side syndrome, and he had to remind himself that he'd had those same feelings when he was on assignment in Paris, Honolulu, Guadalajara, Antwerp, and Cologne with its gorgeous Gothic cathedral. He made a mental note that he had to do some serious thinking about these things.

Karla got off the M25 in the eastern part of London, near Dartford, by the River Thames. They checked into a small motel to shower, separately, and for a change of clothing. Troy and Karla applied topical medications to each other's injuries. Next on their agenda was to locate a small restaurant where they could eat and discuss the next stage. They desperately had to locate Geo-1 and Geo-2.

Karla took the wheel again, with a girlish smirk, while Troy made contact with Admiral Ferris.

"Hi, Admiral? Troy here. We're finally out of that hellish farmhouse in Crawley. Karla and I are pretty banged up but breathing and okay."

"Yes, Troy, we got additional details on that hit on Mr. Graham. Looks like a .50-caliber military round. Could have come only from one direction, and that is a tall building about 500 yards away."

"That sounds professional, Admiral. Any theories?" asked Troy.

"Well, 500 yards, and a direct hit on a walking target. We're not dealing with weekend warriors. This is serious shit that's winning the war for them!"

"But, Admiral, it's obvious that the hit man was waiting for Graham to exit the Embassy building. Who the hell knew Graham was there and that he would soon be going out that door?"

"For starters, myself, my boss, Admiral Chief of Naval Operations Easton Rockwell, and maybe two CIA bigwigs at Langley," said the Admiral almost apologetically. "Do you suspect one of us leaked this information to the assassins in London?"

"Admiral, sir, it's obvious that this assassin group has been ahead of us one, maybe two, steps. They are getting very reliable information. Seems that everything started with the leak at the Groton Submarine Base, wouldn't you say?"

"I can't disagree with you, Troy. There is a deadly leak of information. Remember, too, that I had already expressed to you my suspicion that there is a mole at our CIA station in London. Could be that."

"Would it be possible for you not to provide updates to your superiors or the CIA?" pleaded Troy.

"The way things are going right now, Troy, we know that this case is leading to a catastrophic event against the United States or its allies, and that there will be military finger-pointing afterward, if there is an afterward. My career is basically over, no matter how this pans out eventually."

"Sorry to hear that, Admiral, sir, but I tend to agree with you. Just know that if they let you go or if they imprison you, I will be there with you, taking some of the blame."

"Thanks, Troy, very honorable of you. Okay, as per your request, I will no longer be giving updates to the CIA, but I still have to inform Admiral Chief Rockwell, since he specifically asked me for daily briefings. Let me talk to Karla, please."

Karla was driving, but she had been carefully listening to both sides of the conversation. "Good afternoon, sir, or should I say 'Good morning'?"

"Hi, Karla. I heard you both had a really hard time at the Crawley farmhouse."

"What a hellhole, sir. Those bastards were waiting for us, but we took care of the problem."

"Any significant intelligence?"

"We were able to extract the name of their contacts in London and Brussels, but, more significantly, we got the very strong impression that they didn't easily believe it when they learned that Graham had been shot. They thought it was a lie, a hoax. Wanted him alive. That can only mean that this group of assassins may not be responsible for the hit on Graham."

"Are you saying that there are two independent groups here targeting the United States?" asked Admiral Ferris, almost in a whisper, as if the truth were less harsh if spoken softly.

"No doubt about it," was Karla's definite response.

"Very well. See what you can learn from that contact in London. And, Karla?"

"Yes, sir?"

"Good work in gathering that intel, Lieutenant. You both are excellent military officers. I am proud to work with you. Keep me posted."

They drove a few kilometers, and then Karla made a point. "Shouldn't we be going to Gloucester to see if we can locate Geo-1 there?"

"Well, we could, but my guess is that, if they've already moved Geo-2 out of Crawley, they've probably moved Geo-1 out of Gloucester as well. And, besides, I am pretty sure they would want a second chance to ambush us. Our chances of surviving a second encounter in the woods would be close to zero."

Karla did not respond to Troy's analysis, but, instead, she said they'd better get some food at a drive-through restaurant so they could get on their way to Brussels. Troy felt it was a great idea. The drive to Brussels, in Belgium, across the English Channel, would be about seven hours. They certainly wanted to be fresh and ready for tomorrow's challenge of gathering intel on that contact Gorgin mentioned, Hugh Mitchell of Fernwood Bank & Trust in Brussels.

They ate as well as one can eat in a car dodging traffic and making several route mistakes, but, all in all, Karla was getting the job done. England had its own Dover, and soon they were on the M40 for that British port city leading to France.

Once on the ferry from Dover to Calais in France, Karla and Troy saw the magnificent White Cliffs of Dover. These natural wonders were an incredible 300 feet high and extended about 10 miles up and down the coast of England. Looking like enormous snow-white curtains that completely covered these gigantic cliffs, these wonders were, in reality, white chalk created by fossilized clams and shells from when this landmass was at the bottom of the sea millions of years ago. Karla could really appreciate this beautiful geological phenomenon.

After Calais in France, they got on the E40, which would take them all the way into Belgium and Brussels. They crossed from France into Belgium a short way after Dunkirk and decided that, for the rest of the way, Troy would try to dig up some information on that Hugh Mitchell, about whom they knew nothing besides that he worked at Fernwood Bank and was fingered as being the contact man leading to the main boss, Sanjar. On the device screen appeared some information on Fernwood International Bank & Trust. It apparently was a very potent financial institution, for it had dozens of branches throughout Europe and dozens more in Russia, China, The Middle East, Japan, and Africa. In Brussels alone, it had eleven. When Troy entered the name of Hugh Mitchell in the bank's directory, the search results showed his title as "Treasurer," with his main office at central headquarters near the intersection of Waterloo Boulevard and Rue des Drapiers.

A more general search generated a treasure trove of details. This Hugh Mitchell guy apparently was also on the board of several charitable institutions that provided billions of dollars and euros to charities all over Eastern Europe. That alone was a big red flag. There was no easily obtainable information on criminal records, so Karla and Troy concluded that, if Hugh Mitchell was involved in any nefarious activities, the local authorities were inclined to turn a blind eye to them. No doubt he was also contributing smooth amounts to the locals' favorite charities, perhaps even to their political campaigns or even their kids' college educations.

The biographical page at the bank showed a photo of Hugh. Handsome guy, age 58, full head of hair, seemed trim and fit, friendly face with a disarming smile. Did not mention wife or kids, so it was safe to assume that the man was single. Or was there an ex-wife in the background somewhere?

It was late Monday night when they finally arrived in Brussels, a beautiful city of about one million souls, a city known for its chocolates, beer, and art nouveau grand architecture. That was all well and fine, but when Karla and Troy arrived, they were tired and wanted to have a quiet dinner and then simply just drop into bed. For about 20 minutes, they just drove in a haphazard manner around the downtown section, again to lose a tail if they had one. Then they checked into the cozy Be Manos Hotel — one suite, two beds, please. It was centrally located on Square de l'Aviation, near Waterloo Boulevard and Rue des Drapiers, where Hugh Mitchell worked at the bank.

The hotel restaurant was small, but it was stylish and spanking clean. Throughout the area, a black-and-white theme dominated the walls, curtains, and even the floor. Flowers, flowers, flowers everywhere — they needed that fragrance and relaxing atmosphere after so many hours in the car. After ordering from the French-speaking waitress, it was time to review what was to be done the next day, Tuesday.

"Even if we can determine tomorrow that Hugh Mitchell is the middle-man contact for these assassins, it will be rather difficult for him to confess knowing where the two devices are at this moment, wouldn't you say?" asked Troy as he sipped on his glass of Trappistes Rochefort beer.

Karla took a drink of her ice water. "If he is involved with these assassins, then he will go for broke before he confesses anything to us. His life, his wealth, his reputation are all on the line here. Won't be easy. It will destroy him to give us what we want. There is no middle ground, no bargaining room."

"That means, Karla, that, when we confront him, he will resist to the end, or he'll commit suicide on the spot."

"Yeah, but, if he's such a bad guy, maybe he *should* commit suicide and spare the state the expense of providing an extended trial!"

"What I'm saying is that, when we see him, perhaps tomorrow, Tuesday, it will be like getting into a cage with a ferocious tiger. I figure that, whether we extract the information from him or not, at the end of the meeting, he'll be dead by his hand or ours."

Their steaming food arrived, and they started eating like they had been lost in the forest for days — they hardly spoke. Afterward came the coffee and chocolate-sprinkled waffles, which they wolfed down mercilessly. Still hardly any talk, but both had been contemplating what might be waiting for them tomorrow.

Back in their suite, they took their showers, made sure all windows and curtains were closed, placed some furniture to block the door, and loaded all their weapons with full clips, chambered Sig-Sauers on the night tables. Troy applied more medication to his facial cuts and then to Karla's two long cuts on her back and shoulders. Appeared to be healing properly. Exhausted, they dropped into their beds.

"Good night, Karla."
"Good night, Mr. Navy Intelligence."
It was late Monday night.

CHAPTER 9

Breakfast consisted of scrambled eggs, a passion fruit tart, orange juice, and very strong coffee from Ethiopia. Of course, they kept their eyes fully open and aware of their surroundings, for they well knew that this assassin organization had demonstrated an uncanny knowledge of seemingly everything that was happening or was about to happen in this case.

It was all couples there in the breakfast area of the hotel. Seemed harmless enough, except for an oriental-looking couple in the other corner — they kept looking at Troy and Karla. Korean or Chinese? Karla mentioned to Troy that, although they knew that the first group of enemies was Iranian, they still didn't know anything about the second hostile group. They could be North Korean, Chinese, Russian, or even Cuban, given that country's powerful Direccion General de Inteligencia, with worldwide tentacles. Any one of these countries would gladly kill to possess those two incredible machines that Thompson and Graham had created.

Finishing up her croissant with cream cheese, Karla whispered to Troy, "We should walk over to the Fernwood Bank and check out that Hugh Mitchell."

"I'm almost finished. We *should* walk over to the Fernwood Bank and check out that Hugh Mitchell," retorted Troy.

"Are you mocking me?" she asked with flared nostrils.

"Hell, no, I was just re-asserting my command here. Remember that I'm in charge here, Lieutenant Bloomfield!"

As they were getting up from their table, she added, "Yeah? Nobody told me that. Admiral Ferris didn't tell me that, so, therefore, it doesn't hold here!"

"Women," Troy mumbled under his breath.

"What was that?"

It was a no-win situation, so Troy thought he'd better just let it be. They went out the hotel's front doors into the beautiful Tuesday morning air in Brussels. Just in case, they both looked over their shoulders. No, the suspicious couple was not behind them. But who knew what calamities might come their way soon?

Along the way, they admired the gorgeous architecture of the city, inspired by the rejuvenation at the beginning the 20th century under direction of art-driven architects like Paul Hankar and Victor Horta. Even UNESCO had recognized their unique value and declared these Brussels buildings as world heritage. Too bad that there now was some sinister plot within these cultural treasures.

Fernwood Bank & Trust on Rue des Rapiers had a beautiful and opulent façade worthy of admiration even by rabid socialists with an unrelenting hatred of capitalism. Massive windows revealed promenades on the first, second, and third floors, while gigantic stone blocks provided the main support structures. Intricate bronze statues adorned small ledges on the second and third floors. And, from the outside, one could admire ornate crystal chandeliers that could not possibly fit in any house. It was a sight to behold.

For the next few hours, Troy and Karla separated and worked independently, observing people coming and going, looking at co-workers and directories, and trying to catch a glimpse of their target, Hugh Mitchell. Their separate observations concurred in that many street clients entered his office, something unusual for a bank Treasurer who generally would be expected to be working with numbers, spreadsheets, and bank personnel. In addition, Karla made the interesting observation that Hugh Mitchell appeared to be a self-confident man, taking charge of conversations and always having something interesting to say. But there were too many people there at the bank — they would have to confront him elsewhere, perhaps at his home.

When a Bentley limo picked him up at the bank around 5 o'clock, Troy and Karla were ready in their own car nearby. Troy had had to convince Karla that it was his turn at the wheel; this time she offered little resistance.

Troy followed about 100m behind the Bentley, while Karla fitted all their weapons with silencers. They were going to do dirty work in a residential neighborhood, so they surely did not want all the shots to alert the weapons-phobic locals to call the police. In a few minutes, both vehicles were on the N5 going south, and, as the Bentley picked up speed, Troy decided to pull back a bit so as not to arouse suspicion. Karla kept a discreet but watchful eye on the traffic behind them, just in case a security spotter vehicle customarily followed Hugh Mitchell's car, but there seemed to be nothing of the kind.

Troy and Karla's adrenaline was already starting to pump into their veins, since they were thinking that surely there would be automatic-weapons-equipped security at the residence, and perhaps even invisible sensors that would alert guards if there were unauthorized people on the grounds. A man such as Hugh Mitchell, who handles billions and perhaps trillions of dollars, a man who directs an Iranian death squad, a man who is intelligent and educated and cultured, a man whose goal is to destroy continents and millions of people, is not likely to live without extensive security at his home. The adrenaline should be flowing in their veins. This would not be a farmhouse with a barn.

A few kilometers after crossing over the Flanders line, the Bentley took an exit and headed East on Dreve Saint-Michel in the beautiful Sonian Forest. Two kilometers later, it turned into a smaller, unnamed road. Troy decided not to follow in the car and instead observed on foot just where the car entered a private driveway. Now they knew where Hugh Mitchell lived!

Troy expected that the Bentley might simply drop off Mitchell and that it would be leaving the property shortly, so he and Karla continued driving East on Saint-Michel, just far enough so that they could see if and when the Bentley entered this street again, hopefully going back in the direction of the N5. As soon as they confirmed that, Troy turned the car around and got on Mitchell's street. They wanted a good look at the property while there was still some sunlight. They would drive by without stopping.

"Wow!" exclaimed both Karla and Troy. The man knows how to live. Gorgeous estate with everything one could wish for. Huge lawn in front, the size of two football fields, and tennis courts on one side, huge swimming pool on the other. Massive, two-story brick-and-stone house fit for royalty. No doubt that the five gables on the roof line led to cozy bedrooms or studies. "Troy, I don't think I could afford this on my Lieutenant's salary," lamented Karla. "I know what you mean. Not even on two lieutenants' salaries!" interjected Troy. There was a little bit of odd silence.

But, there were armed security guards. They counted three. It was best to wait 'till nighttime to make the move.

Troy parked the vehicle about three kilometers away, surrounded by the rich foliage of the Sonian Forest. Now, with a little bit of dead time on their hands and the plan already worked out, the conversation moved to the personal.

"Say, Karla, your file says that you joined the military mostly to please your old dad. Is that accurate?"

"You've been checking, eh?"

"Just basics — nothing more."

"At CalTech, I was studying geophysics and seismology when a military recruiter asked to talk to me. Heck, I knew my dad always had wanted me to join, but now he was sending these guys to try to convince me."

"And, given your personality, I'm sure you didn't appreciate it."

"No, that wasn't it. It did not bother me because I have always admired my dad. That's where I get my authoritarian leaning and my sense of independence. But how about you? How'd you end up in military electronic applications? One would think that a Boston native would end up in political science or sociology, but not in the military."

"You got me figured out. My dad is a Boston policeman, even though he's not Irish, so I got the serve-others syndrome from him. I thought the military would be the ideal place for me. I don't regret choosing this career. Well, I do feel the pay sucks." They both laughed and looked at the clock. It was time — it was dark.

Last check on all weapons, vests, in-ear radios, scrambled channel. Troy drove to the dark forest drive and parked out of the way about a quarter-kilometer before the house. The outside wall was really more like a 15-foot-high fence made of steel rods. Using their night-vision binoculars, Karla confirmed that there were still only three guards outside on the premises. Even if they could bypass them to gain access to the house, once the arguing started with Mitchell, they would be alerted and would become a deadly threat to both Karla and Troy. Karla would have to take them out now — there was no other way.

From outside the fence, she used her night-vision scope to center the guard on her cross-hairs and fired one round from her silencer-equipped M-16. Then they both jumped the fence and were inside the property. Neither of the two remaining guards seemed to have noticed anything. As had been previously arranged, Karla would approach the left side of the house and Troy the right, since there was a guard at each end. There were small, thin trees and some shrubbery but not a lot to provide cover on the advance toward the house. Karla was crawling on her stomach, advancing ever so slowly in the almost total silence of the night. Then it happened. She crawled over a small, dry branch on the ground, and it cracked, something the guard on her end of the house heard clearly. She froze. The guard said something on his radio and started advancing slowly in Karla's direction. After the radio contact, the guard at the other end started looking in his direction as if to be on alert in case something were to happen to the guard approaching Karla.

"Troy, Troy, this guy is coming my way," she whispered urgently. Karla was in a compromised situation because she was holding her M-16 across her chest, as is standard procedure in this type of approach. But it also left her vulnerable because, if she dared to move her rifle to point at the guard, he could easily detect the movement and fire his weapon, which was already pointing in Karla's direction. And the closer he got, the poorer her chances of moving, aiming, firing, and hitting the guard before he fired first. Even if she managed to hit the guard, the other guard would notice, and he would sound the alarm before Troy could terminate him.

She quickly thought of an urgent plan. "Troy, hit your guard now — now!" she exclaimed in a whisper, even though it sounded impossible.

"Negative, can't do it. Don't have a clear shot. Trees in the way. Will move." That wasn't the response she wanted to hear. The guard on her side was getting closer, with his automatic weapon pointing in her general direction.

Karla whispered desperately into her mike. "Troy, can't hold off longer. May have to take action within seconds. Am at a grave disadvantage." No response.

Then she heard two silencer shots in quick succession. Her guard turned in the direction of the muffled shots and then toward the other guard, giving Karla that precious one extra second. She moved her M-16 and fired into the forehead of the enemy. She could now breathe again.

"All clear here, Troy. Your status?"

"Troy — clear."

Within 30 seconds, they were both on the left side of the house. "Damn, Troy, you waited 'till the last second. I was starting to shit my pants. As it is, I think I did pee a little."

"Sorry, Karla, the guard on my side was on high alert for any unusual sound or movement. I had to be extra careful, or both of us would have been dead meat. It's over, and we're making progress."

They hadn't counted on this problem, so they were both riled up afterward. To be on the safe side, they did a quick check around the back of the mansion — no more guards. Time to get inside.

After trying several windows on the ground floor, they finally located one that readily opened. If an alarm sounded, they had already planned to do a blitzkrieg inside the house, running from room to room to locate Mitchell and take him into the woods before security personnel arrived. But, no alarm — none they could hear, anyway. Inside they were in awe at the wealth that was evident throughout the house. Fine art, sculptures, expensive Frattini and Nakashima furniture that made Troy and Karla feel they were not worthy to even sit on the sofa. They passed by his closet — maybe a hundred tailor-made suits and cabinets with as many shirts. Troy had to struggle just to keep his attention on potential risks instead of furnishings and paintings.

There seemed to be no sign of women's or children's clothing, or toys — maybe it was true that he lived alone. That was a good sign, for a wife or a child at home would make it extremely difficult to carry out the mission.

No Mr. Mitchell on the first floor. Karla provided cover from the ballroom-sized first floor landing, while Troy slowly went up one of the double set of stairs. He took one quick look down a long hallway. There was a security guard at a desk just outside what appeared to be Mitchell's bedroom. After Karla made her way up the stairs, they put the final step of the approach plan in action. Troy fired one shot at the guard, and they both ran toward the closed bedroom door, slamming their bodies against it. The double doors easily gave way.

Mitchell was lying on the bed reading some materials, but the exploding doors made him run from the bed toward his desk nearby, presumably to get a gun. Karla fired two quick rounds at the desk, causing wood splinters to fly in all directions. In her best Rottweiler snarl, she warned, "Don't you dare!" He stopped halfway there.

"Get on the floor, face down, hands behind your head!" ordered Troy. Karla checked the rest of the palatial bedroom, while Troy kept the rifle pointed at the prisoner.

Then Karla asked, "Are you Hugh Mitchell?"

"You people are going to be very sorry. You are completely out of your league. Damned motherfuckers!"

"Wrong answer, you filthy larva!" shouted Karla and rammed her boot into his ribs. He moaned in pain and reflexively went into the fetal position, trying to catch his breath.

"Answer the question, or we'll go for your other side," ordered Karla.

"Yes, I am Hugh Mitchell. Just take what you want, and I won't report it."

"Well, Mr. Mitchell, first we will tie you over here on this seat…"

Hugh Mitchell interrupted Troy. "It's not just a 'seat', you middle-class moron. That is a very rare Hans Wegner padded Papa chair. You would have to work for a full year just to pay for it on your proletarian salary."

Karla got the cable from the bedroom phone and tied him to the rare Wegner chair.

"Mr. Mitchell, we are not here to steal your expensive trash. If tonight you play your cards right, you just might live. If you don't, you will want to commit suicide," promised Troy.

"I am a very powerful man, you lowly swine. My associates will fillet you both and throw the pieces to the wolves. There will be nothing left for authorities to collect as evidence of your demise."

Karla got serious. "Mr. Mitchell, does the name 'Sanjar' ring a bell in your capitalist head?" His face turned ashen, and his smirk disappeared. Hugh Mitchell knew that his most profound secret was now exposed, that he was now fighting for his future, his wealth, his life. He had to play his cards well, or his international empire would collapse, much like the dancing waters of a Las Vegas fountain after being turned off.

"No, I've never heard that name before. Is that a bank customer who's filing a complaint?"

"Okay, so you want to appear ignorant," said Troy. "Let's play the stupid game for a bit. We know you were getting divorced and that your estranged wife was suing you for 950 million euros, and then she disappeared. Never found."

"Mighty convenient," interjected Karla.

"You idiots are making a grievous mistake by coming into my house, *my house*! How dare you, *how dare you?*" screamed Hugh Mitchell, who was now foaming at the mouth.

Troy continued, "We are aware of some Iranians who take care of stuff like that — you know, make people disappear permanently. For example, Mrs. Mitchell. And they would like to make a bit more money than what you pay them. They're willing to talk to *The New York Times*, seeing that you are such a powerhouse here in Brussels. A man of honor, as the saying goes."

Hugh Mitchell went from ashen to grave to ill to ashen again. He knew that Karla and Troy knew too much and that they could not possibly be bluffing. Their declarations were based on facts. Karla and Troy noticed that Hugh Mitchell was beginning to feel the gravity of his situation.

"So what if I *have* heard of this 'Sanjar'? I'm sure many people have."

"Just think for a moment how it is that we know so much about you. We have met your paid assassins, and they have told us some things about your network."

"'Assassins'? Look here, I am a legitimate banker! I would never have ties to an assassin."

Karla was going through some of Hugh Mitchell's papers on the desk, and then she opened the top left drawer.

"Lieutenant, look what Mr. Mitchell wanted to use against us. It is a Czech CZ-82, 9mm semi-auto pistol, the identical type used to murder Mr. Thompson in London."

"These are cheap pistols. My security personnel bought it on the street, here in Brussels. I don't know anything about this Mr. Thompson you mentioned."

Karla countered, "'Cheap pistol'? Nothing in this home is cheap, and you know it. This is the standard sidearm for many police departments around the world. You like the best things in life, no?"

"Let me take a guess here, Mr. Mitchell. You have been supplying these murderous thugs weapons to commit assassinations all over the world. Do you know how many countries and families would like to get their hands on you to dissolve you alive in a vat of pure hydrofluoric acid? From pulleys above, they will slowly lower your naked body into the vat, and the acid engulfing your feet will dissolve all the flesh down to the bone in about 15 seconds — faster if you move too much. The rest of your body will follow the same fate, until all that's left is a beautiful, clean, bone-white skeleton of Mr. Mitchell," warned Troy.

Mr. Mitchell's initial narcissistic rage at having someone uninvited inside his house, and, worse, at having anyone challenge his secret global plans, was slowly giving way to a silent, unendurable panic, a terror of sorts, an inner explosion of stomach acids and muscular tremors which had to be suppressed no matter what, if he were to continue being the Hugh Mitchell everybody knew and adulated. He had to contain the crumbling psychological structures that made him feel always invincible, inarguably correct, irresistibly convincing, and omnipotent over the stupid middle- and lower-class masses with inferior blood stocks, destined to be his servers forever.

Being tied to this favorite and expensive Papa chair was a profound and painful transgression against his sense of God-given superiority, and it forced a partial unveiling of his fundamental sense of worthlessness, kept furiously at bay by his self-constructed inner psychological empire. This uncovering, much like suddenly losing all of one's garments while in public, required immediate action to turn around, to make whole again. But while a suddenly naked man on the street can quickly put his garments back on to avoid further embarrassment, Hugh Mitchell had already gotten a quick and terrifying look at the fallacy of his invincibility, something that could never be masked a second time.

Almost hyperventilating and sweating profusely, Mitchell spoke. "May I ask what your first names are?"

"This is Troy, and I am Karla. What's your connection to Sanjar?"

"Look, okay, you are probably FBI. You are mad at the CIA, and I understand it. But you seem like a pair of reasonable people. But reasonable people want a long and comfortable life, wouldn't you say?"

"We are here to tear down this nefarious organization and evil plan of yours, so forget it if you think you can buy your way out of this," retorted Troy.

"It's not just my plan. Blame your brothers. But, look, all my life I've been able to use money to solve problems. Your beggar's salaries can hardly compete. For starters, I can give each of you $100 million, deposited to any account anywhere in the world. In America, that would make you wealthier than 99.9% of all citizens. You surely cannot ignore that. Now, untie me, please."

The man was serious. $100 million dollars in a checking account. That was something to think about. But then again, that would be blood money. They had not joined the Navy intelligence service to make money but to do what was right, what their conscience directed them to do.

"Before we even think about money, we want the full story from you now, so we can perhaps trust you a bit more," demanded Karla. "I'm forcing myself not to shoot you in the eye right now, there, where you now sit, in your stupid, ugly, ridiculously over-priced, bourgeois Papa chair!"

"Very well. Yes, I know Sanjar. He is the head of the Iranian organization you mentioned — 'Blue Sparrow.'"

"And what is their mission?" asked Karla.

"They hate you Americans with an unbridled passion. Their principal aim is to inflict damage and death, with the ultimate goal of destroying America as a nation, as a culture."

"Where do you fit in?"

"I was recruited at an economics conference in Bern, Switzerland, about five years ago. We set up charity organizations to receive donation monies from the Iranians, and then we funnel the money where it is needed to local chapters to buy weapons, subvert political figures, pay salaries, and such."

"What's in it for you?"

"They've been paying me a 10% commission on monies I process internationally."

"Not bad. For every $5 billion you handle, you get to keep 500 million."

"And then there are special situations where I get more. Look, there's plenty of money for everybody. Beyond your wildest, most ridiculous expectations! Don't be a fool! Take the money. I lose my patience easily."

Then Troy added, "Why the geophysical devices?"

"I told you, the Iranians hate America, and they will use them to destroy you. Didn't the CIA inform you? They plan to cause earthquakes in the Pacific and in your country. That earthquake in the Northern Mariana Islands? I would say it was caused by them. Not sure, but that is my guess."

Karla interjected, "Doesn't it bother you that hundreds of thousands of innocent people were killed by that earthquake and tsunami?"

"Karla, wake up. I'm just a capitalist. I provide a service to these terrorists, and they're the ones who do the killing."

"But you made it possible!" Troy added angrily.

"Of all people! Both of you are really shortsighted, or maybe even blind. America is one of the world's premier arms producers and exporters. Fighter jets, tanks, destroyers, missiles, automatic weapons, helicopter gunships, RPGs, and tons of other war components — they all go to foreign lands to kill millions of people. But, since both of you are FBI and patriotic, I presume, you are willing to overlook that."

"I'm sure you want to remain alive, so answer this question truthfully: Where are the two geophysical devices right now?" asked Karla, raising her weapon just slightly.

"If I tell you, they will kill me."

"If you don't answer, you will die much sooner, with a bullet to the eye," swore Karla.

Hugh Mitchell was a calculating and rational man. He figured that, to save his skin, he could give them the location in the hope that the devices would have been moved by the time Troy and Karla got there. "My understanding is that they moved them from Gloucester to Rambouillet, just outside of Paris. I had to grease the customs monkeys to let the two crates through with just minimal paperwork and no questions. Set us back 10,000 euros."

"Where in Rambouillet?" snarled Troy.

"Remember, this conversation is not taking place. Listen, you'd better release me before I lose my cool. You cannot do this to me! I am a very powerful man at the bank!"

He was starting to lose his cool, going from resigned acquiescence to impending rage again. Karla detected that he even wanted to cry, to sob, even, but he fought hard not to show it. He was a man on the verge of melting. Karla gave him a cold, hard look to remind him they were waiting for an answer.

"It's called Industrial Leasing & Storage. On Rue du Champ. Block 33-C."

"You'd better not be lying to us, or you'll pay dearly," warned Karla.

"We just might give you a reprieve. Tell us about this mystery man Sanjar," ordered Troy.

"Never met him face to face — just phone calls and messages. Can't tell you more, or he will have me killed. He has eyes and ears everywhere, it seems."

"Too late for that, Mr. Mitchell. When you agreed to work with him, you became his property, in effect. He owns you, even if you don't want to believe that. Tell us about him — that's your best choice," emphasized Troy.

"He's the Iranian master of a group of about twelve dedicated assassins. They do as he says, no matter what. But to stay safe, he channels his orders through me, and his group knows that. He has said before that he would like to destroy America, and finding these two devices was like finding the mother lode for him."

"Alright, where do we find this lunatic?" intoned Karla.

"I did not say this. He resides exclusively in Sofia, Bulgaria. From there, he gives orders worldwide. Last known location was near Battenberg Square, but he moves every seven days to stay ahead of the assassins. He speaks Farsi, Bulgarian, English, and French. Intelligent man."

Troy then asked, "When was the last…." He was suddenly interrupted by Karla, who was peeking out a window.

"Troy, shush! I see lights at the end of the driveway," she whispered.

Troy glared at Mr. Mitchell and asked him accusingly, "Did you send out a silent alarm?" Mitchell just looked at him and did not answer. Troy added, "You stupid fool. Did you think they would come to rescue you? They now know we know your location, and they will assume you gave us important information. They are here to kill you and us, too!"

Hugh Mitchell wasn't talking, but he had a look of terror on his face.

"Karla, what do we have?"

"Well, their vehicle is slowly coming up the driveway; it's a safe bet to say they are here to search and destroy."

Troy and Karla expected the worst, so they checked and re-checked all their weapons to make sure they had full clips and were chambered. Who knew when they would have another chance to top off their ammunition clips? Looking through her night-vision rifle scope, Karla reported, "There are four of them, heavily armed."

Just then, Mitchell cried, "Hey, you've got to untie me. If you are right, then I have no chance of surviving if I am tied to my Papa chair!"

Karla was still checking her window, while Troy was trying to get her attention concerning what they should do about Mr. Mitchell. Suddenly, Karla yelled, "Troy, RPG, now! Quick, under the bed!"

Luckily, the beautiful stained wood floors had a high oil gloss, so Troy and Karla were able to run and dive for the floor under the bed. Their bodies slid the last meter or so and came to rest directly under the bed with a huge, thick mattress and an even thicker box spring. Almost in the same instant, the RPG slammed through the window and exploded near the bedroom ceiling in a thunderous blast, producing a shock wave that Troy and Karla felt painfully around their bodies, in spite of the thick and ruffled bed skirt that surrounded them.

Wood splinters, glass shards, and sharp, deadly metal shrapnel from the exploding grenade flew in all directions, penetrating and shredding anything and everything in the way. Under the bed, Karla and Troy covered their ears and faces as well as they could, and it took about twenty seconds for most of the projectiles to come to rest. They knew they had to get out of that bedroom as soon as possible — most probably the assassins would try to make their way up to the second floor soon.

Keeping a low profile, they crawled on the floor toward the door, trying to avoid the thousands of pieces of sharp glass littered about.

Karla saw that all that remained of Mr. Mitchell was a bloody torso with no limbs or head.

Troy assumed a strategic position at the top of one set of stairs, while Karla did the same on the other set. When the attackers slowly crept in, Troy fired one round at the lead guy and hit the mark. But that shot unleashed a ferocious torrent of automatic fire their way. So heavy was the assault that Troy and Karla could not even look so they could point their weapons at the attackers. Karla figured that the enemies' automatic weapons were firing a combined 30 rounds per second, a hellish assault, difficult to counteract. Wood, glass, fabric, paint, nails, screws, drywall, pieces of copper wires, electrical boxes, insulation, dust and lighting fixtures — all were raining down on Troy and Karla like an indoor tornado, as hundreds of bullets from the attackers were shredding the elegant and beautiful second-floor landing where Troy and Karla had taken refuge.

Karla yelled, "Troy, if they send even one RPG this way, we're dead meat. We gotta retreat!"

"Back to the bedroom!" Troy railed.

Troy fired two aimless shots in the general direction where the assassins were located on the first floor, perhaps to motivate them to keep on firing their submachine guns. Then he and Karla crawled back into Mitchell's once-palatial bedroom. An ottoman, very exclusive and expensive no doubt, had caught fire, so Karla came up with the idea of dropping a full clip of 9mm rounds into the flames, as they made their way to a blown-out window and slid down a rainspout to the ground below. Just about that time, the bullets in the ottoman fire started exploding, and they heard the assassins revive their massive firepower directed at the top of the landing. They decided it was the perfect time to make a run for it toward the woods about 150 yards from the side of the house.

It was a good plan, but they had not seen the attacker guarding the vehicle in which all four men had arrived, so a volley of bullets followed them as they ran zig-zag away from the house. Soon the two attackers inside the house joined the man outside, and all three went after Karla and Troy, who were now desperately running for their lives over a beautiful, manicured, well-fertilized, world-class lawn that offered absolutely no cover at all. Both Troy and Karla felt deep in their hearts that this would be the end of the line, that they had been outgunned and outmaneuvered by these stupid, murderous assassins.

But in spite of their pessimistic feelings, they kept zig-zagging, cringing as they heard bullets buzz by them.

"Shit, Troy, I should be back at CalTech teaching geophysics and enjoying the sun! What the hell am I doing dodging bullets from these assholes?" she screamed, in spite of being almost out of breath.

"And I just remembered that I haven't called my neighbor Miss Lilly in New York to remind her to feed Arturo," retorted Troy.

They covered the final 10 yards with herculean effort and went into the heavy cover of the woods, immediately getting behind a tree and finally firing their weapons at the fast-approaching assassins, who were still about 50 yards from the edge of the woods. Their sudden vulnerability caused the three attackers to retreat, but, just in case they were thinking of using their vehicle, Troy fired several 200-yard shots at the engine and the tires. Now they couldn't follow.

Karla and Troy waited until all three men frantically returned to the house. Then they walked at a brisk pace inside the woods in the direction of the place where they had hidden their car.

"Troy, you okay? No hits? Sorry I didn't ask sooner."

"I feel alright, so that probably means no hits, no bullet holes. And you — are you okay, Karla? Any hits?"

"Oh, no, I'm okay. Smelling like roses. I could easily have done this in my sleep."

In five minutes, they got to their car. Helping each other, they brushed off the considerable amount of debris on their hair, face, and clothing. Troy started the engine, and they anxiously sped away from all that noisy mayhem at the Mitchell estate.

CHAPTER 10

Driving back to the center of Brussels, Karla said, "Seems to me that we should go to Rambouillet before they move the devices, wouldn't you say, Troy? Especially since all hell broke loose at Mr. Mitchell's residence."

"You're right. We'll go to the hotel to wash up and catch the next flight to Paris. If we're lucky, the Industrial Storage place is closed for the evening, so the goons will have to wait until morning to move Geo-1 and Geo-2. We may still have a chance."

Back at Be Manos Hotel, they quickly briefed Admiral Ferris by phone and informed him of their plan to travel immediately to Rambouillet, on the outskirts of Paris, to try to intercept the two devices. They asked him to notify the U.S. Embassy in Paris so they could have a car ready with the usual list of weapons, but this time including two RPG-7 launchers. To destroy Geo-1 and Geo-2, Karla and Troy would need bomb capability, and the devastating Russian anti-tank RPG-7 would be the lethal weapon of choice.

On Tuesday night's short flight to Paris, Karla came up with a suggestion. "Okay, time to take stock of where the hell we stand on this mess."

"I agree, Karla. You have good organizational skills, so go for it."

"We pretty much agree that there are two hostile groups operating here, but it's not clear to me that the Iranians were the ones who fired that shot at me in the hotel in London."

"So what's your hypothesis?"

"Troy, I'm beginning to think that the CIA is involved in this."

"What?" exclaimed Troy, as he now began to pay more attention to Karla. "Our own CIA? That's ridiculous, Karla!"

"Yes, I know it sounds surreal, but I've been thinking about it for the last two hours."

"Karla, watch what you say. Your words are making me feel that I can't wholly trust you."

"Well, is this conversation about the facts and how they connect logically, or about your blind trust in the CIA, Troy?"

"Very well — you have a point. Go ahead. Tell me what makes you suspect the CIA."

"When we were interrogating Hugh Mitchell at his home, he mentioned that he thought we were FBI and that we must be sore at the CIA. Why would those two concepts come up in his analysis of the situation? More importantly, if we were FBI, why would we be sore at the CIA?"

"Are you saying that he felt we were FBI investigating him because he was connected with the CIA, 'Blue Sparrow,' and the geophysical devices?"

"Exactly!"

"And, most damning of all, Troy, were his words, 'It's not just my plan — blame your brothers.'"

Troy reflected on that for a few seconds. "It sounds as if he was saying that this use of Geo-1 and Geo-2 was a CIA plan and that he was involved with them."

"Troy, this is not good. There is something really big happening here besides the use of these machines to create earthquakes. How could our own CIA be involved in killing so many people?"

"Karla, if this is true, we'd better notify Admiral Ferris immediately!"

"Not so fast. This is only one piece of the puzzle. I know you won't forgive me for saying this, but I have to say it anyway. We don't know if Admiral Ferris is involved in this."

A very friendly flight attendant with a beautiful smile approached them and offered them some drinks and some quick snacks, as this was about a one-hour flight. No dinner. Too late for that in addition to the flight being too short. So Karla and Troy doubled up on the offerings, which they began to eat ravenously.

"Karla, how could you ever suspect Admiral Ferris? It's almost like blasphemy — or treason!"

Karla retorted, "There you go again, Troy, letting your loyalties color your analytical thinking. Go back and remember some of the things they taught us in those intel training classes and exercises. 'Trust no one.' 'Suspect everyone.' 'Don't let loyalties get in the way.' 'Go by facts alone.' I could even be a Russian spy, Troy. Are you sure I'm not?"

She was right, but, by then, Troy wasn't exactly sure what he should believe. It was beginning to feel like a hornets' nest, with labyrinthine tunnels and passageways. "So do you suspect me, too, Karla?"

"Nah, Troy — I figure that any man who sings 'Ave Maria' while taking an unnecessarily cold shower every night has to be a good man," cooed Karla.

The airplane chime came on, and the captain signaled that it was time to get ready to land. Forty-five minutes later, they were leaving the Charles de Gaulle airport in Paris, heading for the American Embassy.

Admiral Ferris had done a good job: The Embassy personnel were waiting for them with a modest Peugeot sedan, loaded with weapons, including two RPG-7s, as requested. They filled out all the necessary paperwork, and they were on their way to Rambouillet, just southwest of Paris.

It was 3 o'clock Wednesday morning, so their sleepy disposition did not put them in the mood to enjoy all the beautiful sights in Paris, especially the grand Eiffel Tower. They certainly did not enjoy going on missions at this time — sleepy and all that — but it was top priority to get to those two devices before the Blue Sparrow assassin group could have a chance to relocate them. It had already been several hours since the encounter at the Mitchell mansion, plenty of time to move the two crates if the Iranians had wanted to.

Sleepiness was becoming a problem, so they stopped at an all-night coffee shop for some very strong coffee and perhaps some sugary pastry. It was just off the A10/E5, called Cafe Kromo, a one-waitress joint at that hour. Quite a few people there, couples and loners, all-night partiers, perhaps chronic insomniacs, and some perverts with shifty eyes and hands suspiciously under the table. Lively atmosphere. Besides Troy and Karla, nobody there seemed to be sleepy. After two cups of strong Guatemalan coffee and a shared *eclair du chocolat*, neither were they.

The bald and aging chain smoker near the restroom hallway caught their eye, for they had never seen anyone puff on a cigarette continuously until it burned the front part of the filter. In the ten minutes they had been there, the smoking maniac had gone through seven cigarettes. Incredibly, though, he appeared to be starving for smoke, much like a drowning person gasps for every possible breath of air. And even though it was a bizarre sight to behold, there was something interesting and perverse in witnessing such pathological, self-destructive behavior. It wasn't pretty, since the man was probably already dying of lung cancer, for he was thinner than a skin-and-bones anorexic — the part of his body that held the most meat was probably his earlobes. For just a fleeting second, Troy thought how ironic it was that he and Karla were fighting against the evil in this world, just to make it safer for individuals to piss away their lives like the smoking fiend in this out-of-the-way cafe on the outskirts of Paris at 3 o'clock in the morning. *What a crazy world,* he thought.

The cafe was filling up with more creepy-looking people. Well, these were weird hours, after all. Time to leave.

Rambouillet was a beautiful small city of forests and ancient castles, rich in culture and history. Troy and Karla were eager to see the beautiful architecture but had to be content with general outlines and shadows as provided by street lights, moonlight, and the faint aurora of the new day. Still, despite this minimal ambient lighting, they had no trouble at all in locating the Rue du Champ and, soon afterward, Industrial Leasing and Storage.

ILS was a sizeable storage depot covering perhaps two city blocks. It had very sturdy metal and wire fencing all around and what looked like massive electric gates supported on wheels, wide enough to allow large trucks in and out. There were numerous rows of storage pods or chambers, some large enough to allow storage of a house-full of furniture. Close to the gate was a separate, smaller building that Karla figured was the office, but all lights there were off.

They viewed as much as they could without stopping, for it was possible the facilities were being watched by members of Blue Sparrow, although no suspicious vehicles were spotted in the vicinity. It was clear that they had to get into the facilities now, before the assassin crew arrived.

Karla parked the Peugeot on a residential street, and, fully armed with an RPG in a gym bag, they made their way to the edge of the fence. After cutting away a rectangular piece of the heavy-duty cyclone fence, they entered the premises and began the search for Block 33-C, the one Hugh Mitchell had indicated. It was a good thing that, apparently, the assassins had wanted maximum privacy, because the storage room was located relatively far from the office, facing directly into a wooded area. Even though they were making good progress, they feared that the storage facility might have some silent movement and pressure detectors, so the police might show up soon. Or worse, the storage room might have an explosive booby trap. They had to take that risk.

Since the latch on the storage-room lock had an oversized, hardened steel lock, they opted to cut through the heavy aluminum overhead door instead. As soon as they had made two perpendicular five-inch cuts, they bent the metal corner outward to allow space to view the contents. The two lethal crates were either there or they were not. The moment had come.

Troy bent down closer to the ground and asked Karla for a flashlight. His heart dropped. "Karla — it's empty!"

"Damn that Hugh Mitchell! He must have lied to us!" she exclaimed.

"Or maybe they've already come here to pick the devices up," opined Troy, feeling that they had just lost a very important round against Blue Sparrow. "They've had a few hours' lead time."

"If they were here, who knows where they'll end up next? Supposedly, we know where Sanjar is, but we have no more leads on these laser-energy devices," lamented Karla with an atypical long face.

They were feeling sorry for themselves for less than one minute when they heard the roar of a diesel engine starting nearby, those big, monster motors installed in trucks. It sounded like the roar was there somewhere inside the storage compound, but with so many buildings to reflect the thunder, it was difficult to pinpoint its location. So they picked up the gym bag and started looking. Around the corner, far up ahead, they saw it: a large truck accelerating toward the closed steel gate. It didn't stop — just tore through the steel gate as if it were made of wooden slats, like the ones used in baby cribs.

Karla exclaimed, "They're in a hurry, Troy! It must be them!"

They ran after the truck, but soon gunfire from somewhere near the torn gate came their way. "Karla, can you see where that's coming from?"

"No, but it's coming from near the gate!"

Karla and Troy would be sitting ducks if they continued running toward the gate in the small alleyway, so they had no choice but to seek cover between buildings. Meanwhile the truck was getting farther away. Seconds counted.

"Karla, give me the gym bag."

Karla gave him the bag and a look that said, *You're not thinking of using that tank buster now, are you?*

Yes, he was. He placed a rocket-propelled grenade inside the launcher, aimed at a concrete post in the general gate area, where they believed the shooters to be hiding, and he pressed the trigger. Leaving a trail of smoke, the launcher zipped the grenade warhead to the concrete gate support, and it exploded in a thunderous blast that erased everything within a radius of about 25 yards, sending deadly shrapnel in all directions. Shooters stopped shooting. No time to consider other options. Karla and Troy ran toward the demolished gate, their submachine guns loaded, chambered, and ready to fire. But no shooters. They walked around the giant crater and ran toward their Peugeot.

Karla took the wheel, and Troy loaded another tank-killer rocket grenade into the launcher. Troy struggled with the moral courage it would take to fire this explosive monster at the truck if they caught up to it in heavy morning-rush traffic. He would soon find out what kind of military man he was

Karla wove the small-but-peppy Peugeot through the smaller streets, taking educated guesses as to the direction the large truck might have taken, eventually getting on a small road that paralleled motorway E50. And there it was — the large, orange truck, doing about 130 kph on the motorway toward Chartres.

"Troy, quick — check the map and tell me when and where this dinky little road enters the motorway!" She feared that, if the truck pulled too far ahead on the fast motorway, they would never be able to find it — ever again. Karla continued to drive as fast as she could on this impossibly slow, rural road, all the while watching the truck getting farther ahead.

"No, I don't see any connection to the E50 for another 30 kilometers, Karla."

Karla had to make a quick and risky decision, but that is what it means to be a Navy Intel officer, and she had never backed down before. She turned the wheel sharply and plunged the car toward the no-man's land between the small road and the motorway. The Peugeot started bouncing around, hitting shrubs, weeds, small rocks, old tree limbs broken off years ago, and even trash secretly left there. Some parts of the area were swampy, and the wheels spun wildly. Mud jumped at the car from all directions — Karla turned on the windshield wipers and washers. Troy was holding on to the overhead handle for dear life and started to fear that the wild gyrations of the car would accidentally trigger the rocket grenade already loaded into the launcher. If that were to happen, he, Karla, and the car would all be vaporized by the unforgiving blast. *It would be quick, though*, he thought.

Karla's face was already covered by a hundred beads of sweat, for she knew that, at any moment, the front wheels might drop into a large hole or ravine, and that would be the end of the mission. Her eyes were as wide as Troy had ever seen them, for she was desperately trying to get as much visual information about the area up ahead as possible. It didn't help that the wipers were not doing a good job of removing mud, weeds, leaves, trash, and tree limbs from the windshield. And she was running out of window-washer fluid.

Up ahead, she spotted an opportunity to get onto the motorway, but there was a ravine she had to manage, and she couldn't slow down, either.

"Troy, hold on for dear life!"

The car's nose went down, and she realized that the ravine held some water, like a creek or such. The car slammed into the water, creating a rising water crown all around it, but Karla did not let up on the gas pedal, or they would certainly have ended up getting stuck there. The Peugeot's engine whined with high RPM, and its tires spun wildly as the car went way up on the other side and became airborne, pointing directly at the motorway. If it landed properly, they would make it. Good thing that the traffic on the E50 saw the events unfolding and moved on to other lanes to avoid a high-speed collision.

Karla masterfully landed the car safely but with an ugly thud that indicated that the suspension had bottomed out upon impact with the road surface. The steering immediately felt abnormal, but the car was still running.

The orange truck was about 300 meters ahead.

A nauseating stink quickly permeated the inside of the car as they accelerated toward the truck. Troy and Karla had no way of knowing it, but all the mud that completely covered the car was not mud at all but runoff from a pig farm upstream from where they had gone into the ravine. Yes, it was sickening, and it stuck well to the car, but there was no time to consider the aesthetics of their situation — they had to catch up with the orange truck transporting the two lethal ray devices. In spite of the damaged steering, Karla edged the car ever closer to the truck. Troy fired his pistol at the truck, hitting it twice on the left rear doors, but that really didn't change anything. So Troy prepared the RPG for a devastating hit through the back of the trailer part. He took aim.

But they had not counted on the two snipers riding shotgun on the truck.

Just then, Troy had a clear shot at the trailer, but he failed to take it. He had been ready to pull the trigger on the RPG, except that he noticed that there were too many cars around the truck and trailer. Those would be demolished too, along with drivers and passengers. He waited a few seconds — just long enough for the first two sniper bullets to slam into the car. One went through the windshield and hit Troy in the chest. The other hit a tire, which blew up, making the car spin around twice, ending up on the grassy part of the road shoulder. Another shot hit some metal somewhere in the car, but Karla did not care much by then. That orange truck-and-trailer just sped on over the hill, perhaps never to be seen again.

CHAPTER 11

There they were, on the side of the motorway, almost in a ditch, the car practically destroyed, with Troy not breathing and the loaded RPG launcher on his lap. Just to make sure, Karla unbuttoned his shirt; yes, he was wearing his protective bulletproof vest. Figuring that the impact shock of the bullet had stopped his breathing, she reclined his passenger seat all the way back and began to administer CPR and mouth-to-mouth resuscitation. He was not responding, so she removed his vest, thinking that perhaps the bullet had passed through. But it had not, so she continued. As she was furiously doing the best she could, her mind floated between the task at hand and her realization that the mission seemed to have met its bitter end. The orange truck had driven away, and they had no idea whatsoever where it might be heading. The people with intimate knowledge of the sinister plan were all dead, their own CIA might be hunting them down, she was stranded on the motorway with a broken car that smelled like pig shit, and her partner, whom she was beginning to like, even though he was ornery, might well be dead. She felt lonely, very lonely.

But she was Karla Bloomfield, and she remembered the advice that her dad had always given her: "Karla, on any mission, always give your best to the very end, no matter how impossible a victory may seem." With that thought at the forefront of her mind, she almost said out loud, "Thanks, Dad," and it gave her a re-invigorated will to persist, even if she felt like crying at the same time because of the hopelessness of the situation.

"Come on, Troy, breathe! It was just a little bullet, not like the rocket monster you unleashed against those guys at the gate of the storage depot. Come on, Troy!" She kept at it, pressing down on his chest, and giving air, mouth-to-mouth. Soon she could feel a pulse, and, a few seconds later, he began to gag and cough.

"Sorry, Karla, what happened? Where are we now? Why are we parked in a ditch?" Troy managed to say softly and in broken phrases.

"Don't talk — just concentrate on breathing. Get your breathing as regular as possible."

Yes, he was disoriented, but he seemed to be coming around quickly. Then, he felt the pain in his chest. There was a large, round, bloody wound where the blunt force of the bullet had pressed against it. Karla located the deformed bullet still embedded in the safety vest, and she showed it to Troy. "This almost took your life." Karla slowly re-adjusted Troy's seat to the normal sitting position. Things were beginning to get clearer for him.

"Karla, I was the one who was hit with the bullet, so why are you crying?"

"I was trying desperately to save your life by giving you CPR and mouth-to-mouth, and I just knew I would not feel good if another human being died while I was trying to help."

"So I was asleep when you kissed me?"

"Hey, wait a minute — I didn't kiss you, buddy! It was CPR — that's all!"

"Sure, Karla, call it what you wish. You're a genius. I need to contact that assassin and ask him to shoot me again. Seems that's the only way to warm you up, Lieutenant!"

Troy was feeling better, really better, knowing that Karla had kissed him, or given him CPR, or whatever.

After evaluating their situation, they called the U.S. Embassy in Paris and asked for medical and tow-truck service right away. An hour later, Karla, Troy, and the evil-smelling car were inside the Embassy compound. Doctors treated Troy for the impact wound, gave him strong analgesics, and asked him to take it easy for a few days. *Yeah, but Blue Sparrow's evil plan is just not going to wait,* he thought.

And prescient he was. An urgent call came into the Embassy — it was Admiral Ferris, and he wanted a scrambled video-line to talk to Troy and Karla. Embassy staff provided a secure room for that.

"Hi, Troy and Karla. I hear that things are not going well over there," deadpanned Ferris. They gave him a quick update, telling him they had no idea of the current whereabouts of Geo-1 and -2.

"Well, they've raised the ante, and now we have an urgent national emergency."

Karla replied, "It was already bad enough — now what?"

"The White House received an electronic message today carrying a very ominous threat. A group calling itself 'Blue Sparrow' claimed to have in their possession the device that caused the earthquake in the Northern Mariana Islands several days ago. They underlined the verb 'caused.'"

"Yes, that's the name that keeps popping up over here, and, yes, they do have Geo-1 and Geo-2. So, what do they want?" asked Troy.

"The communication said they want $1 trillion in gold bullion from the U.S. government within three days, or they will unleash a Richter 9 earthquake along the San Andreas Fault line in California."

"What'd the White House say about it?" queried Karla.

"The White House is not up to speed on our current mission regarding the Northern Mariana Islands earthquake, so, of course, they treated it as a baseless threat. But, just in case, they passed it on to the FBI and the CIA. I know we wanted to keep this mission you're involved in covert, especially with regard to the CIA, but, now, they obviously know about the threat."

"And your boss, Admiral Chief Rockwell — what's his role here?" asked Troy.

"The CIA already knew he had you and Karla involved in this intel mission in London, but since I haven't been giving him too many updates, he has consequently not been passing updates to the CIA, either."

"So, Admiral, what is the White House doing about this deadline?" interrupted Troy.

"Nothing, but it only gets worse. The group wants the White House to tell them they will seriously consider the matter within 24 hours. If not, they will attack Alaska first."

"Well, sir," spoke Karla, "you know we don't have to tell you that this Blue Sparrow group is a very professional assassin group, and they have the full technical capability — and no moral restrictions — to carry out those threats. I think that both California and Alaska are under extreme threat right now. What they did at the Mariana Trench was just a warm-up to make sure the machines work. And they work only too well."

"What're the FBI and the CIA doing about this?" asked Troy.

"They claim they've never heard of Blue Sparrow, and they're checking the Internet origin of the message. No luck yet. I'm sure it's one of those disposable email addresses."

Troy warned, "My suggestion, Admiral, is for the White House to reply within that 24-hour deadline that, yes, they will seriously consider the matter. That will buy us some time."

The situation certainly seemed dire, for the United States, in reality, was caught between two equally repugnant alternatives. How could it hand over

$1 trillion of gold bullion to Blue Sparrow? That amounted to a very high percentage of the gold bullion in America. Besides, there was no way to keep that disbursal secret, and, as soon as the world found out, the financial markets would collapse into economic chaos. And if the U.S. government refused to comply, the consequences for California and Alaska would be catastrophic, for the Geophysical Dynamics devices had already proven to be able to melt away the frictional tension along thousands of miles of colliding tectonic plates, allowing for gargantuan land-mass movements, creating earthquakes greater than Richter 9.

Millions of people would die, there would be trillions of dollars of damage, and there would be consequential damage to the economy and the political fabric of the country. It wouldn't stop there, either, for the extortionists would want more and more, with the threat of destroying any continent at will. This was apocalypse, and it was at the door of the most powerful military power in the history of the world — The United States.

As the three of them discussed these points, Troy's mind kept going back to that spot on the E50 motorway, just a few hours before, when he had the orange truck in the scope sight of the RPG-7, and his finger was on the trigger. He had the shot, but he didn't take it. And he hadn't pressed that trigger because he elected to save the lives of perhaps 10 innocent people driving near the truck — the blast would surely have vaporized them, too. Had he pressed that trigger, he would have spared millions of people the potential death they now faced at the hands of the assassins from Blue Sparrow. In retrospect, he felt, regrettably, that he had made the wrong decision.

Yet, in his mind, he was still trying to hedge on the morality of what he had done, accentuating the fact that he had been thinking he could get a better shot but with no nearby vehicles at risk. That opportunity had never come. But, *he should have known* that a soldier takes the shot whenever he can, for he may never get another chance.

So, to prepare himself for the next time, Troy made a mental note he promised himself he would follow: A rule is moral only up until the time it clashes with another, more desirable rule. In this Armageddon struggle he was now involved in, he felt there would be many moral rules he would have to break. He knew he would have to contaminate his soul in order to do the moral job he had accepted to protect his country.

On one level, it was ridiculous thinking, he felt, but, at another level, it made perfect logical sense, because it reflected the morally paradoxical nature of war and conflict.

"Do you have any theories about where the devices are?" asked Admiral Ferris in an almost pleading tone.

"Big probability they're still in France, sir," responded Karla. "And if you put out the word with the U.S. Embassy here in Paris that all ports and border motorways should be on the lookout for these two large crates, we can probably make sure they never leave this area."

"Another thing, Admiral," remembered Troy, "we think it was the CIA that tried to assassinate Karla at the hotel in London. That Brussels banker Hugh Mitchell thought we were FBI and that we were pissed at the CIA for their involvement in this mission."

"Troy, how in the world can you say that? The CIA does not go around killing intel agents in other divisions of the government, much less military intel officers!" screamed Admiral Ferris.

"Yes, Admiral, I know it sounds terrible, but these assassins over here have consistently been ahead of Karla and me one or two steps all the time. They are getting intel from inside the U.S. government somewhere," explained Troy, with an uncomfortable edge of insubordination. "That's why we asked you not to update your commander, Admiral Chief Rockwell — not that we suspect him, but because he is *required* to pass intel over to the CIA."

"But why, Troy? Why would the CIA do such dastardly things? It's hard to accept your theory."

Karla answered, "We don't know yet, but we're trying to get an answer. Now here's another very important point. The co-inventor of the devices, Jacob Graham, told us that a man who called himself Bitor Spinelli went to visit them at the lab, in London, ostensibly to invest, but ended up forcing them at gunpoint to give him the two devices. He described this man as short, stocky, early 30s, three-day beard, did not look Italian. Troy and I suspect that if the CIA was involved, then they would probably have sent an agent to talk to the two inventors. Then Bitor Spinelli showed up some days later already pre-informed of the details."

"So, how do we check up on that?" asked Admiral Ferris.

"Troy and I visited Geophysical Dynamics. Place was a mess, but we did notice security cameras in several sections of the lab. Send a Navy intel agent to see if recordings from those cameras are still on the premises. Hopefully, he'll find them and get those recordings to you right away. See if you can identify an American-looking man who visited the lab a few days before a man with the description I just gave you of Bitor Spinelli."

"Yes, I can get that done right away. We have Navy intelligence personnel at our Embassy in London."

"We would appreciate that, Admiral," declared Troy. "And it might also be a good idea if you sent someone to the bombed-out mansion of Hugh Mitchell in the Sonian Forest just outside Paris. We had to leave the house running, so we didn't get a chance to look at stuff. My guess is that he was working with the CIA, and he might have kept notes on payments, orders, and such. There could very well be a treasure trove there."

"Yes, I agree it would be a good idea. We have U.S. Navy intelligence personnel working cooperatively at the French naval base at Toulon, near Marseille. I can get someone to check out the mansion right away."

Karla added, "Sir, we would love to continue this chat with you, but, right now, time is of the essence. Troy and I had better go to Sofia, Bulgaria. We were informed by Hugh Mitchell in Brussels that the sadistic mastermind of this group from hell lives there. Mitchell said this man, 'Sanjar,' moves every few days for security purposes, but that is the only lead we have at this time — absolutely nothing else. And I would suggest, Admiral, that when we get to Sofia, *you* arrange supplies for us at a Navy Intel safe-house, not the CIA. Please don't inform our Embassy there that we are on a mission — we would like to enter Bulgaria as private citizens."

"Very well. Troy and Karla, best of luck. Only you two can save this country from the calamitous threat that's been thrust upon us. I know I can count on you both."

CHAPTER 12

The 1100-mile, three-hour southeasterly flight from Paris to Sofia took them over Switzerland, Austria, Slovenia, Croatia, Bosnia, and Serbia — they arrived in Bulgaria in mid-afternoon. Passing through customs at the Sofia-Vrazhdebna Airport, Bulgaria's largest, was uneventful. They got into an OK Supertrans Taxi for the short southwesterly ride to the Kempinski Hotel Zografski, not far from the center of Sofia. But, along the way, Karla asked the cab driver to take a short detour so she could get a glimpse of the Alexander Nevsky Gold-Domed Cathedral, constructed over a 20-year period in the early 1900s in honor of the fallen soldiers of the Russo-Turkish war of 1877–78. It was important to the Bulgarians because, through this war, they achieved independence from Ottoman rule.

The Kempinski Hotel was not the tallest or the most expensive in Sofia, the capital city of about 1.3 million souls, but it would serve the purpose. With about 20 floors and all amenities known to Westerners, the hotel provided Karla and Troy with all the comfort they would need. Large suite, two double beds, on a high floor, please. Besides, it had good security, especially for all the floors above the main one.

They decided to spend some time in their room looking at maps, relaxing, and reading up on the geography of the area, for they literally had no idea where they would start looking for Sanjar. In the early evening hours, they decided to go out to dinner to get a better feel for the streets and the general ambience of the city.

One thing that fascinated Karla was the famous Ivan Vazov National Theatre, probably the city's most important historical attraction. Named after the writer of the same name, the building was completed in 1906, had six mammoth columns on its façade and two towers, and was surrounded by beautiful statues and figures etched onto its walls. Even when there were no dramatic works being performed, the building itself was a sight to behold.

To make themselves less obvious to any state security agents that might have been patrolling the streets undercover, Karla held on to Troy's arm as they walked the beautiful streets in the crisp evening air. Well, anyway, that is the story she told him, and it made perfect sense to him. They walked northwest and soon came upon The Spaghetti Company on Alexandar Stamboliyski Blvd, an outside canopied restaurant that offered Italian and other Mediterranean dishes. It was perfect for dining and discussing plans for the next day.

They sat at a beautiful, round ceramic table with an oversized umbrella, barely three yards from the slow-moving traffic. The wafting aroma of pizza, exotic cheeses, and garlic filled the air inside and outside of the restaurant, and, all of a sudden, they were starving.

Even though they were relaxing, they still had to keep their eyes open for any potential agents who might have been following. The locals were not looking at them in particular, since Sofia enjoyed a healthy traffic in tourists year-round, so they were used to seeing outsiders everywhere. No, there was no one who looked suspicious, so they started to enjoy their four-cheese Sicilian pizza, downed with some local red wine.

"Let's say we locate this fiend, this 'Sanjar' guy. Then what?" queried Karla as she was trying to get the stringy cheese into her mouth.

"It's not gonna be pretty, Karla. First, we have to find him, and I'm sure he has more security than our own White House. Second, we have to capture him. There's going to be a lot of dead bodies. And, he's not going to willingly give us the location of Geo-1 and Geo-2."

"Duh. I could have guessed that. Do we have a plan?"

"Because of my hesitation to fire that RPG when I had the orange truck in my sights on the highway, we lost that battle. Now I'm afraid that I will have to force this information out of him. You don't have to participate in what will be a very dirty job. We have this problem because of me."

"No, Troy — we're in this together."

"Thanks, Karla, but I don't feel good about what I know I will have to do to remedy this situation. And I would not want you to stain your heart dealing with this monster."

"Are you talking about torture?"

"Is there any other way?"

She thought about it for a moment. "Troy, we are in the dirty business of protecting our country, and when we go into the pit to fight face to face with the enemy, we are bound to get contaminated. Our only consolation is that we do dirty things to uphold a moral imperative, the safety of our country. That's our duty, and if we can't do that, we should have opted to become hairdressers instead."

"I'm glad you feel that way."

Just then, Troy's phone rang. It was Admiral Ferris.

"Troy, you were right! We sent a Navy intel agent right away to look over the Geophysical lab in London, and he found the video recordings from the security cameras. He said the place smelled terrible."

"Yeah, the bodies are probably still in the supply room downstairs, more than ripe. What's on those recordings, sir?" asked Karla.

"About two days before this strange Bitor Spinelli showed up at the Lab, there was an American-looking male visitor there talking with Mr. Thompson and Mr. Graham. In other shots, he is seen looking closely at the devices. There was no audio."

"Were you able to identify this man?" asked Troy.

"Were we ever!" exclaimed the Admiral. "Our face-recognition specialists identified him as Edgar Wicklund, a CIA agent working out of the consulate there in London. You and Karla were right in your hunch!"

"Damn! The CIA knew of these devices way before the big earthquake struck at the Northern Mariana Islands! Admiral, it's starting to look more and more like the CIA is deeply involved in this attack on the United States. They have murdered innocent people! We need to interview this guy Wicklund right away," urged Karla.

"Can't. We thought of that, but Scotland Yard found him in a trash bin with a bullet to the back of his head," explained Admiral Ferris.

"Just like the three workers at the Lab," remembered Troy.

Karla wondered, "Now, just how does the CIA find out about these Geophysical Dynamics devices? Thompson and Graham were not looking to gloat or to get famous."

"We know that the Agency scours thousands of professional journals around the world on a monthly basis for tidbits that may have intelligence or strategic value. When something looks promising, they contact the author for additional information. I remember clearly, a few years back, when they contacted a professor at Columbia University in New York. He was doing research on how to use voice intonation and facial micro-gestures to detect when a person was lying. Obviously that would have immense value in military interrogations and in field work," explained Ferris.

"So, maybe Thompson or Graham had written some theoretical paper on the technical basis of their devices, and the CIA read it?" Troy estimated.

"I doubt very much that either inventor would have contacted the CIA directly. Both of them appeared to be rather peaceful gentlemen. And remember, it was one of them, Thompson, who sent that warning fax message to Groton Submarine Base," added Karla.

"It's inconceivable that our CIA would be involved in killing hundreds of thousands of people in this manner, but it is irrefutable that their imprint is everywhere," lamented Ferris. "But this also means, Karla and Troy, that you have got to be extra careful. Somebody besides Blue Sparrow is killing people connected to this case. Could be the CIA, a rival terror group, even a foreign government."

"Troy and I were thinking, sir, if you have a local source who can help us get a bearing on the shadowy side of Sofia, that would save us a lot of time."

"While you were in flight to Bulgaria, I was checking out some names of people who have helped us, and there is this informant who has provided us with valuable intel in the past. Rather eccentric. Don't be alarmed; he's harmless — just don't criticize his lifestyle. Name is Yanko Torpolorian, mannequin designer and creator. You can find him at Imperial Mannequins and Design, there in Sofia. He's expecting your call."

"Admiral, one last thing. Did the White House decide to honor Blue Sparrow's 24-hour deadline for an answer to seriously consider the demand?" asked Karla cautiously.

"They basically said for them to go to hell."

Troy expressed what nobody wanted to hear. "We'll know tomorrow morning, if Alaska goes to hell as well."

The rest of their dinner and coffee went okay, although the conversation with Ferris had cast a dark cloud. If the Blue Sparrow group wanted to inflict a Richter 9 earthquake on Alaska tomorrow, there was nothing anyone on Earth could do to prevent it at this time. Hopefully, Geo-1 and Geo-2 were still in France somewhere, so that established some geographical limits. It was certainly much better than having to look all over Eastern Europe for the devices.

"But, Karla, I was thinking — just because CIA sent an agent to Geophysical Dynamics doesn't mean they were involved in the subsequent earthquake in the Pacific, right?" queried Troy.

"Let's look at the broader picture. For sure, the CIA knew of the devices before the Pacific quake. We have that Wicklund guy in the video. Later, Groton base received the warning fax. As a matter of policy, it got sent down the line until it got to Admiral Ferris," explained Karla.

"And the CIA was briefed about it when Ferris reported it to his commander, Rockwell, who was required to send reports to the CIA," concluded Troy. "Bottom line is that the CIA knew the devices were real, they knew about the prediction-warning fax, and they took no action."

"The big question, Troy, is 'Why?' Why did the CIA remain silent and passive concerning the warning?"

"I can't think of any gain that the CIA could achieve from an attack on the Northern Mariana Islands," Troy said pensively. "Then again, maybe they were not so passive if they were the ones who fired that bullet at you at the hotel. At the very least, they did not want us to dig into this case."

"And don't forget that Mr. Graham was assassinated at our Embassy in London. Who knew he would be there? Only the CIA was privy to that info. Another reason Blue Sparrow could not have been involved is that they initially did not believe the news that Graham had been shot. Remember that incident in the barn where that damned fucker had the gun to my head? He wanted corroboration that Graham was alive," added Karla, by now sipping her third cup of Alajuela mountain coffee from Costa Rica.

After thinking for a few seconds, Troy added, "But if an Iranian from Blue Sparrow killed Mr. Thompson when we were there at his hideaway flat in London, why would Blue Sparrow then want Mr. Graham alive?"

"Troy, think for a minute. Maybe it wasn't Blue Sparrow that killed Mr. Thompson. Maybe it was the CIA. They contracted the hit to other, independent Iranians and even supplied them with those Czech CZ-82 handguns, the same type they supplied to that banker, Hugh Mitchell."

Whichever way they looked at it, the situation appeared extremely critical. Blue Sparrow was demanding $1 trillion in gold bullion within three days, or most of California would probably be sliced off the mainland at the San Andreas Fault. Millions of people would die, economic damages would be in the trillions, and human suffering would be incalculable. To make it worse, tomorrow morning, Alaska would probably be split in half, as a prelude of worse things to come. Never in the history of the world had such a small group acquired such enormous power over all the nations on earth. There wasn't much time to play the hopelessly weak hand that Troy and Karla had been dealt.

It wasn't easy to maintain all those details and conflicting theories organized in their heads, Karla and Troy were beginning to feel the exhaustion of the mental acrobatics, not to mention of the travel and the events of the day. Maybe it was time to head back to the hotel.

Once in their room, Karla suggested they call Yanko Torpolorian to set up the meeting for tomorrow morning. Troy volunteered.

"Hello, Mr. Torpolorian? Hi, this is Troy Hamilton. Admiral Ferris in Dover advised us to call you He said you might be able to help us here in Sofia."

"Yes, Mr. Hamilton, I have been advised."

"Well, sir, we were wondering if perhaps we can meet with you at your office tomorrow morning. Is 8 o'clock okay with you?"

"That will be perfectly fine. See you tomorrow." *Click.*

Wide-eyed, Karla asked, "What was that?"

"Remember, Ferris said he was eccentric but harmless."

Since they had already developed a pattern, they took turns taking separate showers. They still required topical medications on their wounds, so they helped each other. Troy's blunt chest wound was now turning colors, but it was still reddish, still oozing small amounts of blood. Karla applied the antibacterial and analgesic cream to his chest. He applied the antiseptic cream to her shoulder and back wounds, which were healing very well.

Then Karla had a thought.

"It appears you are enjoying this too much, Lieutenant. Seems to me you could just as easily apply the cream to your chest yourself."

"Well, Karla, the doctor told me the cream for my chest wound would work a lot better if you applied it."

She gave him another one of her looks, and it was lights out, in their separate beds and with their 9mm Sig-Sauers fully loaded and chambered.

"Good night, Karla."

"Good night, Mr. Navy Intelligence."

CHAPTER 13

They got up very early to make the appointment with Yanko. The address he had given them was on Slivnitsa Boulevard, a bit north of the center of Sofia. The OK taxi took about ten minutes to get there.

Imperial Mannequins and Design was a two-story building with a very interesting façade of various show windows full of mannequins of all sizes, sporting a wide variety of clothing, or no clothing at all, supposedly to show the jointed and interchangeable body parts. Not that it mattered, for the mannequin business was not dependent on great-looking show windows, but on word-of-mouth recommendations between the many retail business managers in Bulgaria and other surrounding countries. Besides, the mannequins in these windows appeared not to have been touched, repositioned, or dusted in quite a long time.

Karla pressed the door button. The intercom crackled, "Yes?"

"This is Karla and Troy. We have an appointment to see you."

The door buzzed, and they entered a surreal world of dozens of naked, standing mannequins staring at them and at each other, made even more creepy by the very poor lighting in the large anteroom. There were tables here and there with mountains of loose arms, legs, eyeless heads, and several containers with nuts and bolts, as well as large porcelain dishes with dozens of eyeballs of all colors. The place had a pervasive, pungent odor coming from several open containers used in the production of the polystyrene and fiberglass material used in the manufacturing process. Troy and Karla were beginning to wonder just where they were supposed to go, when a door at the very back of the anteroom opened.

"Good morning, visitors — this way."

Yanko Torpolorian was a tall, thin man of about 65, wearing a long work-bench apron and a checkered shirt that didn't match his 1960s-type print pants. He looked Eastern European, with strong, pronounced facial features, big, black mustache, out-of-control dark eyebrows, and menacing black eyes.

"Good morning, Mr. Torpolorian. Thank you for agreeing to see us," said Karla, and they walked into the back room. It appeared to be his office.

There really wasn't anywhere to sit, so Yanko motioned them to remove some of the supply boxes that were sitting on the chairs. Then there was no place for the boxes. Yes, it was cluttered, but, for him, it was normal. It was his way of working.

"Chris Ferris called me and said you needed some help. So, tell me, what kind of help do you need?" Even with those cold words, it felt like he was beginning to warm up.

"We don't know how much he told you, but we are looking for a man named Sanjar. We were told that he is in this area, even though he moves around quite a bit," explained Karla.

"Why you want to mess with a psychopath like that?"

"The less you know, the better for you," warned Troy.

Yanko Torpolorian gave each of them a penetrating look — still no smile — as if trying to get a paranormal impression of what they were up to; he moved his jaw side-to-side to assist him in his thoughts, or maybe just to re-align his ill-fitting dentures.

"Chris Ferris and I go back many years. I was with the Bulgarian Intelligence Service, Chris with Navy Intelligence. We were young, in our 30s, idealistic. We became sort-of friends, even though we were on opposite sides of the ideological chasm. Through the years, I discovered that BIS had been lying to us agents for years, while we put our lives on the line. Does Navy Intelligence lie to you, and you?" asked Yanko, looking first at Troy and then at Karla.

Troy said, "Look, Mr. Torpolorian, we empathize with your...."

Yanko exploded. "No! You are *not* able to empathize!" His piercing eyes could cut through steel. "Look what I am now. I surround myself with these polystyrene figures. They're my family. Hopefully, Navy Intelligence will not betray you. You don't want to find out too late that you were just expendable assets to your government."

"Okay, then — where can we find Sanjar?" asked Karla.

"Sanjar is a very sick man, but brilliant. He is devoid of compassion, empathy, love, friendship, and even simple, common, human brotherhood. It is interesting how, in human beings, intelligence and caring are two totally separate, psychological functions." He looked at the floor and then gave Karla a dejected look. "You will not be able to put him down without becoming a little like him. I'm not sure you realize the spiritual danger you are in. Even if he does not kill you, the essence of his evil will contaminate your heart."

"Mr. Torpolorian, we carry out our mission as specified by Admiral Ferris, your friend. We certainly appreciate your concern, but it's a little too late for us to retreat," indicated Troy.

"I can see that you are true believers. You have been warned."

"Please, tell us — where can we find him?" pleaded Karla.

"You are correct in believing that he moves frequently, but he usually ends up coming back to Battenberg Square, here in Sofia. In my line of work, I know many people throughout Eastern Europe, and they have become my eyes and ears. Most recently, he was seen walking around the village of Busmantsi, about 11 kilometers east of here. He and several of his bodyguards went into a white house, number 173-G, on Rodinata Boulevard. Very small village, about 2000 people; foreigners like you are easily noticed, so you have to be careful."

"Can you give us an idea of what he looks like?" asked Karla cautiously, almost feeling they had already bothered Yanko too much.

"Dark man, bushy hair, big, black mustache, like mine, weighs maybe 350 pounds, and, when he sits, he looks more like a ball of putty, slowly oozing and drooping down the edges of the chair. Mean, sadistic face. The only time he cracks a slight smile is when he is causing physical pain to someone else. I really can't see how those bodyguards can work alongside him. They, too, must be demented."

Troy and Karla immediately figured that, if he was 350 pounds, they would not be able to tackle him into submission. And he didn't know fear — or he preferred to die — so pointing a gun at him would not have an effect, either. It was starting to look like a big problem.

"We thank you very much for that information. Certainly we will tell Admiral Ferris that you have been very helpful," declared Troy. "And here's my phone number if you happen to think of anything else that might help us."

As Mr. Torpolorian was showing Karla and Troy the way out through the narrow hallway, he accidentally bumped into a well-dressed female mannequin that was standing nearby, apart from all the others. Quickly grabbing it to prevent it from falling down completely, he implored, "Oh, Vasilka, I'm sorry, I did not see you. Sorry, my dear. I should be more careful, my love. Forgive me." Without any forethought whatsoever, Yanko had let his guard down as he reflexively reacted to the falling mannequin. So, apparently, he did have a heart, but only for those who had not yet betrayed him, and Vasilka had so far been totally honest with him.

Instantly Yanko knew that Karla and Troy had just seen another side of him, and, as he was lovingly fixing her ruffled clothing and her elegantly coiffed jet-black hair, he thought of the best way to explain it.

"Look, Troy, Karla — please don't tell a single soul what you've just seen, or I can lose my entire business and end up on the street. Sadly, I am a very lonely man: No relatives — my wife left me ten years ago — no children, no real friends. I work all day, I don't hurt anyone, and I treat my customers right. My life is a great tragedy. I have no one to talk to, but, Vasilka, well, I sit her at the dinner table with me, and she listens. If it wasn't for her, I would have ended my life long ago. Please don't judge me harshly." By that time, his piercing eyes had lost their harshness, and they were already glistening as he spoke those painful words.

"No, Mr. Torpolorian, don't worry — we won't judge you. Everyone needs a friend, and you have chosen Vasilka as yours. You seem like a decent man, and that is all that matters," sympathized Karla.

"Thank you for your kind understanding," replied Yanko.

Yanko continued walking with Troy and Karla until they reached the front door. "Look, I want to help you more, so I will ask some of my contacts for anything else that may be of help."

"You have already helped us, but, certainly, we will appreciate any additional information you can get," quipped Karla. And, with that, they walked out the front door.

CHAPTER 14

They were practically speechless as they walked away from Imperial Mannequins and Design on Slivnitsa Boulevard. Yes, they were both dying to talk about Yanko and his girlfriend Vasilka, yet Yanko's painfully personal confession had instilled in their hearts a profound admiration and respect that precluded their gossiping about his unorthodox yet harmless solution to a lonely life. Troy and Karla both knew that Vasilka was just a mannequin, but, in their hearts, they had to acknowledge that, to Yanko, she was a friend, a companion. In her, Yanko had found a reason to get up in the morning — to fix her beautiful black hair again.

About two blocks later, they passed in front of a retail appliance store, and the news monitors on display caught their eyes. One was tuned to the BBC in London.

MASSIVE RICHTER 9.3 EARTHQUAKE DEVASTATES ALASKA
EPICENTER LOCATED AT THE ALEUTIAN TRENCH SOUTH OF
ALASKA PENINSULA

Karla and Troy were transfixed by the news monitors. The rest of the story indicated that the seismologists were declaring that the Pacific Plate at the bottom of the north Pacific Ocean had suddenly subducted under the North American Plate at their point of impact, the very deep Aleutian Trench, just south of Alaska. The sudden slippage of the two gargantuan plates had released enormous amounts of energy that were felt as the catastrophic movement of practically all of Alaska. Anchorage, Fairbanks, Valdez, Nome, Dillingham, and dozens of smaller towns were all destroyed. Kodiak, St. Lawrence, as well as the Aleutian Islands were almost immediately inundated. The Pacific

Tsunami Warning Center in Hawaii was declaring a tsunami alert for all of the U.S. west coast, as well as for land masses to the southwest of the Aleutian Trench, including Japan. It was estimated that about 500,000 people were already dead.

Karla barely was able to get her words out. "Troy, people think that this is a natural disaster. If they only knew."

Troy, too, could barely speak. "This will also have a devastating effect on the eastern parts of Russia and China. If they ever found out that our White House was playing roulette with the threats from Blue Sparrow, they might take matters into their own hands."

To get the latest in strategy, Troy managed to call Admiral Ferris back in Dover.

"Admiral, we're watching the BBC news reports on the Alaska earthquake. Were you aware?"

"Troy, this is on the verge of creating a national political crisis, not to mention the tragedy of the destruction in Alaska."

"Yes, Admiral, the animals we're dealing with are not playing games. They don't care how many people they have to kill to make their point."

"The White House, the CIA, the FBI, the NSA, the DHS, and military intelligence are all on heightened security alert. They all know about the demands and threats, and are working to find alternate solutions besides the one you and Karla are involved in. The White House is reluctant to hold many more meetings on the matter for fear of crisis details leaking out to the press. Just imagine if all California residents decided it was time to leave before the San Andreas Fault blows out! Just imagine more than 40 million people attempting to leave, all at the same time. Or worse, imagine the government alerting people of the impending threat, or not alerting them at all! The panic itself will be catastrophic. No matter what the government does, we will have a political nightmare."

Karla chimed in, "Excuse me, sir, but, over here, we're just trying to figure out if any of our security agencies are nefariously involved in these attacks, since we suspect that at least the CIA is. You can't have these organizations working on this problem — they might very well ruin what we are trying to do."

"Karla, I understand your feelings — and your logic — but you know about idiotic government politics. These agencies will try to outdo each other at the expense of finding a suitable solution."

"I suggest, Admiral, that the White House tell Blue Sparrow that they will comply with the demand — and on time. They should start to amass gold bullion ready for shipment — and maybe send these sociopaths a video recording of the progress. Not that the gold will be delivered, but it will keep them at bay and perhaps buy us some time so we can have some success on this side. Is that a good interim plan, sir?" asked Troy.

"Look, Troy, Karla — I will do whatever I can on this side to slow down these damned, self-important bureaucrats, but we are running out of time, and the future looks grim."

Grim, indeed. They knew that even if they could magically destroy Geo-1 and Geo-2 instantly, the damage to the North Mariana Islands and Alaska had already been done. Irreversibly. About one million dead. Unstoppable Pacific tsunami already on the way, going south from the Aleutian Trench. But, even as bad as that was, it would pale in comparison to the threatened loss of California, with its huge population. These cataclysmic losses were nothing the United States had ever experienced since its birth more than 200 years ago. And Blue Sparrow had already proven that it was not bluffing — it wanted $1 trillion in gold bullion. The search for that Sanjar monster was becoming more than urgent.

Troy had an idea to make the search for Sanjar more time efficient. "Karla, here's what we should do. You go to Battenberg Square and perhaps ask some folks there if they know where this guy Sanjar lives, while I go to Busmantsi Village and look things over around that house that Yanko mentioned. We'll meet back at the hotel in one hour." Karla agreed.

Troy got into a Green Taxi and headed to the village; it was a short but pleasant ride on Asen Yordanov Boulevard and then onto Prosveta Street into the center of town. He didn't want the cab driver to think that he was looking specifically for Rodinata Street, so he had cooked up the story that he was looking to buy a quiet place in Busmantsi and wanted to get a good look at all the streets and homes. Without stopping, they passed by 173-G Rodinata several times, and Troy was able to get a good look. Two-story house, one door in front and one in back, all windows covered completely. The house was at a T-intersection, no other houses connected to it. It occurred to Troy that the bodyguards would be peeking out of slits on the edges of the curtains, so he thought it best not to continue going around since it would probably start attracting attention. The rest of the time, he asked the taxi driver to take him around the outskirts of the village. Then it was time to head back to the hotel in Sofia to plan how they were going to approach the house where Sanjar was hiding. It would certainly be very risky, but it had to be done.

It had been a hard morning, so Troy was glad to be back at the hotel. He got there about five minutes before the hour was up, so he did not expect

Karla to be there, and she wasn't. Since it was close to lunchtime, he thought it best that they should have a quick lunch there in the room. He ordered via room service. Twenty minutes after the hour, he began eating his lunch and watching more depressing news on the Alaska earthquake. Casualties and damages were greater than at first noted, and the tsunami was gaining strength, barreling southeast toward the U.S. west coast. Things would only get worse there in the Pacific.

Karla was already one hour late, so he began to formulate theories as to why. Maybe she'd gotten lost. Maybe she'd gotten a great lead and was currently following it. Maybe one local person referred her to another local person not immediately in the vicinity. Just theories. Then the phone rang.

His first thought was that she was calling to excuse herself for being so late. But, no, it was much worse.

He picked up the phone. "Yes?"

"Mr. Troy Hamilton?" the strained voice asked.

"That depends. Who wants to know?"

"I am the psychopath you have been hunting for."

Troy almost froze. This could only mean that Sanjar had abducted Karla.

"Well, that's a good start. And what is your name, psychopath?"

"You are already insulting me, and we just got started. Not exactly diplomatic, are you?"

"Fine. What do you want?"

"Want? I get anything I want, including your beautiful assistant."

Troy hesitated because he knew he had been cornered by Sanjar. Now that he had made contact with him, he could not even savor the moment because of the predicament. His options were now minimal. "Let me talk to her. Hello, Karla — can you hear me?"

"Yes, Troy. Don't bargain with these assholes. Let them kill me, and then run all of them through an industrial wood chipper. Kill all four of them, Troy!" exclaimed Karla with conviction in her voice.

"I believe you can verify that is the lioness Karla, right?"

"So you want to negotiate her release, or what?" asked Troy with a tone of confidence — or indifference, as if he really didn't care either way.

"I figure she means more to you than to me, even though my men here would like to take turns having fun with her."

"Quit the bullshit, Sanjar, and just tell me what the fuck you're fishing for."

"Rule #1 is that you do not talk that way to me! Ever!"

Troy could hear as Sanjar directed one of his men. "Rumen, pull down her pants and panties and apply that red-hot branding iron on her left buttock!"

He could hear Karla curse, and scream, and curse, but these soon gave way to screaming and crying. And then she pleaded with them. Troy was trying to tell Sanjar to stop, that he would be respectful toward him, but apparently Sanjar had put the phone down somewhere — he was not listening. Then came Karla's agonizing scream and the sizzle on her skin.

It turned to wailing, heart-wrenching bawling. No person should ever cause another person to make those horrible, painful sounds. They lasted an eternity, with Troy as powerless as could be on the wrong end of the phone. Then he heard just whimpering. He had tears in his eyes. How quickly Sanjar had converted Karla and Troy from powerful and fearless intel agents to submissive servants of his will. Neither Troy nor Karla was prepared for that shocking turn of events.

Sanjar came back to the phone. "Mr. Hamilton, do we understand each other?"

"Yes, Sanjar."

Troy heard the conversation in the room at the other end of the line. "Miss Bloomfield? Miss Bloomfield? Will you behave and not curse at me, or do you want us to brand your other nice, soft buttock? Gentlemen, put some ointment on the wound, some gauze and tape, and pull up her pants. Respect her body. Mr. Hamilton, shall we start our business?"

Troy was a hardened man, with years of experience, but this had been a debilitating experience for him. Karla's agonizing screams tore at his heart, and he couldn't do anything but listen. Sanjar had brought him to his knees, and he hated himself for permitting that to happen. Yet, if he cared for Karla's welfare, there was nothing he could do but comply. But, he did secretly say to himself that he would make himself enjoy killing Sanjar like he had never enjoyed killing anyone before. Yanko had been right. Dealing with evil eventually corrupts one's soul. Both Karla and Troy were already on that path.

"Yes, what do you want me to do?" asked Troy submissively.

"Look, I gain nothing by killing Karla. Pretty girl, now with a branded butt. But you will eventually have her back. I want to meet you in person."

"And that way you can kill us both?"

"How naive. My men have been tracking you since you arrived in Sofia yesterday. We could have easily killed you at The Spaghetti Company last night — a passing motorcycle could have done the job since you were so close to the curb, no?"

What a realization for Troy! He and Karla thought they'd had a keen eye for agents tracking them on the streets.

Obviously not.

Sanjar was an arch-enemy — the most intelligent, powerful, and sadistic Troy had ever been given the job of bringing down. He was not so sure anymore that Karla and he would be succeeding in this mission.

"What's the meeting for?"

"Meet us at the Cafe Morgan, in one hour, back room. Yes, you can bring your semi-automatic. Just don't try anything that will endanger Karla." *Click.*

It was so anti-climactic to have to meet this evil monster Sanjar in person without having the chance to shoot him on the spot. Troy was a confused ball of conflicting emotions pulling him in all directions, unsure of what he needed to do to continue with the mission. Capturing Sanjar and forcibly extracting information from him about Geo-1 and Geo-2 was a distant goal at this time — or at any time, by the looks of it. But on his conscience were Karla, the tsunami in the Pacific, and the impending doom in California. Gargantuan jobs that needed to be done by one man. It was a crushing, overwhelming, debilitating weight.

Troy arrived at the Cafe Morgan on Tsaritsa Yoanna Boulevard, on the west side of Sofia, on time. As was standard practice, he had asked the taxi to drop him off about two blocks away, so he could pretend to keep a lookout for any agents who may have followed him. The details that Sanjar had provided of his dinner with Karla the previous evening shook his confidence in spotting the enemy. Troy was now almost a broken man.

Cafe Morgan had a beautiful façade of flying coffee cups and pastries etched onto its hardwood finish. Huge, 2-story windows permitted patrons to see the goings-on at street level without having to be outside near the noisy traffic. Inside there were three levels overlooking a large atrium with hanging airplane and air balloon mobiles. It was spacious and clean, and the aroma of always-brewing coffee was a huge delight in itself.

Troy told the lady cashier with the enormous black eyebrows and bulbous nose that he had been invited to a meeting in the back room, and a young, courteous waiter led him to a door marked PRIVATE. He knocked three times, waited, and then knocked four more. The waiter opened the door, Troy entered, and the waiter closed the door. And there he was — 350-pound Sanjar sitting at the table, flanked by three husky, armed bodyguards who were standing behind him and to either side. Just like Yanko had said, he was an ugly, menacing, sadistic, obese monster, with eyes so cold and devoid of brotherhood that they looked like those of Satan himself. *Who the hell gave birth to this horrible, walking cockroach that breathes the same air as we?* Troy wondered silently.

The rectangular, six-chair wooden table in the middle of the room was made of beautiful stained wood and had salt-and-pepper shakers on it in the shape of Bulgarian mammas wearing colorful Babushkas and aprons. There were some light dishes already served — probably appetizers. The walls were adorned with sports photographs — soccer, baseball, basketball, and several of Marilyn Monroe and Greta Garbo. There was another door at the other end of the room, with some kitchen noises coming from it.

Lying on the floor by Sanjar's tight, ready-to-explode black shoes was a well-fed lizard, probably an iguana whose importation was not permitted in Bulgaria. But, what the hell? Whatever Sanjar wanted, Sanjar got. Troy was surprised to see a small cage sitting on a round service table by the wall. It had two golden-yellow baby chicks pecking here and there, quite adorable really, and actually out of place in this surreal and evil meeting room. How in the world could a sinister man like Sanjar take a liking to these two baby chicks? *Maybe the man has a soft side*, Troy thought. He was thinking of how he could exploit that weak point.

He didn't know what to say, as he felt his racing heartbeat inside his ears. For a few seconds after Troy had entered, Sanjar just looked him over, top to bottom.

"Sit over here, Mr. Hamilton." He motioned for one of his goons to bring Troy an appetizer and a drink.

As he continued eating the cheese-and-lettuce on his plate, Sanjar opened the business discussion.

"You look like a sensible man, Troy. Are you?"

"You know I have to be if I'm an intelligence agent for the Navy."

"I don't mean *that* type of sensible. I mean that you know what is really going on between your government and the rest of the world. Are you a sensible man, Troy?"

"My allegiance is to my government, and that's all that counts."

"Then you are not a sensible man. You are loyal, Troy, but so is a dog."

Troy was beginning to feel that Sanjar was trying to corner him into saying or believing something not in Troy's nature. He should resist, he felt, but, on the other hand, he had to go along, to play the game, to let him feel superior, to prevent him from letting his rage come to the surface. He needed to save himself and Karla.

"Excuse me, Sanjar, but I really don't know what you're getting at."

"You probably see me as the enemy, and you, Karla, and your government as the good guys, right?"

"Well, now that you mention it."

"The way I see it, Troy, there are basically two types of people on this earth — those who help me advance my personal goals and those who impede my goals. I like or detest people on that basis alone. Their personalities, their religions, their facial features, their nationalities, their body odors, their likes and dislikes, are all *irrelevant* to me. They can smell like dog excrement and have pus all over their faces, but if they promote my goals, I like them. Am I being clear, Troy?"

"Yes, Sanjar, perfectly clear."

"If I like them, I bestow money and riches upon them, even if they are wicked, cannibalistic men who eat children alive. And if I detest them because they impede my personal goals, I will see to it that they suffer incalculable, inhuman pain. I will keep them alive as long as possible to prolong my plea-sure, but, eventually, they all die from heart failure due to the pain overload. I become disappointed when they die."

"It seems to me, Sanjar, that you know very well what you like. Now can we talk about Karla?"

"Silence! You fucking moron!" exploded Sanjar, the veins in his neck and forehead ready to burst, food spilling out of his mouth, his huge fist slam-ming on the table top. The salt-and-pepper Bulgarian mammas toppled over. "I'm the one who decides when to talk about your bitch! Is that clear? Is that mother-fucking *clear*?"

The outburst caught Troy by surprise. Yet he had no choice — he had to do as asked.

"Perfectly."

Sanjar wiped the food around his lips and chin, and then he used the same napkin to wipe the table area around his plate.

"As I was explaining about people I despise. If I come to despise a person who happens to be a woman, well, the situation is a bit different. My loyal assassin is instructed to first rape her, then mutilate her womanly parts, and finally kill her with a shot to the liver — it's a slow, agonizing death. I like that! I sit and witness her total humiliation and destruction. And people like you, Troy, will never know what total, exhilarating pleasure is like. I become one with God. A truly religious experience."

There was silence, but Troy was not sure if he could talk or not, for fear of interrupting an obviously important point that Sanjar was making.

One of the guards came back from the kitchen and placed a plate of cheese and lettuce in front of Troy. He even brought him a beer, but Troy was hesitant.

"Come on, Troy — eat. I'm not going to poison you. I need you alive. Eat!"

Very meekly, Troy started nibbling at the cheese, by now convinced that, indeed, it was not poisoned. It made sense that Sanjar would want him alive.

"So the question becomes, Troy, should I like you or despise you? Be careful how you answer."

Troy thought that he definitely should not antagonize this fiend from hell. But then he would have to say that he supported Sanjar's goals, and Sanjar would know that he would just be lying to save his skin. He took a risk and opted for some middle ground.

"If you tell me what it is you want me to do, I would tell you if I can do it."

"I want you to rape and then kill Karla. And I want to watch."

Troy was in shock. Sanjar had given him a no-win choice. Troy would never do what that madman had requested. But if he did not comply, he would certainly be killed by Sanjar or his evil henchmen, and very slowly, too. Troy felt he was at the end of the line on this mission. It had been a total failure, and he felt sorry for what awaited Karla Bloomfield after he was dead. No sense in even thinking about the fate of California or the other planned catastrophes. Troy prepared to die.

"Sanjar, if you wanted Karla raped and killed, you could have asked one of your monkeys here to do it. I won't do it, so you can go ahead and kill me now if you wish. We will die without taking any more shit from you. So, go fuck yourself!"

"How dare you disobey, you insolent swine maggot!" Sanjar snapped his fingers, and one of the bodyguards walked over to Troy and struck him across the face with the butt of his submachine gun. "Again!" screamed Sanjar, with foam at the corners of his mouth, and Troy was struck on the other side of his face. Two teeth fell out, and he was bleeding profusely from the mouth and the big gash on his cheek. Sanjar threw a cotton napkin at him.

While Troy did the best he could to contain the bleeding, Sanjar seemed to calm down — he was breathing slower, and his prominent facial veins had subsided. He continued to feed on his cheese and lettuce. Swig of beer. Perfectly comfortable.

"You're right, Troy."

But Troy was still in a daze, blinking his eyes repeatedly to correct his blurred vision. In the back of his mind, he was remembering how right Yanko had been in his warning: "Why do you want to mess with a psychopath like that?" He was feeling it was regrettable that they had not heeded his word of caution, but then again, how could they not go after this demon, this pestilence upon the earth?

"Yes, sir, Troy, you're right. You seem to have some kind of loyal attachment to that Karla of yours, the one with that iron-branding on her left butt cheek. I know now that I can use you for this assignment and that you won't just run away and leave Karla behind with these incorrigible rapists from the sewer."

While Troy was still trying to correct his vision and spit out blood and pieces of tooth onto the cotton napkin, Sanjar was finishing up his appetizer. He snapped his fingers again. Troy cringed, expecting another blow, but this time the signal was for one of the brutes to bring the cage with the two beautiful baby chicks to the table. *Peeuu-peeuu-peeuu, chirp-chirp-chirp, peep-peep-peep* — they just wouldn't keep quiet. With the corner of his eye, Troy saw that now the baby chicks were on the table, and he thought again just how a fiendish vampire like Sanjar could have space in his putrid heart for these beautiful and harmless pets.

He didn't.

His assistant brought another plate with a pita pocket-bread, more cheese, tomato, and lettuce. Sanjar himself cut the oversized pita in half, opened it to make a pocket, and placed the tomato slices, cheese, and lettuce inside. "This is one of my favorite meals, Mr. Hamilton, but you are too culturally constrained to understand it, much less to appreciate it."

And with that, Sanjar opened the small cage and took out a chirping baby chick, which he forced into the pocket pita bread. The baby chick kept struggling and chirping, but it was of no use — it was firmly secured by the pocket and by Sanjar's huge, evil hands. The irredeemable glutton then opened his enormous, cavernous mouth and took a bite of his live-chick pita bread sandwich, as the sound of crunching bones and desperate chirps of the poor chick permeated the otherwise totally quiet room.

Chewing on the bird, Sanjar explained. "You know what makes this sandwich even more tasty? The dying baby chick's last desperate chirps and its moving body inside my mouth! It's an incredible experience! Better than sex with one's sister! Oh, God!"

Troy was aware of what was happening, but he was not fully conscious. He just knew it was something very disgusting. *If he does this to a baby chick, what'll he do to Karla?* was his lingering thought. He felt he had to bring this to its conclusion, whatever that might be.

"Look, Sanjar, I'm glad you enjoyed your lunch, but we have to conclude our business here — got to see the doctor quickly, losing too much blood."

"There's still one more chick — would you like to give it a try?"

Troy shook his head, and he noticed that Sanjar had a small feather sticking out of one of his teeth, but he was not about to tell him about it.

Guzzling the rest of his beer, Sanjar spoke. "Fine — here's what I want. You probably know by now that your CIA contracted my men, through that double-dealing banker Hugh Mitchell in Brussels, to obtain the machines from the inventors in London — I believe they were 'Graham' and 'Thompson.' The CIA didn't say it, but they wanted those machines to achieve absolute clandestine superiority over all nations. I figured they wanted the ability to cause massive earthquake destruction over any country that dared challenge them militarily, politically, or even economically. All without having to use your country's mighty military. The enemy would see the destruction as an act of God!"

Of course, Troy had guessed — but was not sure — that the CIA had been involved all along, but now he knew.

Sanjar was eyeing the second chick, which was still chirping innocently, but instead he asked his bodyguard to bring him something sweet. Soon the guard returned with a very large piece of banitsa sweet bread and a large cup of very black Bulgarian coffee.

"So why did the CIA go to Mitchell and not to you?" queried Troy.

"I thought you knew all these things, Troy. Simple reason. I have always kept a low profile in all countries where my men carry out their assignments. So I used Mitchell as a middleman. My guess is that the CIA found out that my men always got their orders from Mitchell, and they assumed he was their leader."

"So, why do you need me and Karla? You seem to have all the answers."

"I've been tolerant of you, Agent Troy — don't press my buttons unless you want another two teeth knocked out, you ignorant Navy man!"

"Okay — sorry."

"You need to know these things so you can perform your assignment properly, but, if you question me one more time, I will have to hammer a chopstick completely into your ear. Don't force my hand — do you understand?"

"Yes, absolutely."

"Through my ring of spies, I found out that the CIA was paying Mitchell S5 million for the job, but Mitchell told me the contract was for $2 million. I knew I had to have him killed, because I could no longer trust him."

"Did you hammer a chopstick into his ear?"

"You know, Mr. Hamilton, I'm having a hard time keeping my cool, so I'm using my tension energy to think of things I will do to Karla, since you don't seem to care about your personal welfare. Did you know that a nail gun can send a large nail all the way into a person's brain? And there's virtually no pain, so I can hammer many more nails just as easily. I've done it. Thoroughly enjoyable activity — it relaxes me. After about 10 nails, I would say that a head of lettuce would have more neurological activity than Karla's."

"You've made your point. I will listen. Sorry, no pun intended. Sorry," moaned Troy.

"So this Mitchell was cheating me out of $3 million. About two days ago, when my backup men in Brussels received a distress call from the Mitchell estate at night, I figured it was the CIA who was there to close the books on Mitchell. Being a coward, he would tell them everything. So I ordered an RPG into his bedroom — all that was left of him was his torso, and it was well done, too. Unfortunately, the two CIA agents escaped. I wanted to fry them, too. This goes to show that, when someone crosses me, they don't live long."

"Yes, I can see that." Troy was a bit more coherent. He picked up his two teeth from the floor and placed them in a paper napkin — an orthodontist might want to re-implant them.

From what Sanjar was saying, it was clear that he did not know that it had been Karla and he at the Mitchell estate that night. If Sanjar had known, he would already have killed both of them.

"But why did you have Thompson and Graham killed? They were harmless," voiced Troy.

"Heard about that, but that was not me."

"So, if it was not you or your men, then who?"

"Man, you are dense! The CIA! Your fucking CIA did those hits."

"But it was Iranian-looking men who were shooting at us. We killed one of the assassins who killed Thompson. He was Iranian and was using a Czech pistol."

"He might have been Iranian, but he was not working for me, Mr. Hamilton. We wanted both Graham and Thompson alive, just in case something went wrong with the machines."

Troy was trying hard to assimilate what Sanjar was saying. Now, he wasn't so sure just who the enemy was.

"So you see, Mr. Hamilton, your own government has been betraying you right from the beginning. Par for the course, since all governments eventually betray their citizens one way or another, but things move right along because most people are kept in the dark — ignorant, if you will. But once you open your eyes, you will find yourself adrift, not feeling allegiance to any government. That's why I am like I am, and that is why I have an essentially hopeless life."

"But if it was the CIA's plan to acquire the devices, why did they turn against everyone? You're not making sense."

"They found out I was the real leader and that I wanted a lot more than the $5 million they had given Mitchell. Once we had the machines in our possession, I ordered that they should not be delivered to the CIA agents running the operation. I wanted those machines for myself, because I want all the gold bullion in the world! All of it, Mr. Hamilton, all of it, all of it, all of it, all, all, all the gold bullion! Yes, oh God, Oh God!"

Troy noticed how Sanjar's demeanor had changed. For a few minutes, he had appeared more lucid, more calm, even more normal, if that was possible. But the thought of the gold bullion had effected some type of personality change in him. His face metamorphosed into a satan-like radiance with a creepy, sadistic smile and sepulchral eyes that one would not want to see, even in broad daylight. Sanjar was in some type of self-induced rapture — he was trembling, his face and smile evidencing his internal manic high, unreachable by regular human beings, who had to be content with mortal happiness. Troy knew that this man possessed the subjective manic feeling of invincibility and omnipotence of a manic-depressive who fed his obsessive mania with vulgar activities in sadism, sex, violence, and brutal abuse of human beings and animals. When he was in this state, Sanjar was practically Lucifer incarnate!

It was better to wait a few moments. The security guards were at ease; for them, it was business as usual.

After a few seconds, Troy proceeded slowly. "So what happened when the CIA found out that you were not going to hand over the devices?"

Sanjar could not answer promptly, for he appeared to be wrestling against and pushing back against some evil, green vomit that wanted to explode out of his mouth. He kept swallowing and gagging alternatingly. After several attempts, things seemed to quiet down.

"Please forgive me, Mr. Hamilton. Ah, yes, when your CIA found out that their plan to dominate the world with these machines had gone terribly wrong, they started killing everybody connected with it, to destroy the evidence of what they had attempted to do. They shot the three workers in the lab; we killed one. And they hit Graham and Thompson, your CIA did. And the CIA has tried several times to kill you and Karla."

"Well, if word had gotten out, it would have been the CIA scandal of the century," Troy added. "Still, it seems like a drastic step to take."

"Not really, Troy. The damage they inflicted is much greater. After we had acquired the machines, the CIA insisted that they be deployed at full power to cause an earthquake. They wanted proof."

"Like a test run? But why not do the test on some remote area with minimal population?"

"Yes, a test, but they were thinking several steps ahead in their plan. The wanted a tsunami to hit America's west coast, just to let the world know that your country suffers, too, from earthquakes and tsunamis. They were preparing to unleash catastrophes in other countries, so your country could legitimately claim to be suffering, too."

"So, they wanted many people dead?"

"Well, not such a big sin. It was rather fun reading the news reports of the destruction. It made me feel alive and powerful!"

"On the other hand, you, and not the CIA, were responsible for the earthquake in the Aleutian Trench south of Alaska, right?"

"Oh, most definitely. I had to let your America know that I'm in charge."

"Is that because you hate America?" Troy was thinking of what Hugh Mitchell had said, but he couldn't bring that up without revealing that Karla and he had been there the night of the RPG attack on the mansion.

"No, Troy. Ironically enough, I would say I love America, but not for the same reasons you do. Two things I love about your country are its incredible wealth in the form of gold, and the limitless stupidity and hypocrisy of your government. Makes my work easier. But enough of explaining. I need you to carry out an assignment."

"I've been afraid to ask."

"By now, you should know that I would love to do a lot of terrible, terrible things to Karla."

"That would be in your first nature."

Sanjar's bull-type nostrils flared to three times their size — one could easily have rammed a garden-hose into them. But he stayed calm.

"I want bullion. I will not trade intense sexual pleasure for gold bullion, and that is why I would rather not kill you and Karla. You are more valuable in carrying out the assignment."

"Just tell me what you want me to do."

"Your government most probably does not believe I have the power to do terrible things with these machines. And, besides, they would not want to part with $1 trillion worth of gold bullion. Your job is to convince them to take my offer. Quite simple."

"In the greater scheme of things within the government, I am just a lowly Navy intel agent. How could I ever make the top echelons in government listen to me?"

"Don't belittle your stature, Mr. Hamilton. You may not have physical or resource power, but you have political media power — the power to create huge embarrassment and political chaos within your government."

"What are you getting at?"

"*The New York Times.*"

Troy searched his imagination for a few seconds. "Are you saying I should go to *The Times* and let them know about this operation?"

Sanjar nodded without saying a word.

"Even if that could be of benefit to you, you are asking me to be an accomplice to something that would be very detrimental to my country. Besides, how do I know you will release Karla afterward?"

"What are your options?"

"I could just refuse."

"I would not just kill you both. I would inflict unimaginable pain and suffering. Karla would be first, so you can enjoy watching. Every three minutes, I would ask you if you want to put a bullet through her eye to end her suffering. You would have to make a series of agonizingly painful decisions. Then it would be your turn to suffer and die. Not exactly the future your mother would have wanted for you."

Sanjar's words painted horrible images in Troy's mind. He thought, *What price loyalty, how much suffering can one take for his country? Maybe this demented Sanjar is right.*

"Alright, no more pussyfooting — I'll do it. What exact steps do you want me to take?"

"Wise decision, Troy. Soon you'll be a very rich man, and both you and your branded-butt Karla can be enjoying the good life here in Bulgaria, instead of dodging bullets for a living. I want you to contact your President, Federal Reserve Board chairman Winston Steinberg, and CIA director Kirk Weatherhouse. Let them know that you have assembled a very detailed file on the international crimes of the CIA on this matter and how they ordered the deliberate destruction of the Northern Mariana Islands in the Pacific. Say that the CIA is directly responsible for murdering several hundred thousand innocent, non-combatant people. Tell them that the CIA murdered the three workers at the lab, plus Thompson and Graham, and give them some details so they know you are not bluffing."

"It sounds almost like blackmail."

"Damn it! Don't interrupt — don't fucking interrupt! Do you hear, do you hear? It's damned painful!"

"Yes. Sorry."

Sanjar had to wait for the spontaneously engorged veins on his neck and face to subside. After a few seconds, he continued. "You will tell them that you are aware that the White House received a communication from Blue Sparrow demanding gold bullion, with the threat of destruction of landmasses if the White House did not comply. Tell them that you and other Americans believe that it is in the best interests of the country to comply with the demands. If the American government refuses to comply, you will be sending the full report with details to *The New York Times*. And, just in case they might strong-arm *The Times*, the report could also go to the BBC in London — they don't like the American government, either. Russia and China might retaliate in some manner when they read that the White House ignored the warning that devastated the eastern sections of those two countries. Might want monetary compensation in the billions if not trillions."

"Fine — I'll do it." There really wasn't much to think about. There were no other options.

He got up, with his two teeth in his front pocket, and started for the door. Sanjar cautioned him. "Don't try to look for Karla. Besides, we placed her in the basement, so you would have to go past four of us to rescue her. Not advisable, Mr. Hamilton."

"Just don't hurt her anymore. You'll have your gold bullion."

No good-byes — Troy just left.

CHAPTER 15

Troy's face was all bloodied, and the holes in his gums were still bleeding, so his first priority was to find an orthodontist who might be able to reimplant the two teeth safely tucked away in his pocket. But maybe not — his priority was to find Karla. Was she at the house there in Busmantsi Village, #173-G, or maybe elsewhere? Could he positively rely on what Yanko had told him about that address? Could he trust Sanjar's promise to release Karla after this was over? There was no time to consider the many alternatives, so he opted to keep an eye on Sanjar and his henchmen from a distance, just in case they might leave for Busmantsi. Troy was determined to start an all-out war against the psychopath who sadistically hurt Karla. There could be only two outcomes, he felt: Karla would be saved, or they both would be dead.

He stood unobtrusively about a block away, using the cotton napkins to clean his face and creating paper balls to plug the holes where his two teeth used to be. Then he had a scary thought. He was one man only, armed with a semi-auto Sig-Sauer pistol. Was it realistic to think he could just walk into the house spraying bullets everywhere to rescue Karla? His heart was in the right place, but he had to keep that at bay and think more like a soldier in the battlefield against a psychotic, implacable enemy.

Yanko! *Yanko might help*, thought Troy. But help with what, or how? Yanko was a peaceful man who enjoyed working with inanimate objects — his mannequins. Why would he want to help Troy with the violent and dirty business of rescuing Karla? Every minute, Troy's desperation was increasing and was getting the best of him. He felt a growing urge to run into Cafe Morgan and blast away at all the miscreants in the back room. All of them! Dead! *No more crimes against humanity, you perverts!*

"Hello, Yanko? It's me, Troy. Do you have a minute?"

"Yes, Troy. Don't tell me you drove by the house and they spotted you and Karla."

"Much worse. Sanjar kidnapped Karla, and they've been torturing her. I met with the monster at the Cafe Morgan."

"Every minute you talk to that animal, your soul gets darker. So, what do you want?"

"I think that Karla is in the basement of the house you indicated to us in Busmantsi, but I can't go in there alone to rescue her. Do you know some people who could assist me on this?"

"Troy, you are incredible. You want locals to help you in a shoot-out with Sanjar and his evil bastards?"

"I'm just desperate, Yanko. I've nothing else, and I feel they will kill her. You gotta help — please."

"I'm telling Chris Ferris he owes me a big favor."

"Karla and I would be indebted to you forever. Thanks, call me as soon as you have something for me."

Just then Troy spotted a van that stopped right in front of Cafe Morgan; the driver opened the vehicle's sliding doors, and out came Sanjar and his three bodyguards from the cafe and right into the van. Troy knew he could not lose sight of the van, for this was probably the only chance he would ever get at hitting Sanjar right where he was staying.

He flagged down a taxi and told him that he just wanted to look at real estate in the area, so he would direct him when and where to turn. The cabbie did not mind it at all, as he was a big talker. In just a few minutes, the van was east of Sofia, heading toward Busmantsi, so Troy had to orchestrate a series of innocent-looking turns so as to prevent the taxi driver from suspecting that they were following a van or that they had a keen eye for house 173-G on Rodinata Boulevard.

Yanko had been right! From two blocks away, Troy could see that the van stopped at the house, and four men stepped out of the vehicle and into the house. One of these figures was very obese, like Sanjar. Karla had to be in the basement of that house! Now all that was needed was for Yanko to come through with some significant help.

Still, something could go wrong, so Troy thought it better to hedge his bets. He opted to do what Sanjar had asked of him — to send a written communication to those honchos in the U.S. government about following through with the delivery of the gold bullion. He asked the taxi driver to take him back to Sofia.

In their hotel room, he prepared the letter addressed jointly to The President of the United States, Federal Reserve Board Chairman Winston Steinberg, and CIA Director Kirk Weatherhouse. As Sanjar had instructed him, he urged these powerful men in government to heed Blue Sparrow's threat and to deliver the $1 trillion dollars in gold bullion on time. Troy detailed that the organization had proof of the crimes committed by the CIA and other government agencies, including the wanton murder of several hundred thousand innocent, non-combatant people with the deliberate use of the geophysical devices at full power to effect the sudden movement of the Mariana Trench in the Pacific.

Toward the end of the document, he warned that Blue Sparrow would transmit this document, together with more details, to *The New York Times* and the BBC in London if the American government did not comply on a timely basis with their demands. He added, "Gentlemen, it is in the best interests of the United States that you comply with this request, for failure to comply will result in inestimable economic, political, and financial losses, as well as in millions of casualties throughout the west coast, for the moment." He signed the document as Lieutenant Troy Hamilton, U.S. Navy Intelligence Division, Temporary Assignment, Dover, Delaware. He transmitted the letter to the three persons and hoped that his government would be prudent and deliver the gold bullion.

While he waited for Yanko's call, Troy decided to shower and change the paper plugs he had in his gums. Afterward, he applied some medications, checked the readiness of his Sig-Sauer, put on his bulletproof vest, and looked for orthodontists in the local phone book. It was already dark, early evening, and he was getting panicky. Had Yanko failed to find anyone willing to join him in a shoot-out? He wouldn't be surprised. Then, the phone rang.

"Yes?" was Troy's anxious answer.

"Were you expecting someone else on the phone?" It was Sanjar.

"Don't know quite what to expect these days."

"Did you send the letter I requested?" rumbled Sanjar in a scary, guttural drawl.

Troy almost made a fatal mistake: At first, he was going to answer honestly to show Sanjar that he was keeping up his end of the bargain. But then he had an immediate second thought: *What if he feels that, once the letter has gone out, our usefulness has come to an end?* Troy had to delay whatever terrible plan the evil Sanjar had in store for Karla.

"I am following your specific suggestions, and I'm including much detail to make the letter more convincing. This will definitely go out this evening."

"Don't fail me, Troy," uttered Sanjar in a hellish, threatening tone. *Click.* Troy didn't get a chance to ask how Karla was doing.

He was congratulating himself for the split-second decision not to reveal to Sanjar that the letter had already been sent. It surely would have been a monumental mistake, especially for Karla's chances of getting out of this alive. The phone rang again.

"Yes?" asked Troy apprehensively.

Finally, it was Yanko. "Troy, listen, I have a plan. Meet me three blocks north of your hotel, ten minutes." *Click.*

Troy's heart was racing, because he knew this was it — his only chance to rescue Karla. Many things could go wrong, and Karla would be dead. And, Yanko and himself, as well.

He put a few more paper balls of assorted sizes in his pocket and went out into the street, arriving about two minutes later at the assigned spot, but no Yanko. Was he supposed to be there on foot, or in a van, car, truck, or what? He didn't have to wait long for an answer.

The rumble on the surface of the street said it all: Something big is coming this way. About two blocks away, he saw the outline of a large vehicle, and, a few seconds later, he saw that Yanko was at the wheel and that there was a passenger, too. It was a Manitowoc 16-wheel, 300-ton mammoth crane with the boom pointing forward like a battering ram. Nothing could stop this beautiful, red behemoth when it was in gear, and that was the idea

Troy was about to ask Yanko to introduce him to his co-driver when he took a closer look. It was Vasilka — in full camo uniform, cap, and fire-engine red lipstick! Troy was so happy to see that Yanko had come through that he forgave him on the spot for his peculiarities. Harmless, he felt. She did have her seatbelt on. Not only that, but now he noticed that, over the entire gargantuan crane Yanko had secured other mannequins in uniform, and they were holding wooden rifles. Incredible. Troy was beginning to get an idea of what Yanko had in mind.

"Hop in, Troy. Vasilka told me she likes you, so it's okay."

"Well, tell her I like her, too. Looks cute in that camo uniform."

"You tell her, Troy. She's sitting right next to you."

Troy felt really strange. He could carry on with this innocent play for the sake of Yanko, but now he had to talk to a mannequin, even though it was a special one.

"Good evening, Vasilka. Nice to see you again. You look very nice in that uniform." Troy caught himself foolishly waiting for an answer. *Very well She's pretty, but enough of that.*

"Okay, Yanko — what's the plan? No soldiers?"

"Sorry, Troy. This is all I could find. I figure that we would ram the house with this Manitowoc, 2-engine steel monster. The house sits at a T-intersection, so that allows us to gain speed and plow mercilessly into it. That wood-frame house doesn't stand a chance against 300 tons of steel at high speed. I figure that, at this hour, we will catch them relaxing, and we'll completely destroy all the protection around them. This super-crane here will easily flatten everything. Whatever the 16 wheels don't eviscerate, we'll have to take care of ourselves. For that, there's a Cherkashin sub-machine gun under your seat, with several extended magazines. It will stop a charging brontosaurus. Let's get going."

A powerful, 8-cylinder Daimler engine allowed the Manitowoc to move through the streets like a nimble whale, and soon they were on the outskirts of Busmantsi.

"Excuse me, Yanko, but I noticed that the car behind us has been following us; it has made the same turns we have."

"Oh, I forgot. That's my wig supplier, Olga. She said she would not participate in any shooting but that she would gladly drive the car we'll need afterward."

Yanko positioned the crane on the street that formed the bottom part of the T-intersection, about three blocks from the house.

"Okay, Troy, all hell will break loose in less than one minute. After impact, we both will come out shooting at anything that still moves. Hopefully my uniformed and armed mannequins attached to the crane will confuse and distract these goons in the dark, just long enough for us to shoot them first. I'll cover you as you go to the basement and search for Karla. Let's hope for the best."

Yanko put the monster in gear, and the Daimler roared with 8 industrial pistons pushing and pulling, getting the crane up to speed. Half a block from the house, the Manitowoc super-crane was roaring at 50 miles per hour, and then it mercilessly slammed into the front of the house, with a horrible cracking explosion created by the thousands of wood beams and slats that met their destiny in front of 300 tons of barreling, unstoppable steel. Like a sledgehammer striking a long line of delicate wine glasses, the crane penetrated deep into the house, as millions of pieces of wood flew in all directions — like toothpicks, really. Main support beams were no match for this locomotive-sized destroyer —they cracked and exploded like dry twigs. Ten seconds after initial impact, the crane had gone completely into the house and had come to rest in the back yard. There was no more house, but someone was shooting.

Troy and Yanko quickly jumped out of the crane and came out spitting automatic rounds from their Cherkashins, pointing them at anything that moved or showed muzzle flash. The enemy was at a grave disadvantage, really, since there was nothing left to provide cover, and the shooting quickly came to an end. Cautiously Troy approached what was left of the house, and he counted three bodies — the bodyguards. He looked for an obese cadaver but could not quickly locate it. So his thoughts shifted to finding a basement entrance; he had to locate Karla.

Yanko lifted some broken slats and found a floor entrance that had a lock and chain — nothing that a quick burst from the sub-machine gun could not handle. Yanko offered to stay at the entrance to provide cover. Troy used his flashlight and slowly went down the creaky steps. The smell was nauseating — maybe a sewer pipe that had been broken for months — and poor Karla, if she was there, had been forced to endure this inhuman condition. There were old boxes piled everywhere, but their crunched condition indicated they had been there a long time.

"Karla, Karla — can you hear me?"

He heard something move, but there was no Karla voice.

"This is Troy — can you hear me?"

"Troy, Troy, oh, my God, Troy — I'm over here, I'm over here. Oh, God!" Karla answered, starting to weep.

Troy could see her now and rushed to her side. She was on the floor. He knelt and took her in his arms.

"Troy, I am so happy to see you, happy to see you, Troy." Her arms were tightly locked around him, and she was wailing from the center of her heart. Troy felt her pain, too, and tears filled his eyes and overflowed. "Karla, I'm happy to see you, too. I am so happy we found you alive. I am so happy to see you!"

Yanko ended their tender moment. "Okay, you love birds, cut the crap. We have to get the hell out of here before the bribe-hungry Bulgarian police show up. Come up, come up!"

Karla could barely walk, so Troy assisted her up the stairs. "Glad to see you again, Karla. Sorry about your ordeal," consoled Yanko. She nodded acknowledgement.

By this time, Olga, in the car, was a knot of nerves, for she had never seen such destruction and gunfire in her life. She was eager for Yanko and friends to get in so she could drive away. Both men helped Karla into the back seat.

Yanko said, "Be back soon — got to turn off the Daimler." One minute later, he returned and got into the front seat. He had placed Vasilka in the middle section, next to Olga. "Good evening, Vasilka, I hope that all this noise has not frayed your nerves." They drove away.

During the short trip to the hotel, Troy supported Karla's head on his shoulder. She seemed very weak and probably would need medical help. At the hotel, everyone helped in getting Karla to the room and into a bed. Olga offered to take care of her.

Olga had gotten into the wig business when she was in her twenties and was ousted from the university for being a "rabble-rouser," as they say. She was now 45, a few pounds under plump, about 5'6", short, dark hair, bushy eyebrows, and a little bit of a mustache, which she was proud of. She had trouble making friends, so, like Yanko, she made friends with the mannequins who appreciated the wigs and hairdos she provided to them. Never married, no kids, didn't hurt anybody, and if she bumped into a mannequin, she always said, "Excuse me."

"Yanko, you helped save Karla's life. We are very appreciative. But I must ask you if what you have done tonight will endanger your life here in Bulgaria."

"No, I don't think so. I was able to acquire the super-crane using another name, with the full permission of the owner-company. They owed me a very big favor. I hope the insurance covers all the damage to that great machine."

"Yeah, but you also risked your life."

"As I said before, Chris Ferris and I have been doing favors for each other for a long time. This is one of them. You don't owe me anything in return. But I do think that you and Karla had better plan on leaving Bulgaria tomorrow, if possible. Police will start checking things. It will be hard to leave once the system ensnarls you."

"Well, okay. We thank you for the greatest of favors, Yanko."

"Yeah, just don't get mushy on me — Vasilka might get jealous."

Olga told Yanko that he should take the car and that she would take a taxi tomorrow after she had cared for Karla overnight. Yanko left.

Karla was in bed, slipping between groggy and unconscious. Olga made her as comfortable as possible and said she would be going downstairs to get a whole new set of clothes for her and maybe some soup and orange juice.

Troy pulled up a chair to Karla's bedside and held her crusty hand, thinking how Sanjar had turned this fiery Navy Lieutenant into a whimpering patient. Surely, for this reason alone, he deserved to die. He was probably already buried under tons of decimated wood chips, where his hideout used to be.

Lieutenant Hamilton was feeling low. Depressed because Karla and he had had a run of terrible mission failures in the last 48 hours. Of course, he was happy to have Karla back, but that was the personal side. On the professional side, things were not looking too good.

He was startled when his self-flagellating train of thought was interrupted by the phone. He discovered that, now, he was afraid even to answer it.

"Yes?" he meekly asked.

It was Admiral Ferris, and, from the sound of his voice, Troy knew he was very angry. "Troy, what the hell are you doing? The CIA, the FBI, the NSA, Interpol, and the Department of Homeland Security are all looking for you and Karla!"

"Admiral, we're just doing our job."

"You need to know that you and Karla have been declared highly dangerous enemies of the state."

Troy was shocked, maybe even infuriated. Karla and he had been risking their lives, and they were now declared to be enemies of the state? He looked at Karla on the bed and thought of how she had been abused and tortured in her efforts to accomplish the mission defined by her government. And now she was an enemy of the state? *Damned ingrates*, he thought.

"The FBI, the NSA, and Interpol want to arrest you both, but from the remarks made at the meeting moments ago, I believe the CIA and Homeland Security are looking to kill you both and not even bother with any questions. They didn't actually say that, but that is my hunch."

"But, Admiral, why is this happening? We are working as hard as we can to find Geo-1 and Geo-2."

"It's the threatening letter you sent to The President, the Chairman of the Federal Reserve Board, and the Director of the CIA! Troy, level with me, I can't defend you over here. Why did you threaten the U.S. Government by saying you would reveal mission specifics to *The New York Times*? You're an intelligence agent, Troy — you can't be saying those things!"

"Admiral, I wasn't threatening our government. I was just relaying a...."

Then it hit Troy like the crane had hit the house. His spirit shriveled, and his heart sank low, real low — broke into a thousand splinters. Sanjar might have been an irredeemable, sadistic psychopath, but he was also brilliant, more astute and calculating than Karla and Troy combined. Troy dejectedly realized all of a sudden that Sanjar's real motive in asking him to write the letter to those three important persons in the U.S. Government had not been to make them see that Blue Sparrow was serious in its threats to unleash another earthquake, but rather to compromise Troy and Karla's integrity in the eyes of U.S. law enforcement and to create the suspicion that, in reality, both of them were at the head of the terror group demanding the gold bullion! Sanjar had set the trap, and Troy had naively fallen right into it! He felt he was now worth less than a stupid cockroach.

"Troy — are you still there?"

"Yeah, just thinking about something."

"Well, dammit, did you and Karla cross over to the other side now? After all I've done to help you in this mission?"

"No, Admiral, we have not. Please believe me when I explain that I wrote that letter because I believed that it would help save many lives."

"That's not the tone of it, soldier! The CIA, and especially the Department of Homeland Security, are foaming at the mouth with venom. They're saying that Karla and you are military traitors worthy of the death penalty. Especially because hundreds of thousands of people are dead in the Northern Mariana Islands earthquake and the Alaska earthquake as well."

"I'm sorry, Admiral. There's nothing I can say or do right now to correct this situation. Our mission is still to find and destroy Geo-1 and Geo-2."

"That's if you live long enough to locate those devices."

"What do you mean?"

"Those five law-enforcement organizations I mentioned are looking for you right now, as we speak, presumably to arrest you. But the CIA and the DHS have mobilized their web of international assassins to terminate you and Karla."

"Look, Admiral, believe me when I tell you that Karla and I are not working for the enemy. We are still under your command. What can you do to help us with this mission under these dire circumstances?"

"If you're lying to me, Troy, they will assassinate me as well for helping you. I don't think they want explanations. Very peculiar."

"Admiral, I will follow all your orders and return immediately to Dover if you ask me to."

"This is a leap of faith. We must all take risks in the right direction when we don't have enough information for a thoroughly logical decision."

"So, is that a 'Yes'?"

"I will help you and Karla. First thing you need to do immediately is to stop using your passports and credit cards. They're probably already checking hotel and credit card records, so your current hotel room is, more than likely, compromised."

"Okay, but Karla needs at least a few hours to recover from our last encounter with Sanjar. She's in bad shape."

"It's life and death, Troy. Did Yanko's assistant Olga help you out today?"

"How did you know?"

"All the help that comes your way is not because of your good looks, Troy."

"Yes, she's helping me care for Karla. Downstairs getting some soup and new clothing."

"I will send Yanko a message right away to request that he help you with new passports, credit cards, IDs. In turn, he will message Olga and ask her to get another room using her own prepaid credit cards, maybe there on the same floor, so you can determine if any CIA hitmen go to your current room."

"Do you really think all this is necessary, Admiral?"

"If you had been at this meeting moments ago, Troy, the hair on the back of your head and arms would have stood up. I can't explain why the CIA and the DHS showed such intense desire to hunt you and Karla down — not to arrest you and bring you to trial, but to put as many bullets into your heads as possible. It was horrific."

"Well, I think I know why the CIA wants us dead, but, right now, our concern is the mission. Where do you stand on this, Admiral?"

"What was the last verified location of the two devices?"

"For sure, they were on an orange tractor-trailer heading southwest from Ramboiullet, France, on the E50 motorway, about 48 hours ago. There can't be that many orange 18-wheelers in that part of France. You did send lookouts to all ports and border points as I had suggested, right?"

"No luck at those points. Must still be in that area."

"I suggest, Admiral, that you mobilize all your Navy intel agents to look for truck storage depots that may have an orange vehicle southwest of Ramboiullet. There is nothing else we can do here in Sofia."

"So, change rooms as soon as Olga comes back, Troy, and get out of Sofia first thing tomorrow morning. We'll talk again when you and Karla are in Paris."

Troy was feeling sorry for himself for having been duped by Sanjar. After all, Troy had a university degree and intensive intelligence-officer training. Worse, still, it was not just some ordinary manipulation that Troy had been the victim of. No, it was a matter of life and death for him, and for Karla, who had nothing to do with it. And this had been his second major failure on this mission, the first being his hesitation at firing the RPG when he had the orange truck dead center on his sights — he'd had a good, clean shot. That would have destroyed the two devices and saved hundreds of thousands of lives. So he saved ten innocent lives and lost several hundred thousand. *Rotten deal, bad decision*, he thought. The record was piling up against him, and, now, he was being considered a traitor by his own country.

The doorbell rang. It was Olga with soup and some clothes for Karla.

"Mr. Hamilton, I have to get a room under my name on this floor. Why don't you try giving Karla some soup?"

Karla was able to sip the soup from the spoon. "Who's the woman?"

"That's Olga. She's Yanko's wig supplier — and partner in clandestine activities such as these."

"Troy, I'm not sure what happened or what's going on, but it looks like we're up shit creek. What kind of bomb blew up Sanjar's house? Was that a bunker-buster? Did you get the motherfucker?"

"Look, Karla, we're in a critical situation right now, so we have to change rooms because the CIA and the DHS are out to kill us both. I'll explain later. Please finish the soup while I pack our few things here. And, sorry, but we didn't find a fat corpse at the house. I doubt that anything could have survived the crane impact, the collapse of the two-story structure, and our machine-gun fire afterward. He was so fat, he could have burst like a water balloon dropped on concrete if the crane's tires rolled over him."

"What happened to your teeth? You seem to have some paper over them?" asked Karla, without looking up from the soup bowl.

"Broken. I'll have to get them fixed in Paris, maybe tomorrow."

Olga came back and hurriedly took them to a room not far down the hallway. They were careful to make sure that there was no one watching them.

"Karla, I'm glad you are feeling a bit better. I bought some nice, clean clothes for you. Hopefully, I guessed correctly at your size. Let me assist you in cleaning you up. Looks like you will need some help," said Olga. She supported Karla by the arm as the two women went into the bathroom.

But Troy was on edge because he had gotten a very clear picture from Admiral Ferris of the danger they were in if the CIA and the DHS were trying to carry out a hit on them. He kept his door open just a bit to get a look at their former room's door and the elevator further down the hall. In the bathroom, he could hear the bathtub filling with water, and the two women talking. He was beginning to like how Olga treated Karla in a very motherly fashion.

The elevator bell dinged. He took a peek out his door.

Three suited men wearing latex gloves stepped out, looking left and right at room numbers as they walked toward him. He knew they were looking for his former room, and that is exactly where they stopped. One of them had some form of electronic gadget that silently unlocked the door. In a lightning strike, all three rushed in, and Troy heard their silencer-equipped automatic pistols as they made that metallic *crack-crack-crack* sound with each detonation. Obviously they weren't taking any chances, because they must have fired about 15 rounds inside the room. There was silence for about 30 seconds, and then two of the three men walked out of the room, closed the door, and went down the fire-escape stairs. One of them was putting two pistols away — one into his holster, the other one inside his pants belt in the back.

Something was wrong, very wrong, Troy thought. Through the small slit of his slightly open room door, he kept looking and waiting for the third man, but no one came out of the room down the hall.

Troy realized that Admiral Ferris had been right! His suggestion to immediately change rooms had saved their lives. Troy closed the door and applied all three locks. He checked his Sig-Sauer, just in case, and took a peek out the window. The two CIA assassins got into a black van, but it did not immediately drive away. Were they re-evaluating? Were they homing in on telephone signals? Were they waiting for updates from headquarters, given that they had not found their targets in the designated room? Most terrifyingly, were they now getting info on Olga — information that would lead them to their new room? Troy knew that if these two men came up again, he might be able to hold them off for a couple of minutes, but they would soon ram their way in, and Olga, Karla, and he would be summarily executed, each by at least five hollow-point bullets to the head to ensure total brain-tissue destruction and, consequently, non-survivability. Death was never far behind, it seemed. It was a relief, though, when the black van finally drove away.

He left the window and went back to the door, again opening it just enough to get one eye looking down the hall. Nothing — other door still closed, no one in the hall. He was disconcerted and perturbed, almost in a panic, given the real danger they were in. Why had only two men exited the room? Did the third one stay behind, waiting in the shadows for when Karla and he returned? Was he there to assassinate them? But then, why was one of the men who left carrying two guns? Did one belong to the man who stayed behind? If the plan was to liquidate Karla and him, wouldn't it have been better for all three men to have stayed, lurking in the shadows of the room? Back to the window he went.

Nothing unusual outside — no sign of the third man. Besides, why would the van have abandoned him? Like a creeping octopus, Troy felt an obsession taking hold of him from all angles. He felt an urgent need to know where the situation stood. Were they going to die tonight? Was there a CIA hit man barely 25 feet from their new room? Was it better to let it be or to confront the threat on one's own terms? He would not be able to sleep tonight knowing that death might be so close by, so he decided to go check the situation in his former room. Once again, he checked his semi-automatic pistol, fully loaded, and chambered, no safety lever to worry about. It *had* to fire on less than one second's notice, if needed. He made sure he had the electronic keys for both rooms, and stepped out into the hallway. Carefully he placed his ear on his former room's door but heard nothing. Very slowly and quietly, he inserted the electronic card-key to unlock the door, and, in one huge push, he slam-opened the door and rolled on the floor to avoid any potential bullets coming his way. His eyes were as wide as they had ever been, rapidly scanning left, right, center, and back again. He hurried to check on the bathroom, barely avoiding pulling the trigger when he saw his own image in the mirror.

Yes, the third man was still there. He was on the bathroom floor with about five bullet holes on his face and his brains coming out the back of his head. Beautiful white-and-blue bathroom tiles were almost totally covered by a large pool of crimson. CIA ID in his wallet. Quickly Troy checked the messy bed with lots of pillows and balled up blankets — it had about ten holes in it. It was clear that the man on the floor had been murdered by one or both of his CIA partners.

Thinking about the grim scenario brought chills up Troy's spine. Since this was his room, he would now be associated with this cadaver. Should he move the body to another room or perhaps the trash bin? Nope, too much blood and brain-tissue splatter everywhere — even without a body, this would readily be declared the scene of a crime by the police. Besides, moving the cadaver would imply a desire to cover up the killing, and that would work against Troy later on.

He was feeling a noose tighten around his neck as he pondered what had happened there in the room. The three CIA assassins came to kill Karla and him, but, after the initial 10 shots, they discovered that the bed and the room were empty, so they must have had a Plan B. One of them must have already been pre-designated by the CIA as the sacrificial lamb, to be killed in the event that Troy and Karla, for whatever reason, were not liquidated that night in their hotel room. In this manner, Troy and Karla would be implicated in the grisly murder of a federal agent, further reducing their options in hiding from the CIA and other police authorities, and increasing the intense psychological pressure on their lives. Clearly, there were few human beings on the planet who could escape, for even a few days, the tenacious and ferocious desire of the CIA to eliminate them. The Agency had just executed a brilliant, yet dastardly, maneuver against Karla and Troy, and it was looking dim for them in Sofia.

He kept on thinking, or, rather, his growing paranoia compelled him to consider his situation. If the CIA was willing to murder one of their own loyal agents with five savage, close-range shots to the face, then they would be will-ing to do anything to track down and kill Troy and Karla. No wonder — the information that Sanjar had provided him corroborated many aspects of what Karla and he had lived through in the last few days. The CIA had been the instigator of the theft of Geo-1 and Geo-2, and had demanded proof that they worked properly, proof that had resulted in a destructive earthquake and tsunami in the Pacific and killed hundreds of thousands. Then they'd killed three employees in the lab, plus Thompson and Graham. The secret CIA operation to acquire these powerful devices had gone horribly wrong when Blue Sparrow decided to keep the machines for themselves as weapons to bargain with for gold bullion. Directly as a consequence of dealing with underworld terrorists, the CIA had lost control of the devices, and the CIA's former criminal associates used them to create the disastrous movement of the Aleutian Trench just south of Alaska, resulting, once more, in the loss of hundreds of thousands of lives and trillions of dollars in damages. All in all, the CIA was directly guilty of murdering several people and indirectly guilty of the deaths of approximately half-a-million more. The CIA was a clear case of a sociopathic organization.

But it was worse than that, thought Troy. While, on the surface, it might appear that the CIA was hunting down Karla and Troy as part of their duty to protect the United States, the real truth of the matter was that the viciousness of the hunt was to protect the internal interests of the CIA, especially the reputations, careers, financial status, and comfort of the members of the CIA directorate that had approved the criminal and felonious mission in the first place. This was not just a criminal theft gone horribly wrong — it was a mission that demonstrated the moral turpitude of highly decorated station chiefs and the big-ego CIA leadership in Langley. The last thing they wanted was for this evidence to reach the halls of Congress via an exhaustive research news article by *The New York Times*. Many careers would be doomed by the resulting international uproar; some senior officers might end up in prison. Some countries might sue the U.S. to recover damages. It was clear to Troy: The CIA had a huge problem, and the most effective solution was to find Troy and Karla, and to make them disappear forever, no questions asked. The sooner, the better.

Troy's mind had covered all the angles, so his paranoia was as strong as ever. Maybe he shouldn't stay too long there, close to the cadaver. Troy felt he could not do anything else in the old room, so he discreetly walked out and closed the door behind him. When he entered his new room, Karla and Olga had already emerged from the bathroom, Karla looking clean, brighter, and more alive.

"Where were you?" inquired Karla.

"I'll tell you in a minute," he replied, almost exhausted.

"Troy, that's a nasty branding burn that those motherfuckers inflicted on Karla. I applied some burn salve on it and covered it up with plenty of cotton gauze. Here's the burn kit — you're going to have to change the gauze every 4–6 hours. Apply more salve, sparingly," suggested Olga. "I'm sorry, Karla, that they did this to you, but these animals are dead now, and they won't bother you ever again."

"Thanks for your help, Olga," replied Karla.

"And, Troy, I was going to apply the cream to the stitched cuts on her shoulders and upper back, but she said that the doctor had told her that the medication would work better if you applied it," coughed Olga, with a playfully suspicious eye to them both.

"Wait, Olga — don't leave. I need to tell you both what has happened in the last few minutes." Then, play by play, Troy gave all the details to both women, who listened without uttering a single word. "Had we been there when they arrived, we would have been dead meat," exclaimed Troy. "Now, there is a murdered CIA man on the bathroom floor."

Olga responded, "Yanko told me you were in trouble, but I had no idea."

"The reason I wanted you to hear this, Olga, is that I feel you have to discuss this with Yanko. He will advise you if he thinks you personally are in danger. I can't say if these assassins or the CIA know of your involvement here, or even of your existence."

"I appreciate the advice. I will discuss this with him." Olga gave Karla a warm hug and said, "Karla, take care of yourself, dear. Don't be like me. I'm 45 now, can't have babies anymore, my time is past. Don't have a husband, wasted my youth fighting for stupid political causes that didn't make the world any better. You're young and pretty, and you have this scared hunk-of-a-man here who's an eligible bachelor. I want you to call me from America and tell me that you have a baby who will call me 'Aunt Olga.' I'll pack my bags in a jiffy. No more wigs! Be well, both of you." She squeezed Troy's hand, and, with watery eyes, she closed the door behind her.

It had been a warm moment, but now Karla and Troy were left feeling a bit awkward. Troy opted to get down to business. "Very nice person, this Olga. But, Karla, we have to plan our getaway from Sofia tomorrow morning. Our situation is deteriorating by the hour."

Yanko had already been contacted by Admiral Ferris, and he came over later that night with new British passports and credit cards. Just in case, he brought some wigs, eyebrows, mustaches, pastie moles, and other stuff he used to make his mannequins look beautiful or manly, as the case may be. Who knows? Maybe the CIA was keeping a lookout at the airport. "Whatever you don't use, put it in a bag and discard it after you leave the hotel tomorrow. Don't leave any evidence here. All trashcans should be empty of real trash. Just put a bit of unused toilet tissue in each of them." warned Yanko.

They spent a quiet evening in their room, giving Karla time to recover from her ordeal. They applied each other's medications — doctor's orders. Exhausted, they prepared for bed. All of a sudden, they both realized that there was only one bed — queen size. Olga had just assumed. No time to change. They got in bed, not exactly sure what configuration they would assume, but Karla took care of that. "Troy, could you just hold me for a little while?"

"Sure will, Lieutenant," was his eager reply. And when they were ready to doze off: "Good night, Karla."

"Good night, Mr. Navy Intelligence."

Very early in the morning, they phoned Yanko to thank him again for all his help and asked him to relay their thanks and gratitude to "Aunt Olga." An hour later, they were in the air, on their way to Paris.

CHAPTER 16

The flight back to France was uneventful, but it did give them an opportunity to evaluate their serious situation.

"One thing that is up in the air, Troy, is the status of the threat to unleash the San Andreas Fault in California. If Sanjar is dead, who will manage that threat? In fact, who will manage those two devices?"

"How I wish we had conclusive evidence that he was blasted out of existence. It's hard to imagine that anyone could survive that explosive impact without at least many serious injuries."

"The three-day deadline established by Blue Sparrow expires tomorrow about noon. There's no reason to suspect that they're bluffing. They weren't with Alaska. It's unrealistic to expect that we will find the two devices quickly in an area as big as all of France, so we should prepare for a catastrophe."

"As far as I know, Karla, we are the only ones looking to find and destroy those devices. None of the law-enforcement agencies that Admiral Ferris spoke of are looking. It would seem to me that priority one should be finding those two machines!"

Karla added, "You also had said that both the CIA and the DHS are looking to kill us. We have very damaging criminal info on the CIA, so I can understand their desire to save their own skins. But we don't have a shred of evidence or suspicion about DHS. What's their problem with us?"

"Keep in mind that, when things started to go wrong with their plan, the CIA began killing people left and right. Heck, they even killed CIA agent Edgar Wicklund, the guy whose face showed up on that security video at the Geophysical lab. Remember? If this international CIA conspiracy were to be investigated by Congress, his testimony would have placed the CIA at the very center of this felonious mess. They had to kill him, too. So maybe the DHS, with its ever-expanding international security mission, is trying to protect the CIA," elaborated Troy.

"So, Troy, what's our future?" demanded Karla.

He did not want to offer a ready-made, naively optimistic answer to her legitimate question. While he was seriously thinking about the issue, he was also looking at an American man who was sitting about five rows ahead of them and who had turned to look at the back of the aisle several times, chancing a glance at both of them every time. Was he CIA? Troy and Karla were still wearing the minimal disguises provided by Yanko, so was this guy working hard to figure out if they were his targets? Well, as long as Troy and Karla were in a crowd, there was little chance that he would try to kill them. On the other hand, the CIA had already proven it was willing to do desperate things. Troy thought it better to keep one eye on the suspected assassin.

Finally he answered Karla's query. "Not good, Karla. Both of us have sustained injuries, but I acknowledge yours were worse when you were in captivity. Keep in mind that we are intelligence agents sworn to protect our country, and that is what we will do, even if it costs us our lives. Do you still agree with your oath to protect the United States?"

She didn't know quite what to make of Troy's accusatory question, so she fell silent. Maybe he was the type of agent who would blindly stick to an oath under all conditions, an oath taken under the seductive and patriotic environment of the government training center, where everything was rosy, and the government promised that it would support and protect its agents. But that was *not* what was happening here. On the contrary, their government was out to kill them. A hit man's bullet had barely missed her at the hotel in London. She had suffered incredible torture and abuse at the hands of Sanjar and his brutes, and instead of giving her help, her government had sent three assassins into their hotel room in Sofia who fired ten rounds into their beds. The government would like for them to think they were safe, but Karla felt that a more accurate description of their desperate situation was that they were "terminally safe."

"Look, Troy, I am all for protecting our country and all that — that's why I became a Navy intel officer. Yes, our first priority should be finding and destroying those two devices. That's our mission. But what I am asking is what we'll be doing after that. You and I have a huge personal problem — they want to kill us. What are we doing about that?"

It seemed that Troy had not gotten that far in the planning process. He simply had invested all his time in figuring out *what* actually was happening.

"The simple answer to your question is this. If they want to kill us to prevent this information from getting to *The New York Times* or the U.S. Congress, then we should provide that information as soon as possible so there won't be any reason to kill us afterward. Well, maybe for revenge only. Am I on the right track with this?"

Karla's CalTech mind, honed by years of deep study in the vagaries of geophysics and seismology, thought about the implicit proposal in Troy's remark. It seemed simple enough on the surface, but there were still various unanswered questions that cast some doubt on that plan to save their lives. One of them was that even if all the details were to be sent to Congress, Troy and Karla would continue being a huge liability for the CIA because they could, at any time, be asked by the House Judiciary Committee to testify in person. That certainly would be more dramatic and damaging for the CIA. No, there was no easy or obvious solution on what to do about their personal safety. And they still had to worry about the DHS — it might yet spring a surprise hit on Troy and Karla.

After the short flight, they arrived at Charles De Gaulle Airport in Paris, and their first order of business was to keep a close eye on the suspicious American they had spotted on their flight. Karla got the impression that he was still trying to look at them at the airport but was trying hard to appear discreet, maybe because he had become aware that he had been made. Nevertheless, he made one call and sped off in a taxi. It was cause for concern.

Troy was readily able to locate an orthodontic clinic near the airport. Unfortunately, the doc there told him that the teeth could not be re-implanted, but that he would able to utilize most of the two teeth in a bridge configuration to provide a temporary repair that could easily last a month or two. It was better than nothing.

They went around several blocks a number of times, just as a precaution, and then they got a room with one queen-size bed at the Paris Regal-Greene Hotel, near the center of Paris, using their new identities. Troy thought it might be a good idea to call his elderly neighbor, Miss Lilly, back in Manhattan, just to touch base with her.

"Hi, Lilly — this is Troy!"

"Oh, you scoundrel-about-the-world! You left me all abandoned. Where are you now in your business ventures?"

"I'm traveling all over Europe. How have you been holding up?"

She told him about all her ailments and such. "And that dirty super, Antonio Colon, keeps asking me if you really just want to be my boyfriend to get to my money. Ha! I told him that, actually, you are just one of my hot lovers. He had this look on his face!"

"How is Arturo doing? Eating okay?"

"He's fine. I think he misses you a lot. When are you coming back to New York?"

The conversation was cut short by a call that came in on the other line. They quickly said goodbye.

"Hello, Mr. Hamilton. Recognize my sweet voice?"

Incredible but true! It was the vile and malevolent Sanjar! Both Troy and Karla were shocked. So the monster was alive after all. The beast was alive!

After a bit of silence to recover from the initial shock, Troy responded, "Sanjar, you share one admirable quality with the German cockroaches that plague New York."

"And what would that be, Mr. Hamilton?"

"After 300 years of liquid poisons, smoke bombs, roach traps, and biological powders, they're still alive, they're still here! They're nasty, filthy, and durable. That's you, Sanjar. You are a durable cockroach. Now, what the hell do you want?"

"Oh, you know I get what I want. I must tell you, though, that I did not appreciate your dramatic show destroying my little house and killing three of my best assassins. Well, that's okay, I suppose, because I have plenty more."

"Yeah, well, I am sorry we didn't get that big crane to roll over your filthy body and make it into a dog-shit pancake. Get to the point, fat man."

"You are probably wondering how I managed to survive. I'm not stupid. I have alternate places, but I did err in not killing your bitch. I was going to do it after you sent the letter."

"I'm glad I didn't send it. Are you still keeping that deadline for the San Andreas Fault, you pig?"

"You might as well accuse me of having cooties, Mr. Hamilton. That would be in line with the other adolescent insults you keep sending my way."

He did have a point, Troy thought. Yet there was no other way of expressing the anger that Karla and he felt at him. "You're right, Sanjar. Okay, is your threat still active?"

"Absolutely, and with a vile vengeance because of you!"

"Hopefully the Treasury Department is getting that gold bullion ready for you," Troy mentioned, halfway serious.

"Oh, that would be glorious! I will be waiting for the transfer. Will let you know."

"Yes, I'm sure you will," replied Troy, knowing that Sanjar would be gloating about it.

Almost as if it had skipped his mind, Sanjar uttered, "Troy, listen. I did notice from my window next door the woman who was at the wheel of your getaway car when you and that other guy rolled over my house. Here's a digital photo she is sending you. Will talk later."

Shocking! That could only mean that Olga was now being held captive by Sanjar, that she would be suffering the same torture and sexual abuse that Karla did. They felt they now had no choice but to travel back to Sofia to try to rescue her. How could they not? She had been so kind to them. But then again, wasn't it their duty to stick to the mission plan? Then the digital image arrived.

Odious and disgusting! It was "Aunt Olga's" severed head on a very large, oval plate, with a baby chick standing next to it! Troy and Karla almost vomited at the image, and they took a few minutes trying to compose themselves. Was there no limit to the evil coming from this man? Was this reprobate cannibal even human?

"Troy, when this is all over, we have to search for this sombitch and kill him slowly. He doesn't deserve to live — he is not part of humanity," bellowed Karla. She had personal reasons, too, for wanting the beast dead. While in captivity, she had suffered in a way that she had not dared tell Troy.

"Yes, but we have to keep focused on our mission. Karla, get the Admiral on the phone while I get a notepad. We have to search for those truck depots."

Still shaking from having looked at the photo, Karla dialed the secure number.

"Hello, sir — this is Karla."

"Karla — nice to hear your voice again. Are you recovering well from your wounds?"

"Well, sir, everything hurts, but, here I am, doing my job. Were your agents able to get some hits on depots?"

"Good news. First of all, I have to reiterate that officials kept a keen eye on all points of entry into, and exit from, the country, and there was no orange truck leaving or any other vehicle with large crates."

"And the truck depots?"

"We had more than twenty agents working around the clock, checking depots, and they located seven truck station-depots that had an orange truck, two of them very close to E50, the motorway you last saw the truck traveling on."

"And how do we get that list?"

"I am sending a digital image to you as we chat. Look, Karla, the situation over here is still critical. I don't know how, but the CIA knows that you both are in Paris right now, at the Regal-Greene. Don't confirm or deny — just get out as soon as we finish the call. Don't stay at big-name hotels, don't use credit cards; use a disguise if possible, and while in the big city, walk separately and not as a couple. Let me talk to Troy, please."

"Yes, Admiral. This is Troy — I heard the conversation."

"What's the latest, Troy?"

"The CIA was deeply involved in the original theft of the geophysical devices, and they have murdered many people involved in this case. That's it in a nutshell, Admiral."

"That's what I feared. No wonder they're out to get you. They have no desire to bring you and Karla to trial for treason and over the letter you wrote. And they have Homeland Security on their side, looking for you. I don't know exactly why they, too, say they prefer you put up a fight so they'll have to shoot you."

"What's the latest over the tsunami from the Marianas Trench and the earthquake in Alaska?" inquired Troy.

"The tsunami has already hit the west coast and caused extensive damage but minimal loss of life, since people were warned in plenty of time by the Pacific Tsunami Warning Center in Hawaii. In Alaska, the Aleutian Trench earthquake caused catastrophic losses over the entire state. It's now a disaster area, and casualties keep climbing by the hour. One of the worst in U.S. history, Troy."

"That's why we have to find those two devices. The sadistic ringleader, Sanjar, is demented. If he doesn't get his gold bullion by around noon tomorrow, I figure he will initiate the fault slippage — he'll enjoy watching the news about California splitting off the mainland and going out to sea. He would really love to see that."

"If I get any more intel on this side, I'll let you know. Now get the hell out of that hotel room!" ordered the Admiral.

But it was too late. Karla had just looked through the peephole and signaled to Troy that there were two suited men just outside their door. Most probably, they were planning on breaking the door down and start shooting, so Troy and Karla quickly took positions on opposite sides of the room, waiting for the men to break in. They heard noises outside the door, like objects clinking against each other. Were other assassins joining the original two? Did they have fully automatic weapons? Did they have a snake lens camera, like the one used when Thompson had been killed by a barrage of bullets in London? But there was nothing coming through the small slit at the bottom of their door. What were they waiting for? Troy and Karla's only chance for survival was to fire their weapons as rapidly as possible. If they took the time to assess the nature and the size of the threat, it would be too late. One second would just be too much. What they did not count on was that the assassins had a C-4 door-buster explosive with them.

They had sweat on their brows when the hotel door exploded and sent a shock wave that stunned them for a moment, but the dust and smoke at the door blinded the intruders' line of sight, so the rounds they fired into the room did not find their mark. Karla and Troy, being a bit farther from the center of the explosion could easily see the silhouettes of the two figures and fired their weapons, hitting their marks about three times each. Two figures dropped to the floor, like dead weight. There were no more shadows or figures, and no more hostile fire. But just in case, Troy and Karla quickly changed positions within the room and then remained immobile, with one eye on the door and the other on the two bodies on the floor.

While Karla checked the hotel hallway for other potential threats, Troy checked the dead men's IDs. Yes, CIA. Silencer-equipped regulation semi-automatic Glocks.

They had to get out of there quickly before the police or hotel security showed up, so they opted for the back entrance to the hotel. Before they opened the glass door, they looked carefully at the parking lot. Everything looked normal, except for a white step-van with furniture-store lettering and a motionless driver at the wheel. Was he on standby? Were there other agents inside the van? They had to take the chance, so they exited slowly and leisurely, walking away from where the step-van was parked. Troy managed to look at the mirror of a parked car and detected that four men were coming out of the back of the van. No coincidence — it was time to run!

In a few seconds they were out of the parking lot, but, as they turned the corner heading southwest on Rue du Cherche-Midi, a bullet hit the edge of the building and spread pieces of brick and powder all over them. The shot had been very close. There were many stores on that street, but the question was how to elude the five assassins after them — the driver had joined the chase. It was clear that they could not hope to outrun them, for both Karla and Troy were still trying to recover from their injuries, and all body movements were exceedingly painful. They opted to go into a supermarket, adopt some strategic positions, and return gunfire. Each of them chose a position with a clear view of the main entrance — Karla behind the beer cooler, Troy on the side of the cosmetics counter.

As the men hurriedly entered through the main glass doors, they were greeted by a furious barrage of gunfire from Troy and Karla's Sig-Sauer semi-automatics. There was so much gunfire that the whole store shook from the high-powered detonations. Glass from the very large windows in front of the supermarket shattered and rained on the CIA hit men still near the entrance, desperately trying to locate the source of the gunfire. The assassins returned fire, but Troy and Karla were well covered by merchandise or heavy shelving. What the CIA's bullets were doing was exploding cans of tomato sauce and corn, milk and orange juice cartons, and all sorts of aromatic cosmetics bottles. Troy, in fact, had gotten all wet with the creams and skin moisturizers raining down on him. After about 30 seconds of this mayhem, the hit men retreated a few feet outside the main door and just around the edge, but not before one of them fell, mortally wounded. The gunfire stopped. It was time for a very quick assessment.

A terrible thought came to their minds. As it now stood, the situation was at a virtual stalemate: The CIA agents could not come in, and Troy and Karla could not go out. But what if two of the four hit men had decided to go around the block to the alley behind the supermarket and enter the store from the rear? Troy and Karla would have to fight the battle on two fronts, something they probably could not win. They concluded they had to get out at that moment! Without any further analysis, they quietly ran to the very back and entered the storage section, looking for the receiving gate, where, undoubtedly, the trucks came to unload their shipments. Out the huge doors they went, into the alley, and, right away, they saw two assassins running toward them about 100 yards away, guns already ablaze. Troy and Karla ran in the opposite direction, dodging bullets and desperately looking for an open door. They knew that the other two hit men would soon be joining the pair running behind them, and the situation would get much worse. As they were running past a large, steel garbage bin, they took cover behind it to catch their breath.

Breathing like people who had never run in their lives, they turned to face the enemy and fired a new volley of 9mm bullets in their direction. Their tormentors, caught by surprise and with nothing for cover, went to the ground to reduce their effective target size, but Karla took her time in aiming and hit one of them in the forehead, and something behind his head went flying all the way to his feet. He fired no more after that. His buddy slid rapidly onto the ground and used his friend's cadaver for cover while he kept firing.

Just about that time, Troy saw that, at the very far side of the alley, the two other assassins had appeared, running furiously to catch up with their buddy, who was pinned down on the ground by Troy and Karla's gunfire. Knowing that their advantageous position could not last more than about half-a-minute, Troy and Karla decided to run again, this time in zig-zag fashion, and the barrage of bullets zipping and buzzing past them began again. They were tired, they were desperate, they were injured, and they were in pain. They were running low on ammunition, so they went through an open door. For one split second, they thought they should wait in there to ambush the assassins after them. Just as quickly, they abandoned that idea.

It was a multi-level department store. They made the split-second decision to run toward the second floor and hide for maybe two minutes to reload and catch their breath again — they were panting beyond control, almost like people who have been rescued from drowning. Sure, they wanted to hide, but there were lots of personnel in the store whose commotion would alert the hit men. Yet they managed to make it to the third floor, where there were few customers and workers.

One reloaded while the other kept watch. Time to go, but where? Certainly not down. They weren't sure where the assassins were. Now they were at an extreme disadvantage if they were to try to go down to the first level. An ambush would be all but certain.

With a look of resignation, Karla said, "Troy, it doesn't look good. I feel that the stitches on my back are opening up, and my branding burn hurts like hell — I have blood running down my leg. Try to save yourself. This is the end of the line for me."

"No, Karla, no! We're a team. I would never run to save myself and just leave you here because you can't run as fast. We make it together, or we die together, Lieutenant! Is that clear enough?"

"Thanks, Troy — I needed to hear that from you. I am leaking blood down my leg, so they'll be able to track us that way. Let's give it one more big push — I'll do the best I can."

Troy squeezed Karla's hand and motioned for her to follow him. What he had in mind was for them to make their way to the back area of the third floor, the supplies and inventory backroom. Once there, Troy started looking for a window leading to the exterior fire escape stairs. He found it, but it had a large padlock on it. Undoubtedly, that was a huge fire code violation and a fire hazard, but he was not about to argue with the store management. He aimed his Sig and fired one round dead-center on the steel lock, and it went flying in pieces. "Let's hurry. I'm sure they heard that shot."

Once on the fire escape, they took turns covering and going down a few steps, for they expected that, at any moment, someone would start firing at them from the open third-floor window.

That's exactly what happened. They selected the area on each step that afforded them the best cover from the shots coming from above. There were so many steel members and trusses that it was hard for the hit man to get a clear shot, yet Karla and Troy knew that he could just get lucky one time and it would be over for them. Finally, they were on the ground level, and it was time to run like hell again, flying bullets digging pockmarks in the asphalt surface of the alley.

They needed to get out of the alley for good, so into another door they went. It was a hardware store, with a clear shot toward the front door. Once on the main street, they grabbed a cab. They took many looks behind them, but they were not being followed. It had been a true nightmare.

The cab ride afforded them the opportunity to rest and catch their breath. Karla almost fell asleep, exhausted, with her head on Troy's shoulder. They told the driver to drive around, that they just wanted to catch a glimpse of Paris. But in spite of their exhaustion, they managed to change cabs twice, just to reduce the risk. On Rue de Bagneux, Troy spotted a small medical clinic but said nothing. A block later, they got out of the cab and walked to the clinic. Karla needed medical attention. Troy asked her to hand over her Sig Sauer.

Even though they were both wet with perspiration, the staff was very accommodating and gave them a quick, superficial cleaning. Karla's stitches on her back had opened up, so they were replaced, and new healing ointment and gauze were applied. The branding burn on her left buttock was quite another matter.

The doctor removed the old, disheveled, and bloody cotton gauze and found the branding was still oozing blood. He couldn't quite make out what symbol had been burned onto her buttock, but he asked her, "Are you two into some type of S&M or rough sex? Is he forcing you to do this?" He fixed her wound, but Karla knew that the doctor had a high degree of suspicion about the situation. Unfortunately, it was time to flee again. They paid the bill, and, on the way out, they heard the doctor talking to the police.

They were in no condition to hunt for the orange truck at that point, so they got a take-out Chinese lunch and went to a park to eat and rest. Troy returned the Sig-Sauer to Karla.

"You know, Karla, I believe that Admiral Ferris is doing all he can to help us out with the internal goings-on inside the government, but I feel there is a lot we don't know. We can't ever do our jobs because of the assassins on our trail."

"Yeah, it's starting to feel like a thankless job."

"Do you know anybody in other branches who might be able to point us in the right direction? Anyone who has access to information not available to us or to Admiral Ferris?"

She looked up as if mentally reviewing a list of persons known to her and discarding everyone down the line. Except one. "Well, I had this friend — we were at CalTech together, and she was studying international relations. We were close, but my field was too 'stifling,' she said, given that she was in the social sciences. Both of us thought of working for the government, and, after graduation, we sort of grew apart."

"But you're still on speaking terms, hopefully?"

"Last time we spoke was about six months ago. She's not a field agent, but she compiles intelligence analyst reports for Homeland Security. I bet she might know what's going on."

"Would you feel comfortable asking her for help?"

"She owes me a few favors, so we'll see. Her name is Elizabeth Eisner. Works out of Washington. I'll try her now."

Like Karla, Elizabeth was in her early 30s, had dark hair, and had always dreamed of serving her country. But while Karla had more of a hard-science mind, Elizabeth was more inclined to spend all her free time reading about politics, culture, diplomacy, economics, and geography. Unmarried, but not by choice. Men just felt intimidated by her whiz mind. While at CalTech with Karla, she had been a loyal and true friend.

Karla fumbled around a few moments with her digital directory. Then she pressed the entry. "Hello, Elizabeth? Hi, it's me, Karla! Yeah! Is this a good time, or am I interrupting?"

"Oh, no, this is fine. So how have you been? You just disappear for long periods!"

They chitchatted for a while with a few formalities and old college gossip. "OK, Karla, you Catalina Hall genius, I know you called me for more than just girl-talk, so what's up?"

"Very perceptive, Elizabeth, as always. Look, you know, please keep this confidential. I'm on assignment with my colleague Troy here in Europe. We're in terrible trouble."

'Karla and Troy'? Yes, I've been hearing your names pop up. What kind of trouble?"

"Well, I'm sure you've heard and read about the terrible earthquakes in the Northern Mariana Islands and Alaska. Our work is connected to an investigation about that."

"Yes, it's on all the news channels around the world. People here, that's all they talk about," responded Elizabeth.

"Look, I'll be honest. The CIA and Homeland Security are out to kill us. They say we are working with the enemy to extort gold bullion from the U.S. government. Does that sound ridiculous, or what?"

Whispering, Elizabeth continued. "They say you're asking for $1 trillion in gold ingots, but there is something strange about it, Karla."

"Strange? Like what?"

"Well, DHS Director Michael Hartwell — I'm sure you've heard of him — he says that he wants the FBI to bring you in — alive, Karla, *alive*! But, at other times, he says that agents should shoot you first and then ask questions. Mighty strange. Don't quote me."

"Elizabeth, we know for a fact that the CIA has made several attempts to kill us, and they've killed other people connected with this case."

"Wait! Stop, Karla. You did not say that, and I did not hear it. Dammit, Karla, in college you used to get me in trouble with the guys we dated, and now you want to ruin my career?"

"Sorry, Elizabeth, got out of hand. Please help us!"

"So what do you want me to do?"

"We can understand why the CIA might want us dead, but we are perplexed and worried by the stories we've heard about the DHS wanting to kill us, too. There is no information that we have that is damaging to them, so why not just arrest us if we've done something wrong?"

"I've heard rumors, but I don't have a definite answer for you. Give me a little bit of time, and I'll send you a message when I have something."

"Thanks, Elizabeth. I'll be waiting."

Troy had heard the entire conversation. "So, the key here seems to be DHS Director Michael Hartwell. Maybe he is trying to juggle two incompatible objectives here. Fact is, we haven't seen any Department of Homeland Security assassins after us."

"Yes, and I think that my friend knows more than what she told us, but maybe she's trying to figure out how to tell us and not involve herself too deeply."

They tossed the subject around a few times but didn't reach any more major conclusions. Then Troy suggested, "Time to get back on our feet. Let's look at that list of depots with an orange truck. We have less than 24 hours until Armageddon is unleashed against California and practically the entire western half of the U.S."

CHAPTER 17

They prioritized Admiral Ferris's list of the seven depot locations that had been observed with at least one orange truck. It was possible that the two devices had already left France, but the list was all they had at that point.

In a rented car, they started driving southwest from Rambouillet and quickly found out that the first three depots they checked had orange trucks that were vastly different from what they remembered from the violent encounter a little more than two days earlier. The fourth depot on the list, however, was a bit more promising. It was called Mediterranean Uniport, and was located in Marseille, a port city about 425 kilometers south of Paris, by the Western Mediterranean Sea.

Karla and Troy parked their car about two blocks from the depot's fenced parking area and assumed a good and secluded lookout post on some bluffs.

"Karla, I think we've hit the jackpot!" exclaimed Troy as he looked through his binoculars at the lone orange truck in the depot.

Looking through her own, she replied, "I'm looking at it, but how can you be so sure?"

"Remember two days ago, when we were chasing the truck going south on the E50?"

"Yes — I know it sort of looks like it, but you're saying you're sure," mumbled Karla, with a look of confusion.

"Well, Karla, this orange truck-trailer has two bullet holes on its left rear door, at exactly the same spot where I hit the orange truck on the highway! There's no doubt — this is the truck!"

"Hallelujah! I was beginning to think that we would never find it in time," expressed Karla. "Now, the next step is to find out if the two machines are still inside."

Just then, an uncomfortable thought hit Karla. What was the truck doing at a depot in a port city by the Mediterranean Sea? It was easy to see that the depot was no more than 400 meters from the giant cranes that loaded and unloaded the ships and boats of all sizes at the dock. Was the plan to load these machines onto a ship or boat? That would complicate the mission considerably. She shared her thoughts with Troy, who agreed that it was now a matter of urgency to take quick action. All well, except that now Karla and Troy were armed only with their Sig-Sauer 9mm semi-automatics — hardly a neutralizing weapon against reinforced crates, and at a distance, to boot! To make matters worse, there were about ten security guards in and around the depot, armed with automatic weapons. They were obviously guarding something very valuable.

Troy took a closer look through his binoculars. The ten guards did not look French at all. They looked like Americans, with German-made Heckler & Koch MP5 automatics like the ones in use by the U.S. Secret Service and the Department of Homeland Security! What were armed American guards doing at a French seaport? Was it just a coincidence they were armed with the same weapons in use by DHS? Troy had been taught long ago not to believe in innocent coincidences.

Just then a message marked HIGH PRIORITY came through: KARLA, CALL ME RIGHT AWAY. URGENT. ELIZABETH.

So, Karla called Elizabeth immediately. "Hi, Elizabeth — this is Karla. What's up?"

"This is heavy shit, Karla. Don't be surprised if they find me in a ditch tomorrow," said Elizabeth in a subdued tone.

"I'm afraid to ask," replied Karla. "Just to let you know, Elizabeth, my colleague Troy is connecting to this call."

"Hi, Troy. Nice to meet you."

"Same here, Elizabeth."

Elizabeth continued with her report. "I've been going back to old intel summaries I've compiled and checked files not meant for my eyes. Homeland Security has been working on a secret project called 'HAARP' for years."

"Yeah, I've heard of the anagram with those letters, but what is it?"

"The letters stand for High Frequency Active Auroral Research Program. Nothing more and nothing less than the attempt by DHS to actively control the weather, Karla!"

Karla was stunned for a second or two. "How would they do that?"

"You have probably seen those chemtrails high up in the air. But more important is that they are using very high-power radio signals aimed at the troposphere of the earth's atmosphere to, in effect, create the kind of weather they want in any part of the world," explained Elizabeth, with a bit of a tremor in her voice.

"It's easy to see that this type of research can have incredible military applications. Any country having control of the weather of any other country in the world can effectively control that country. Tornadoes, hurricanes, lightning, monsoons, floods, droughts — all of these are more powerful than the biggest military in the world! Elizabeth, this is huge!" cried Troy.

Elizabeth continued to explain. "I also found out something else, something related to what you two are doing."

"I can see where this is going," guessed Karla.

"It seems that these earthquakes and tsunamis of the last few days were not simply natural phenomena. Am I right?" quizzed Elizabeth.

"You're on the right track, so I'll admit it. Yes, these were caused by very sophisticated devices, but this is supposed to be classified," advised Karla. "Since these two devices are not under U.S. control, we are trying to locate them to destroy them. That's our mission. Now you know. We're trusting you."

Elizabeth hesitated a bit, and then she dropped a bomb. "Have you asked yourselves why Homeland Security would want you to destroy those devices when, in fact, they fit perfectly into their plan to control natural phenomena? They would control the weather, climate, earthquakes, and tsunamis. The DHS would have more power to control nations than all the military forces on earth, combined!"

Karla and Troy were stunned. Yes, if Homeland Security controlled weather, climate, earthquakes, and tsunamis, they could easily control the world!

"But, Elizabeth, does this then mean that Homeland Security, with such enormous power under their control, could then decide not to be answerable to the U.S. government, to the people?"

"You read my mind, Karla dear."

Another piece of the puzzle materialized in Troy's mind. "Maybe that's why we haven't noticed any Homeland Security assassins on our trail — just vicious CIA hit men."

Throughout the very revealing conversation with Elizabeth from DHS, Troy and Karla continued to keep their eyes on the depot — especially on the orange truck-and-trailer with two bullet holes in the rear. They noticed that two rather large and identical fishing boats had docked. That seemed odd because this port was not for fishing vessels.

Elizabeth asked, "So how is it that Homeland Security located or became aware of these geophysical devices you talk about?"

"It wasn't Homeland Security. It was the CIA that got a whiff of them through their professional-journal research. Then they stole the devices from their inventors in London, killing quite a few people who got in their way. Elizabeth, these murderous bureaucrats at the CIA are directly responsible for the Marianas Trench earthquake that killed hundreds of thousands of people. This is unprecedented in the history of intelligence services around the world!" answered Troy.

Elizabeth chimed in, "Well, that explains some ridiculous things here at the DHS center that have not been making sense."

"Like what?" Troy asked.

"For years, our director, Michael Hartwell, has had a venomous dislike for the CIA, especially for director Kirk Weatherhouse. He walked around here calling CIA people all sorts of bad names and saying that the DHS has a more important mission than that of the CIA."

"But isn't that just part of the normal inter-agency rivalry within the government?" quipped Karla.

"You decide. About a week before the Marianas Trench earthquake, our director started having numerous daily conversations with Weatherhouse at the CIA — and in a nice tone, too. Don't know what they talked about, but I bet it was about those devices."

Troy thought about it for a moment. Then he barged in, "In Belgium, we spoke to the banker who handled the contract to steal the devices. The CIA paid him $5 million. But the banker tried to rip off the boss of the henchmen who did the actual stealing, and the deal went real sour."

"Our, guess, Elizabeth, is that the CIA has been trying to kill us because they know that we know they contracted to steal the devices and that they killed all those people," explained Karla.

"Now it makes sense! Hartwell has been feigning support for the CIA, but he would love nothing more than to see the CIA go down in flames for this fiasco that involves assassinations, which have been prohibited by Congress for several decades now," observed Elizabeth.

"So that's why they don't want to kill us — they want us alive to testify against their nemesis, the CIA!" added Karla.

"And if that happens, Homeland Security would be left as the premier security and intelligence agency for the U.S. government. That damned Hartwell is a power-hungry bastard!" roared Troy, as he was signaling to Karla to look at the depot and the port.

Dockworkers had opened the trailer's back doors, and heavy-duty forklifts had made their way there. With their binoculars, Troy and Karla could see two tall crates inside the trailer — the devices!

"Listen, Elizabeth, we're in a situation right now — gotta go. We're very much appreciative of your info. I'll call you in a couple of days with an update. Stay safe!" urged Karla.

Of course, Troy and Karla had made the connection that the crates would be loaded onto the two fishing boats that had docked earlier. So close, yet it seemed almost impossible to try to destroy the machines, given that Karla and Troy had only two relatively small firearms while the ten security personnel had fully automatic weapons.

"We should call the Admiral. Maybe he can help us," opined Troy.

Karla agreed.

Troy made the call. "Admiral, Troy here. Arpeggio 103. Karla is on the line, too."

"Nice to hear from you, Karla and Troy. I hope you have good news for me — I'm drowning in bad news over here."

"Admiral, a confidential source has given us some information that makes us conclude that the CIA wants to kill us because we know they are responsible for the earthquake."

"Yeah, we were leaning in that direction. Anything else?"

Karla added, "Yes, in spite of what Director Michael Hartwell at the DHS has been saying, we don't think that Homeland Security is out to kill us — they want us alive to testify against CIA, their nemesis."

"So what have we here, a struggle for power?" asked Admiral Ferris, almost incredulously.

"We believe it's more than that. It looks like Hartwell wants Homeland Security to rule over all the intelligence agencies in the U.S. government, even if he has to destroy some of them along the way," articulated Troy.

"Our situation was grave even before this, and now it appears that the enemy is within us!" exclaimed the Admiral. "How can we effectively fight Blue Sparrow when we are being eaten alive from the inside by this cancerous grab for power?"

After a few seconds, Karla added, "Look, sir, the crisis between the CIA and the DHS is something you might have to handle yourself. Troy and I are looking right now at the two geophysical devices being loaded onto two large fishing vessels, here at the port of Marseille in southern France. We have located them!"

"My Lord! That is spectacular news, especially because the deadline for the San Andreas Fault earthquake is so near. Good work, you two, good work!"

Troy then gently continued, "But we need help. As you know, we have only our 9mm Sig-Sauer semi-automatics, and there are at least ten security guards with automatic weapons. It would be suicide to attempt to hit the devices."

"Any idea where they're heading?"

"Our best guess is straight south to the Port of Annaba in Algeria. Sanjar may want the devices to be completely out of Europe, out of the reach of possible interference by NATO forces later on. And in addition, since he is asking for so much gold bullion, we guess that an African country might be more receptive to his plans for the future. Just a guess," surmised Karla.

The two bright-yellow forklifts had picked up their cargo and had made their way to the edge of the dock, where large overhead cranes were moving into position above them. There was a lot of activity on the two fishing vessels, perhaps indicating that they were readying to accept the large crates. Workers began to tie heavy lifting straps around each of the crates. And the ten security guards had now positioned themselves in the dock area near the fishing vessels.

"Sir, it's one thing to work undercover trying to destroy these machines in Europe, but things can get politically messy if these devices get to Algeria," warned Karla, with an edge of urgency in her voice.

"OK, Lieutenant, so what are our realistic options? What are you suggesting?" retorted the Admiral.

Karla was caught unprepared by that question, for she had not given any thought whatsoever to a possible plan of attack.

Troy submitted, "Well, there are basically two lines of attack. We hit them by air or from another boat. By the time we put into action whatever it is we decide upon, they will be out at sea."

There were a few, long seconds of silence. The Admiral spoke with a firm decision. "The two closest air bases we have in that area are the U.S. Air Base a few kilometers outside of Seville, in Spain, and the Aviano NATO Air Base in Italy."

"Are you thinking of a helicopter attack on the two boats?" asked Karla.

"Karla, this might start some international political incident, but we can't worry about that now, when so much is at stake. Yes, a helicopter search-and-destroy mission against the two boats."

"OK, so how long will it take to get that helicopter here in Marseille?" uttered Karla.

"Give me a minute," pleaded the Admiral. After taking into account several logistical considerations like availability, range, speed, armaments, and likely scenarios to be encountered deep in the Western Mediterranean Sea, he answered. "The area of likely engagement is just outside the range of the best attack copter we have, so it might just be a good idea to deploy two of our Black Dragon BD-303M units. Given the area of engagement, the probability is more than 40% that one unit will not have sufficient fuel to return to base and will have to be ditched in the ocean. I will have to answer for that."

"The bureaucrats in Washington would not complain at all if they knew that we're only trying to save the entire state of California," wailed Troy.

"Well, what do they care? Everything they say and do is simply for show, to fluff themselves up in the eyes of the voting public," lamented Admiral Ferris.

Karla added, "Sir, make sure these copters are equipped with Gatling cannons — we want to rip those devices to shreds."

"Karla, I always knew you had fire in you! Yes, in your honor, I'll ask that they come equipped with the awesome destructive power of the General Electric seven-barrel, 30mm monster that spits out a furious 70 rounds per second. At 4200 heavy rounds per minute, Karla, this weapon can level a whole house, so the fishing boats will be no match!"

"I like that!" she yelped.

Troy was getting impatient. "Very well — let's get this plan moving. We will take cover in the nearby areas awaiting further details on the arrival of the two choppers."

By then, the crates had been loaded, and the fishing vessels had started out to sea. Now it was a race against time.

CHAPTER 18

It was already nighttime, and they received a disturbing message from the Admiral.

SHIPS HEADED SOUTH AS ANTICIPATED BUT ARE NOW 110 NAUTICAL MILES APART. PLEASE ADVISE.

Obviously, the Admiral was tracking the fishing vessels by satellite. One would think the vessels would travel in file, the rear one about 1–2 nautical miles behind the front one. So why were they so far apart?

Then it hit Troy like a thunderbolt. "Karla, they're getting ready to activate the devices to use while at sea!"

She thought about it for a few seconds. "That's right! Remember when Jacob Graham told us that the devices had to be a little more than 100 miles apart for proper functioning? And 110 nautical miles is about 127 statute miles. Yes, they're getting ready!"

Immediately they sent a return message to the Admiral.

BELIEVE DEVICES GETTING READY TO OPERATE. STATUS ON CHOPPERS?

It was already early morning, and just a few hours to doomsday at 12 noon, assuming that the members of Blue Sparrow onboard the fishing vessels would not decide to throw the switch earlier, as a vengeful lesson to America. Was it not enough of a lesson that Alaska now lay in ruins? Another message arrived via the encrypted line.

CHOPPERS ENROUTE, DELAYS IN GETTING FRENCH GOV AIR SPACE PERMISSION, ARRIVE 1–2 HOURS.

"Those damned Frenchmen!" exclaimed Karla. "I had forgotten they don't even allow any U.S. military installations here."

"That's too bad, because what we are doing here is getting rid of Blue Sparrow, which, sooner or later, would threaten the French government, too," added Troy.

Karla had a thought. "Look, Troy, we have no chance of winning here if Blue Sparrow does not at least expect that they will be given the gold bullion. If they know that getting all that gold together is in the final stages, then they will delay the threat until the time they originally indicated, which is about three hours from now. We need to know if we have a chance at this." They opted to talk to the Admiral directly.

"Admiral, this is Troy. Arpeggio 103. We need to know if the government is readying to deliver the bullion to wherever Blue Sparrow indicated."

"Fortunately, yes. Michael Hartwell of Homeland Security has been working around the clock with the White House on this. The President, the Federal Reserve Board, and the Treasury were all initially skeptical about the plan, but Hartwell must have said all the right things. In the end, they all approved the plan."

"So where is the bullion now, where is it going, and has Blue Sparrow been informed?" asked Troy.

"Over the last few days, gold bullion has been trucked in from Kentucky and Washington to this military airbase here in Dover. It has been loaded onto a C5 Galaxy transport plane. My understanding is that Blue Sparrow ordered in the original electronic message sent to the White House that it be delivered to El Dorado International Airport in Bogota, Colombia. Yes, they have been notified that the U.S. government is complying with their demand. Blue Sparrow has had their own observer here at the base who will verify to them when the loaded plane leaves in about five minutes. In fact, he will accompany the gold bullion on the plane."

"At least that allows us some time to catch u p with them. Anything else, Admiral?"

"Remember I told you I was sending some agents to check out banker Hugh Mitchell's bombed-out estate? Well, I just got a quick report indicating that they found a loose, burned notebook page. The only things decipherable on it were several figures that appeared to be sums of money in multiples of 25,000. We don't know whether it was dollars, euros, or some other currency. At the top of the page, incredible enough, was a partial name, we think: 'twell.' This is worse than what we had imagined, if that stands for 'Hartwell.'"

Troy and Karla were confused at what that could possibly mean. Was the squeaky-clean Homeland Security Director Michael Hartwell paying Hugh

Mitchell for something? But if that were true, why did Mitchell implicate the CIA and not Homeland Security when Karla and Troy interrogated him — especially because Hartwell would have been paying him far less than what CIA was?

Karla and Troy began to hear the faraway, *plop-plop-plop*, pulsating sounds of helicopter blades and prepared to drive to a nearby open field as previously instructed by Admiral Ferris. They quickly said goodbye to him.

But, just then, an urgent call came in on Karla's device. It was Elizabeth Eisner at the DHS. "Karla, Elizabeth here. Are you planning on chasing some fishing boats in a helicopter?"

"Yes — how did you know?" answered Karla, somewhat flustered.

"Well, *don't*! I overheard Hartwell talking about getting some fighter jets up in the air and attacking a helicopter that is threatening the security interests of the United States in the Mediterranean. I figured that would be you and Troy."

"Oh, my God — *everybody* is against us! What the hell are we doing wrong, Elizabeth?" shrieked Karla.

"It's just par for the course, Karla. We work for the good guys and the bad guys at the same time, hoping that, at the end of the day, we did what was right," cooed Elizabeth. "But, listen — I've got less than one minute. It skipped my mind to tell you during our last call that, for some time now, we have been gathering information on Colombia, even though we have few assets in that area. Hartwell has been asking for secure-line connections for phone calls he's been making. That's odd too, although I don't know what it means. I hope that helps. Got to go. Bye."

Troy and Karla didn't have time to think about this. After parking their rental car near the helicopters' landing site, Troy and Karla ran to different aircraft, got into their flight suits and helmets, and climbed into the pilot's seat. Right away, they connected their communications gear. They already knew that there would be two independent but simultaneous attacks on the fishing vessels.

"Ready, Lieutenant Bloomfield?"

"Affirmative, Lieutenant Hamilton." Both heavily armed helicopters lifted flawlessly from the field there in Marseille, and headed south over the Western Mediterranean Sea.

Within a couple of minutes, they were able to get a radar and satellite location on the two fishing boats carrying the geophysical devices, which, at that time, were 125.43 statute miles apart. Karla locked her navigational system onto the vessel traveling on the left, and Troy locked onto the other.

They had now reached the desired ideal altitude to avoid being detected by the Blue Sparrow assassins on the vessels.

"Troy, do you copy?"

"Affirmative, very clear."

"Do you realize that we have about 35 minutes before 12 noon, and that they are traveling at a speed much too high for a fishing vessel?"

"Yes, I realized that too, Karla. I think those are modified watercraft selected for this operation. They have too much lead time. I'm afraid we'll have to increase our speed, even though we are close to maximum already."

"My navigation says we will intercept them in 41 minutes; that will not cut the mustard, Lieutenant," warned Karla.

"I hope these Black Dragons have been maintained properly, because we will have to increase our speed by about 15%. Here goes."

Both massive helicopters roared and shook as their engines were being pushed to their limit. Yet there was no other way. Troy and Karla were the last chance that the people in the western half of the U.S., and especially those in California, would have to escape a cataclysmic Richter 9.6 earthquake in the next few minutes. The loss of life would be in the millions, and it would take 30 years to repair the infrastructure. And that was assuming that Blue Sparrow wouldn't come up with additional demands later, even if they got the gold bullion en route to Colombia.

The two helicopters were now about 85 miles apart, on their way to their two targets. Admiral Ferris called on Troy's helicopter's encrypted shortwave radio.

"Admiral Ferris calling Troy. Do you copy?" The transmission was weak and full of static, but decipherable.

"Troy here. I copy."

"I see from satellite information that you're getting close to your targets. Urgent new information. The C5 Galaxy has changed course and is no longer heading for Colombia. The Defense Intelligence Agency claims that the Air Force did not order or authorize any changes, so we're in the dark. Communications to the C5 are interrupted. Do you copy that?"

"Yes, I'm afraid so," responded Troy. "Karla, did you hear that, too?"

"Affirmative, Lieutenant."

Admiral Ferris continued with more bad news. "Troy and Karla, we have to assume that Blue Sparrow is also aware of the change in course and that they probably are thinking that we are out to trick them."

The helicopter engines were overheating due to the extreme speed and the mid-day sun over the Mediterranean, so they had to pull back slightly on the controls. Karla and Troy started feeling that this was a battle they just weren't going to win — too many things were going wrong. The odds were against them by a decisive margin.

Karla prodded the conversation to bring it up from its negative tone. "Sir, I guess that all bets are off in trying to appease these bastards. We just have to get there in the next few minutes and incinerate their sorry asses, sir "

"Yes, Karla — well put. We'll figure out later what to do about the wayward C5, but, right now, I'd bet that Blue Sparrow is readying those two speeding devices for immediate activation," yelled the Admiral.

"But, sir, we got a piece of intel that indicated that some fighter aircraft might try to blow us out of the sky. Is there any truth to that?" asked Troy.

There were a few seconds too many of silence. Troy and Karla knew that they might not make it out alive from this mission even if they succeeded in blowing the two devices to smithereens.

"I'm afraid so, Troy and Karla. Two supersonic F-25 fighter jets are screeching toward you at full speed right now. Departed from the American Incirlik Air Base in Turkey. I can't prove it, but I believe these were ordered under pressure from that damned Hartwell at Homeland Security."

Troy and Karla knew that these top-of-the-line jets wouldn't even have to get close to their Black Dragon helicopters to blast them out of the sky, for they were equipped with deadly Nebula 100XM air-to-air missiles, which flew much faster than the jets themselves.

An uncomfortable and eerie silence fell over the radios as the helicopter engines dutifully roared toward their doom. Admiral Ferris was still connected, but he was not talking, either. It was not in his heart to order Troy and Karla to continue on with what had degenerated into a suicide mission. Yet it was his professional and military duty to urge his soldiers into battle, no matter what the cost, for that is what it meant to be a loyal soldier. After a few more seconds of soul searching, the Admiral spoke.

"Karla, Troy, you are en route to saving the lives of millions of people, but, most likely, you will lose your own. It is my responsibility to urge you to complete the mission even if you will die in the process, but I will understand it if you abort and try to save yourselves somehow. I will claim later I ordered you to abandon the mission."

In a very subdued tone, Karla replied, "Thank you, sir. It has been a great honor working with you on this mission."

"Same here, Admiral. A soldier could not ask for a better leader," added Troy.

All the red alert indicators on the instrument panels were lit, for the Black Dragon choppers were being flown with total disregard for safety precautions and procedures, speed being the ultimate and only goal. Engine-coolant over-heating and overflowing out of the safety valve, engine and transmission oils hot and getting to their frothing temperatures, overhead rotors hot, vibration near the aircrafts' destruction point. It was a miracle that these machines had not yet disintegrated under this extreme abuse.

"Troy, thanks for applying the cream on my back and for rescuing me from that horrible dungeon. Enjoyed working with you," said Karla solemnly.

"You know the best part of this mission, Karla? That was when you asked me to hold you for a little while. I'm sorry we didn't get to know each other longer, Lieutenant."

Admiral Ferris interrupted. "Missiles from the two interceptor aircraft have been launched, heading to you at hellish speed, will hit you in four-and-a-half minutes! We are beyond the point of no return. May God bless your souls for your brave work."

About 30 seconds later, the dreaded news came in from Admiral Ferris. "Troy, Karla — some tremors have begun on the southern part of the San Andreas Fault! Whatever you're going to do, do it, do it! We are losing California and the western part of the U.S.! God help us all!" Karla started to tremble, for things didn't look good and were getting worse by the second. Yes, Geo-1 and Geo-2 were beaming their complementary and satellite-coordinated rays to the tectonic plates deep under California, and the Apocalypse had begun.

To add to Karla's distress, the helicopters' radar instrumentation confirmed two new objects locked on to them and approaching at great velocity. They also showed that the helicopters' distance to the two boats would probably not give them enough time to destroy them before they themselves would be blown out of the sky. There was no other way but to further increase the last remaining ounce of speed on the throttles, even at the risk of causing the disintegration of the two choppers. Smoke from the engines started to fill the main compartments, while the jarring vibrations were causing some rivets to pop and the tempered glass windows to crack. Both Karla and Troy knew what they had to do: Pass the controls over to the copilots and strap themselves in over at the position of door gunner, with their hands on the Gatling guns.

Not too far in the distance, Karla was able to spot her objective. The helicopter pilot pulled back on all the controls as the aircraft approached the boat on the portside and matched its speed. And there it was — the reason for all the pain, anguish, and frustration. The reason why Troy and Karla were losing their lives.

She opened the helicopter's right-side door and readied the General Electric seven-barrel 30mm cannon. She could not believe her eyes!

Fat man Sanjar came out of the bridge and started shooting at her heli-copter with a submachine gun. Some bullets were hitting the aircraft. Her simple, moral dedication to the mission turned to rage, as the despised symbol of her suffering re-appeared unexpectedly. Yes, it was the hated sociopath!

"Sanjar, you motherfucking sadistic maggot. You deserve to die because of all the innocent people you have killed. Because of how you hurt Troy. Because of your threats against my country. Because of how your henchmen abused me. Because of all the poor baby chicks you have eaten alive. But especially because of what you did to Aunt Olga! Die, you fucking cockroach!"

And, with that, Karla activated the ferocious 7-barrel cannon, which unleashed a continuous and hellish barrage of 70 rounds per second at the hard-to-miss fat man Sanjar. Spent casings flew out in a long, almost unbro-ken string, by the hundreds, forming a neat, parabolic arc over the side of the helicopter and down to the water below. Hundreds and hundreds of these large, unstoppable anti-tank bullets hit the sociopath, turning him first into hamburger meat and then simply into an ugly, reddish, lumpy stew on the fast-disappearing deck.

The seven rapidly rotating barrels glowed orange-hot as Karla concen-trated on the cabin, the crate, the engine room, the hull, and what was still visible of the deck. Soon what was left on the water looked just like sawdust and nothing more. Karla had completely obliterated the objective.

"Troy, do you copy? Troy, can you read me?" She waited five seconds and tried again. "Troy, this is Karla!"

"Give me a second!" screamed Troy over the radio. Karla heard the rapid-fire whine of Troy's Gatling cannon over his voice.

"Karla, did you get the boat?"

"Yes, Troy — did you get yours?"

"Affirmative, Lieutenant! We've got about 45 seconds until the two mis-siles hit us. Great working with you, Karla! I wish it could've ended differently for us."

"Troy I've got one last idea. Quickly — get the chopper near sea level, set it on autopilot at full speed ahead, and jump out with your crew immediately. Will do that now! Do it now! Now, Troy!" she screamed.

Karla had not calculated too well, so she and her crew must have fallen about 50 feet before hitting the cold Mediterranean water. She reoriented herself quickly to see her Sikorsky Black Dragon BD-303M helicopter roaring and accelerating away under full power, with its faithful but dying engine smoking more than ever. Ten seconds later, she heard the awful crackling whine of the incoming missile, and the poor chopper was blown into millions of marble-sized pieces, sprinkling the sea surface like heavy raindrops over a still pond.

A minute later, the smoke had cleared; both fishing boats and two geophysical machines had been obliterated. The threat of the earthquake-inducing devices had been decisively eliminated.

Karla quickly asked her crewmembers if they were okay and accounted for all. She knew that Troy had destroyed his assigned target, but she didn't yet know if he and his crew had managed to bail out before the missile hit. Besides getting an answer to that question, she also needed to know if the devices had inflicted too much earthquake damage in the area of the San Andreas Fault in California. The third problem at hand — and the most pressing one for them — was getting everybody back on land as quickly as possible.

Karla turned on her waterproof VHF marine radio to emergency channel 16 and asked for help; a merchant ship not far from the area agreed to pick her and the crew up, and, soon enough, they all were onboard. But no word on Troy and his crew. She had been monitoring the emergency channel, since that was the one he would be using to call for help — but, nothing. Just in case, her radio was scanning all the international marine channels, and, although she heard all the ship-to-ship and ship-to-shore conversations, she didn't detect Troy's voice or anything related to him and the crew. Hopefully, he had jumped out of the chopper on time and was now aboard some other merchant ship in the Mediterranean.

She was anxious to know about the status of California, so she called Admiral Ferris. "Hello, sir — this is Karla."

"Oh, my God, Karla — it's good to hear your voice again! I was 99% sure that you and Troy hadn't made it out alive! Our satellite indicated that both fishing boats and both helicopters were destroyed! How is he?"

"My crew and I jumped out 20 seconds before impact. I had asked Troy to prepare to do the same, but we have had no contact since. My gut feeling is that they're okay on a ship somewhere and we'll hear from him soon."

"Mission accomplished, Lieutenant!" gushed the Admiral.

"Thank you, sir. How's California?"

"Your attack on those two devices could not have been a minute later. Initial reports indicate that the quake definitely was centered on the San Andreas Fault, began very mildly, and in less than a minute had grown and peaked out at Richter 4.4. Damage was not catastrophic, although the public will never be able to thank you both and the crew for your services."

"And the C5 Galaxy with the gold bullion?" asked Karla.

"Diverted, for unknown reasons, but let's not discuss this over this line. Where are you headed?"

Karla had to encode her response, for the Admiral's caution indicated that perhaps he suspected that his line was not entirely secure anymore. "Well, sir, we're going to the same city where I drove the car on three wheels on a previous case."

"Got you. I will see you there within 24 hours."

A short time earlier, the captain of the merchant ship that had rescued her and the crew had informed her that it was headed for the port of Barcelona.

She had been in a little-known hotel for about 15 hours when she decided to call Elizabeth Eisner at the DHS again to thank her for her great help.

"Hi, Elizabeth, it's me again. Is this a good time?"

"Karla! You're alive! Hold on a moment." Apparently Elizabeth wanted to carry on the conversation in another section of the large analysis room where she worked. "Okay, don't talk loud. What the hell happened? I heard that the fighter jets destroyed the two helicopters and that the twin fishing boats disappeared from the radar. Did you and Troy just not go onboard?"

"It's a long story, Elizabeth. I was just calling to thank you for all your help. You might have actually saved our lives."

"Damn! I think you involved me in some nasty stuff going on here at Homeland Security. The grapevine says that the airplane with the gold is missing and that Hartwell has not been heard from in almost 24 hours. Don't know if these two things are related."

"Liz, the DHS is not what you think it is. You might have to do some serious soul searching before you get contaminated."

"Your making contact with me again with this case has opened my eyes. It makes me sick to my stomach, and I haven't been able to sleep too well. But, Karla, I'm a patriot just like you, and I'm here for the long haul. I'll clean up this mess from the inside, even if they kill me in the process! I'm not running, girl!" exclaimed Elizabeth.

"Oh, Elizabeth, you are tops! Will contact you later. Watch your back. Bye."

After the phone call, Karla was left feeling that Elizabeth had always been a great person to associate with. *Too bad we haven't maintained as much contact as we should have*, she thought.

A message from the Admiral flashed on her device. TROY OKAY. WILL MEET AT CAFECITO MIROSLAVA 6 P.M. TODAY. She was so relieved to read that Troy had made it out of that inferno in the middle of the Mediterranean. For the rest of the day, nothing else mattered — Karla could hardly wait for it to be 6 P.M.!

It was 5:55 P.M. as she walked down the last 100 yards on that cobblestone road to the cafe. No outside tables, a run-down façade with lots of nailed-on signs announcing the delicacies in the bakery, and the wonderful aroma of strong coffee. She walked inside, where all the walls were covered with dark-wood paneling, and spotted them at a table far away from the windows.

"Glad to see you, Troy, and Admiral Ferris!" She hugged both of them. "Truthfully, I never thought the day would come when all three of us would be able to sit down for coffee," she exclaimed. "This is incredibly special!"

"I'm happy to see you too, Karla," said Troy. "For a long while there, I really thought it was the end."

"Happy to see both of you safe and sound, and on dry land," uttered the Admiral.

Troy ordered *cafe cortado*, while she asked for a *cafe doble*. The Admiral wanted the serious stuff, so he ordered *cafe carajillo* — add brandy, please.

After a few minutes reviewing the hair-raising near-death experience involved in destroying the devices and bailing out of the helicopters, the Admiral turned the subject to the analysis of what the underlying facts were about the overall mission.

"You both probably know that the situation, as it stands right now, is that the C5 Galaxy aircraft with the $1 trillion in gold was ordered off course and is nowhere to be found. To make matters more mysterious, Michael Hartwell of the DHS is considered missing."

Karla added, "Remember that originally we thought that Hartwell wanted to sink the CIA, and that's why he wanted to bring us in alive — to testify against the CIA and their murderous trail after their plan to acquire the devices went bad."

"Yeah, but I believe that being so involved in this terror case and having so much control over the delivery of $1 trillion in gold must have made him think that maybe having the gold bullion was even better than destroying the CIA and being king of security services in the U.S.," contended Troy.

"There is something far more ominous here," said the Admiral. "We don't know for sure who ordered the fighter jets against your helicopters, but I believe it was Hartwell. He clearly did not want the two devices destroyed. Maybe he cut a deal with Sanjar, but both of you blocked that. Like you, I believe that the twin fishing boats were headed for the Port of Annaba in Algeria. That would have complicated matters."

Karla added emphatically, "Sir, I have a contact inside the DHS, and this contact assured me that she heard Hartwell order two jets on standby at our base in Incirlik, Turkey. He wanted us dead by that time."

"And at the dock at Marseille, the ten security guards assigned to watch over the devices looked American, probably supplied by Hartwell," noted Troy.

"That bastard wanted the geophysical devices for his own plans for the future. It wouldn't surprise me if he took all the HAARP weather-management technology with him," warned Admiral Ferris. "If my hunch is right, he will be 100 times more dangerous than Blue Sparrow and Sanjar — and wealthier than all of the world's billionaires combined."

"And you, sir, are you still on good footing over at Navy, given that you have been helping us all along?" asked Karla.

"Not sure, Lieutenant. I went out on a limb several times, and they didn't like it. But I'll tackle my political problems with those bastard higher-ups as they materialize."

"You know we're on your side, Admiral."

"One thing, Troy and Karla. You can't come back to the States at this time. The CIA still sees you as major political threats with all the damaging inside information you have over their involvement in all those assassinations. They will stop at nothing to kill you both, claiming you were traitors and foreign agents. They're even saying that *you* killed that CIA agent in your hotel room in Sofia, Bulgaria."

"We figured as much, Admiral, but we're broke," mentioned Troy.

"Not to worry. I will have periodic deposits made to your accounts, and I'll provide you with new passports, IDs, and credit cards. Here are two new communication devices. My encrypted phone number is already in their directories. Karla, your code name is Kilohertz, and, Troy, yours is EchoTree. Mine is WaterStone. Change hotels often, and don't stay at the same place for more than three days. For the moment, just take some time off and rest from your ordeal."

Concerned, Karla asked the Admiral, "But, sir — how long will we be doing this?"

"Look, Karla, the way things are right now with Hartwell and the gold bullion missing, things are bound to get much worse before they get any better. I have this gut feeling that all the power bestowed on Hartwell, ostensibly to *help* with the security of the United States, has exacerbated his underlying pathological need for power, wealth, and influence. He may yet re-surface as a delirious and unpredictable madman, the likes of which the world has never known," replied the Admiral in a somber tone.

For the next minute, they sipped their coffees in silence, looking carefully at their surroundings. Then Admiral Ferris said, "I have to get going. Wait ten minutes, and you leave, too."

They shook his hand, and the Admiral walked out of Cafecito Miroslava into the dark, cobblestone street. They had no idea when, if ever, they would again see their leader, their kind mentor, Admiral Christopher Ferris.

"You know, Karla, I really wouldn't mind it too much if we spent the rest of our lives chasing terrorists together," crooned Troy near Karla's ear.

"Listen here, Troy! Working with you, I've gotten shot at and blasted in the dungeon of a house. I've had to drive a car into a creek full of repulsive pig shit. I've had to learn how to say 'Excuse me' to a mannequin. I've gotten deep cuts on my back and shoulders, and I got my butt burned until it got crispy. And to top it all off, I even had to jump out of a flying helicopter into chilling waters to avoid being vaporized by a screeching missile! But you know what, Mr. Navy Intelligence? These last few, dangerous days with you, have been the best of my life!"

----

www.ingramcontent.com/pod-product-compliance
Lightning Source LLC
Chambersburg PA
CBHW020127180626
46810CB00004B/1439